OF MORTAL FURY

A MEDIEVAL ROMANCE
PART OF THE EXECUTIONER KNIGHTS SERIES

BY KATHRYN LE VEQUE

© Copyright 2022 by Kathryn Le Veque Novels, Inc.
Trade Paperback Edition
Text by Kathryn Le Veque
Cover by Kim Killion
Edited by Scott Moreland

Reproduction of any kind except where it pertains to short quotes in relation to advertising or promotion is strictly prohibited.

All Rights Reserved.

The characters and events portrayed in this book are fictitious. Any similarity to real persons, living or dead, is purely coincidental and not intended by the author.

KATHRYN LE VEQUE
NOVELS

WWW.KATHRYNLEVEQUE.COM

ARE YOU SIGNED UP FOR KATHRYN'S BLOG?

You'll get the latest news and information on exclusive giveaways, exclusive excerpts, coming releases, sales, free books, cover reveals and more.

Kathryn's blog followers get it all first. No spam, no junk.

Get the latest info from the reigning Queen of English Medieval Romance!

Sign Up Here

kathrynleveque.com

When Morgan de Wolfe, commander of Richmond Castle, is called by his liege Caius d'Avignon, (*Winter of Solace*) into the full-fledged world of the Executioner Knights to go deep undercover, a de Wolfe becomes a Wolfe in sheep's clothing, all for the sake of William Marshal and his spy ring.

Will a de Wolfe be the greatest Executioner Knight of all?

Morgan de Wolfe, nephew to Edward de Wolfe, Earl of Wolverhampton, finds himself the perfect man for an Executioner Knight's job. Assuming the identity of a dead man, he makes his way to the Welsh border to infiltrate his way into a castle stolen from a Marshal ally. His task is to use the dead man's identity to reclaim the castle.

What he didn't count on was a woman who could quite possibly ruin his mission.

And possibly even his life.

Amarantha de la Haye's father had laid siege to Mount Grace Castle in Yorkshire twenty years earlier in a dispute of honor. She has grown up at Mount Grace, an educated and clever young woman who finds herself ruling the house and hold because her father is slipping increasingly into dementia – a rather guarded secret. When a chance meeting with Morgan sees sparks fly between the two of them, she has no idea that she will be the key to Morgan's mission… and her own destruction.

The Wolfe fangs are sharpening.

Join Morgan and Amarantha on a journey of lies, deceit, betrayal, and, ultimately, the power of love. Will Morgan obey William Marshal? Or will he obey his heart?

Of Mortal Fury is part of the USA Today bestselling Executioner Knights series.

Executioner Knights Motto

Milites umbrae et immani

Knights of Shadow and Savage

LIST OF EXECUTIONER KNIGHTS/SPIES
FOR WILLIAM MARSHAL
As of 1215 A.D.

(Note: some later Executioner Knight tales take place years after this story is set, so as of 1215 A.D., this is where these knights serve and/or are in command of. Also note that while some Executioner Knights may be mentioned, not all appear in this story.)

William Marshal – Earl of Pembroke, Pembroke Castle and Farrington House

Christopher de Lohr – Earl of Hereford and Worcester, Lioncross Abbey Castle

David de Lohr – Earl of Canterbury, Canterbury Castle, Bellham Place

Peter de Lohr – Lioncross Abbey Castle, Lord Pembridge/garrison commander Ludlow Castle

Gart Forbes – Dunster Castle, Devon

Caius d'Avignon – Richmond Castle, North Yorkshire – also Hawkstone Castle

Maxton of Loxbeare – Chalford Hill Castle, Gloucester

Kress de Rhydian – Seton Castle, Scotland

Achilles de Dere – Caversham Manor, Berkshire

Susanna de Tiegh de Dere – a Blackchurch-trained knight, wife of Achilles

Alexander de Sherrington – Lioncross Abbey Castle/garrison commander, Wigmore Castle

Bric MacRohan – Narborough Castle, Norwich Castle, Norfolk

Dashiell du Reims – Ramsbury Castle, Wiltshire – also Thunderbey Castle, East Anglia.

Sean de Lara – King John's personal bodyguard

Kevin de Lara – Canterbury Castle (in the service of David de Lohr) – also Hyssington, Caradoc, and Trelystan Castles – Welsh Marches

Cullen de Nerra – Rockingham Castle, Northamptonshire

Cole de Velt – formerly William the Lion's personal guard, now at Berwick Castle

Addax al-Kort – service to Christopher de Lohr and William Marshal

Essien al-Kort – service to Christopher de Lohr and William Marshal

Morgan de Wolfe – in service to Caius d'Avignon, Richmond Castle

Gareth de Llion – in service to William Marshal

Morgan du Bois – in service to Christopher de Lohr/after 1201 living in France under an assumed name

Keller de Poyer – in service to William Marshal at Pembroke Castle/Nether Castle (Keller is more of a knight for William Marshal than he's actually a spy)

Garran le Mon – technically, he's believed to be dead after 1201 A.D.

Marcus Burton – Lord Somerhill and Dunnington, Somerhill Castle

Ashton de Royans – serves Ajax de Velt

Beau de Russe – serves Ajax de Velt

Tristan de Royans – serves Juston de Royans

Juston de Royans (*Lord of Winter*) – an original Executioner Knight. Too old to be active at this time, but has trained most of the men listed

REBEL WARLORDS AND OTHER NOTABLES

This is only a partial and mostly fictional list

"The Northerners" (this was actually a term for warlords from the north who rebelled against King John)

Juston de Royans – Bowes Castle

Ajax de Velt – Pelinom Castle and Berwick Castle

Yves de Vesci – Earl of Alnwick

Alastor de Bourne – Castle Keld

Marcus Burton – Somerhill Castle

Allies of The Northerners:

Christopher de Lohr

David de Lohr

Duke of Savernake, Bentley de Vaston/Dashiell du Reims

House of de Lara (Kevin, Sean)

Maxton of Loxbeare

Alexander de Sherrington

Caius d'Avignon

Morgan de Wolfe

Siding with John (though still secretly allied with de Lohr and the rebellion):

Daveigh de Winter/Bric MacRohan

Valor de Nerra/Cullen de Nerra

William Marshal, Kress de Rhydian, Achilles de Dere

AUTHOR'S NOTE

Welcome to Morgan de Wolfe's tale.

I love the Executioner Knights. They've quickly become one of my favorite series, mostly because they're just so different. They're not a family but, in a sense, they are. They act like a family and work like a family, and that means when one is inducted into their group, he's part of the Executioner Knights for life.

Enter Morgan.

Though he is a de Wolfe, he's NOT part of the de Wolfe Pack. Not at all. Let me explain – Morgan lived prior to the de Wolfe Pack really getting started. William de Wolfe and his group. I was ambiguous in the beginning about Morgan's relationship to the de Wolfes we know and love, but the truth is that he is a nephew to Edward de Wolfe (*Rise of the Defender*), who is William de Wolfe's (*The Wolfe*) father. Morgan is the eldest son of Edward's youngest brother, Arthur. If you want to find out more about his life and relations, here's a short family tree of Edward de Wolfe and his brothers:

Edward de Wolfe

Robert

Jonathan

William (*The Wolfe*)

Henry de Wolfe

Meredith

Cecily

Gavyn

Arthur de Wolfe

Morgan

Owen

Reese

Drew

It was mentioned in another book that Edward had to wait to marry because his bride was a child (literally) and had to grow up, so Arthur and Henry married well before he did and had children, meaning Edward's sons were the youngest of the three brothers. Henry and Arthur de Wolfe have never been mentioned in any other book, so you are reading about them for the first time here.

Now, back to Morgan – interestingly enough, we first met him in *Winter of Solace* as the second in command to Caius d'Avignon. Morgan was never a spy or assassin in the Holy Land like so many of the Executioner Knights (Caius d'Avignon, the Britannia Viper, included). He was simply a knight who had been too young to go on crusade, but he swore fealty to William Marshal and that's how he ended up with Caius at Richmond Castle. He kind of got sucked into the Executioner Knight lifestyle and now, as a full-fledged agent for William Marshal, he has his first "mission".

As Morgan himself says in the book, he has always been part of the support team for the main agents – Maxton, Kress, Achilles, Caius, Alexander, etc., etc., so with his first mission where everything depends on him, he rises to the occasion. He's a de Wolfe, after all. But he makes the fatal mistake of falling for his enemy's daughter, a rookie mistake, actually, and has to get himself out of a jam.

Just remember – he's a de Wolfe – and they don't fail!

Just a quick note about the location for the vast majority of this book. We're just inside of the Welsh border, not far from

Jax de Velt's property. If you recall from *The Dark Lord*, he had six castles along the mid-Welsh Marches, so he's close by. Much of what takes place is near a village called Bronllys, which does exist. It also has a castle that has been there since the 12th century, upon which the castle in this novel, Mount Grace, is loosely based. Bronllys Castle had a litany of owners, including de Clifford and de Braose lords, one of the main castles on the Marches that has a vivid history.

Lastly, there is a very small mention later in the book about an ancient (love) poem and our heroine recites a couple of lines. Those lines actually come from the oldest known love poem, called *The Love Song of Shu-Sin*. It comes from the ancient kingdom of Ur and was thought to have been spoken from the high priestess to the king. Very interesting reading if ancient history is something that interests you.

Now, on to our usual pronunciation guide:

Amarantha – Am-uh-RAN-thuh
Gere – Gear

And with that, allow me to present the tale of Morgan and Amarantha. It's a good one!

Hugs,

Kathryn

PROLOGUE

Year of Our Lord 1214
London
The Pox Tavern

A BODY WENT sailing past him, crashing out into the street beyond the entry door.

There was a fight going on.

That wasn't unusual in this place, the seediest of establishments down by the River Thames. It smelled of unwashed bodies and hopelessness, and William Marshal had told his agents they were never to visit the place, but that was one order they almost always disobeyed.

One could have anything one wanted at The Pox... for a price.

Accompanied by the Earl of Hereford and Worcester, Christopher de Lohr, and the greatest warlord in Devon, Lord Gallox, also known as Gart Forbes, The Marshal pushed into the very crowded Pox, stepping out of the way when someone threw a fist at him. Such things happened in a fight, men throwing punches when they did not even know who their opponent was.

The Marshal was untroubled as the offending man ended up plowing a fist into Gart's left arm. Gart's response was to plant a ham-hock sized fist into the side of the man's head and he went down like a stone. Christopher, bringing up the rear of the trio, started to chuckle because no sane man would ever challenge Gart Forbes in any kind of fight, ever. The man known as "*sach*" on the battlefield, Gaelic for "*mad*", was not a man to be opposed if one wanted to keep all of one's teeth.

Gart saw Christopher laughing and he fought off a grin.

"Having fun?" Christopher asked.

Gart narrowly avoided being hit by another flying body. "Completely," he said drolly. "I had no idea we'd be walking into a party."

"Did you not receive an invitation?"

"Sadly, I did not."

"You can still join the fun."

Gart wriggled his brows. "*After.*"

Christopher's smile faded. "Aye," he muttered. "After."

They caught up to William, who was midway through the establishment at this point, past the fight at the entry. Now they were in the seedier real estate where deals were brokered, prostitutes engaged, or any number of other less moral situations unfolded. Women were scattered in the shadows, waiting for customers, spreading their legs and flashing their goods when Gart and Christopher passed by. But they didn't notice the women.

They were focused on something ahead.

The Pox had several private rooms where men could go to engage in whatever struck their fancies. Christopher and Gart pushed ahead of The Marshal, yanking back the curtains of a few of those rooms to see who was on the other side. They came across hemp smokers, drunks, a couple of prostitutes and clients engaging in the activities of their trade, and still more people who were evidently sleeping off their extravagance.

As they came to the last chamber, which was the largest one and with a door that opened into an alley, they heard a good deal of laughter and shouting. Recognizing more than one voice in that room, they pulled back the curtain in time to see someone lighting a man's arse on fire. Or, more correctly, they were lighting his fart on fire and the man was trying very hard to see how far he could shoot the flame. It shot several inches out into the air of the room and men began cheering and exchanging money.

The Marshal, Christopher, and Gart recognized a few of those gamblers.

"Caius," The Marshal barked. "Maxton, Achilles, and Morgan. For God's sake, come out of there."

Without question, the knights immediately began to move, following The Marshal and de Lohr and Forbes out into the common room where the fight had mostly ended at this point. Men were picking themselves off the floor and a few dazed individuals were being hauled away, slapped, or otherwise revived. The Marshal headed straight for the table in the very front of the room, positioned in the oriel window that overlooked both the street and the river. There was one table there, and several seats, and it was the prime seating spot because one could see everyone coming in and going out of the establishment.

Unfortunately, three men were already sitting there and Caius and Maxton moved in, tossing them out. Achilles got involved and literally threw the men out the front door. Achilles had always been the emotional type, less able to control his impulses than some. He may not have always been levelheaded, but he was entertaining. As the others sat down at their newly confiscated table, Achilles stood at the entry to The Pox to make sure those they'd so recently stolen from didn't try to come back inside. When he was certain that they were running off, he returned to the table.

"Sit, Achilles," The Marshal said, but he pointed to the room beyond. "And make sure no one hears our conversation."

Achilles planted himself at the end of the table obediently. "We would have better luck with that if we were at Farringdon House, my lord," he said, referring to The Marshal's town home. "Why did you come here? You hate this place."

The Marshal's shrewd, yellowed eyes fixed on him. "I came because I knew degenerates like you would be here," he said, watching the others grin. He glanced at the group. "I must say that I am surprised to see Cai and Maxton here."

"Achilles forced us," Caius said, casting blame. An enormously tall man with black eyes and black hair, he'd been known during his days in The Levant as The Britannia Viper. "He would not take 'no' for an answer."

"And what was so important that Achilles had to be in the middle of it?"

"Lighting farts on fire," Achilles said as if it were the most normal thing in the world. "Men were betting big money that they could shoot a flame further across the room than any other man, so we bet on it. Cai has made at least twenty pounds from it, so do not let him fool you. He was a willing participant."

As Caius shot Achilles a withering glare across the table, Achilles smiled triumphantly and Christopher put up a hand to stop the inane conversation.

But he was fighting off a grin.

"Enough," he said. "The Earl of Pembroke did not come here to listen to your foolery, so cease your prattle. He came because he knew he would find you here even though he has forbidden you to come."

There was a rebuke in that statement but The Marshal snorted softly, an unusual sound coming from the usually serious man.

"If there is only one order they disobey, let it be this one," he said. "I suppose I cannot genuinely control a man's sense of recreation, so let us not mention it again. I have indeed come on a serious matter. So serious that I dare not speak of it at Farringdon."

All eyes turned to him. "Why not?" Christopher asked, intensely curious. "You did not tell me why you wanted to speak here, only that you did. It seems a strange place to carry out business."

The Marshal shook his head. "I fear I have a spy in my home," he said. "I am not sure who it is but I am sure who has sent him. The only person who would have any reason to spy on me is the king, but let us dwell no more on that. Sean de Lara is trying to find out who it is."

He was speaking of the spy known in inner circles as the Lord of the Shadows, a spy buried so deep in King John's retinue that he was deeply trusted by the monarch he had been assigned to watch by none other than William Marshal himself. Every day, Sean's life was in danger, but every day, he did his duty. No man was more greatly respected for it.

"De Lara will discover the spy," Christopher said, his tone tinged with distaste. "This is not the first royal spy you've had in your midst and it will not be your last."

The Marshal shook his head. "Nay," he said. "That is the unfortunate part of this business we engage in. Everyone has spies and everyone has a price. It is a business where one can never be complacent. Sometimes, we must go above and beyond what is usually expected of us and that is why I've come. We have an opportunity to break John's foothold in Wales which, as you know, is becoming increasingly strong. I know this is not the usual conversation we have about him because we have enough worries with the French mercenaries he is bringing to our shores, but we have a legitimate worry in Wales. In fact, I…"

He stopped when he caught sight of an enormous figure coming in from the darkness outside. His halt caused everyone to see what he was looking at and they all saw the big, cloaked figure enter. The Marshal was on his feet.

"De Velt?"

The figure turned to them, quickly, as his name was called. Men near the doorway were starting to wrestle and slap each other around again, one of them falling back into the figure. It was enough to jostle him and he reached down without hesitation, grabbing the man by the neck. In a swift move, he threw an elbow into the side of the man's head, snapping the neck, and then tossing the man onto the ground as if nothing in the world was amiss. As if he did that sort of thing every day, which he did. In the same motion, he pulled back the hood of his cloak and approached The Marshal's table.

Ajax de Velt in the flesh had arrived.

Everyone was on their feet at the sight of the legendary Dark Lord. There was no man more feared, nor more brutal, in all of England, as evidenced by the man he'd so smoothly killed. Christopher, a good friend of de Velt's, moved around The

Marshal and extended his hand to him in greeting.

"Jax," he said incredulously. "I've not seen you in months. Why did you not tell me you were going to be in London?"

Jax smiled at his old friend as he took Christopher's hand. "Because I was not sure when I would arrive," he said. "I've been at my Welsh properties, gathering intelligence at The Marshal's request. He is the one who asked me to meet him on this very night at this fine establishment."

There was irony in his voice as he glanced around the packed common room, shaking his head in disapproval. Christopher grinned.

"Our sons come here from time to time," he said. "I have always chastised Peter for it, but here I am."

"Here *we* are."

Jax snorted, as did Christopher, before Christopher pulled him to the table where everyone was still looking at him with a bit of awe. Jax wasn't looking at them, however. He was looking at William Marshal.

"My lord," he greeted. "I hope I've not kept you waiting."

The Marshal shook his head, indicating for him to take the seat next to him. "Nay," he said. "We only just arrived in time to stop Achilles and Caius from lighting men's farts on fire."

Everyone started chuckling and even Jax grinned. "Is that so?" he said. "I've heard about this place from my sons. They say a man can bet on anything here. Nothing is forbidden."

Christopher was seated on The Marshal's other side. "Nothing, indeed," he said. "Peter has told me about gambling on men to see how far they could vomit or how much they could drink before falling to the floor. Although he will not admit it, I do believe he has participated in some of those games as more than just a gambler, but as a willing participant."

No one was going to speak of what they knew about Christopher's eldest son because they were all Executioner Knights. There was a brotherhood there and that did not include tattling to a man's father. Christopher realized this by their expressions, mostly Achilles' expression, and he simply chuckled, looking to The Marshal to begin their conference without delay.

William took the hint.

"All discussions of wild knights aside, let us come to the point of this meeting," he said, lowering his voice and sitting forward so the men around the table could hear him better. "Now that de Velt is here, we can begin in earnest. Before I start, however, I would like to ask if any of you have heard about *Mynydd Gras*."

Immediately, Christopher and Morgan, the two men who had properties on the Welsh Marches, nodded.

"Mount Grace Castle," Christopher said. "Of course I've heard of it. It's to the northeast of my holdings. The place is legendary."

The Marshal turned to him. "Tell me what you know."

Christopher shrugged. "It is one of the rare castles built by the Normans on Welsh soil," he said. "Back in the days of the Duke of Normandy, he sent his son, William Rufus, into Wales to push hard for conquest. Mount Grace was built as a landing point for the Normans in their quest to subdue Wales and although they were not entirely successful, it has been held by the same family since the days of old until a few years ago."

"Exactly," The Marshal said, returning his attention to the group. "A few years ago when John pushed into Wales to subdue Llewelyn ap Iowerth and his fellow warlords, he took the opportunity to lay siege to Mount Grace because he felt it had become too 'Welsh'. Over the decades, the le Marche family had become more Welsh than English and John used that excuse to take the castle, claiming it was a hive for Welsh rebellion."

Christopher shook his head. "But that was not true," he said. "The le Marche family has always been loyal to England, but they have the unique position of having married into noble Welsh families so many times that they are kin to many great warlords."

"They've been able to help the English negotiate many a treaty."

"Exactly."

"Then why did John want Mount Grace so badly?" Achilles asked.

Christopher looked at him. "Because Mount Grace has a vast silver mining operation that makes it quite wealthy," he said. "They call it the *Brenin Arian*, or the Silver King. It has been a point of contention between the le Marche family and John, and Richard before him. I believe Henry even had issues with it. The le Marche family is richer than God because of that mining and whoever holds the castle holds that mining."

"And an unlimited supply of wealth," The Marshal finished grimly. "We have been wondering how John has been able to pay these tides of French mercenaries and it is partially because of the Mount Grace mine. He now has an unending source of coin and that is going to create a critical problem for us."

Now, the gravity of the situation was starting to become clear. An immoral king with endless wealth to pay for his war against his own barons was an intimidating prospect, indeed. It was bad enough dealing with John and the continuous issues they had with the man, but unlimited wealth had never been a concern. In fact, John needed money badly and he always had.

But no longer.

The men began to shake their heads in disgust at a greedy king having access to, of all things, a silver mine, using it to fund his war chest against his very own warlords. They had been fighting the man for the past several years and it was a problem that was only growing worse. Everyone knew that John was moving more mercenaries into England by the day.

And now, with the benefit of a silver mine at his disposal.

"You must have a solution for this, my lord," Caius finally said. "You have us gathered to remediate this situation?"

The Marshal nodded. "I believe I have a solution," he said. "The problem is that we have far too much to deal with as far as John goes without taking on the additional burden of wresting Mount Grace from his clutches. I cannot simply mount an army and lay siege to the castle because John's garrison commander could destroy the mine or otherwise damage it. We need that mine intact."

"Then what is the solution?"

The Marshal held out a hand to beg patience while he explained. "When John took Mount Grace about five years ago, he went in under a flag of peace," he said. "The le Marche family had no reason to believe John had come to take the castle and they naturally admitted John's army. Once inside Mount Grace, John's men took the castle over and tried to kill the le Marche family. Only Lady le Marche and her eldest son escaped. After this happened, I spoke with Gere le Marche, the eldest son and heir, and he told me that he was going to raise an army to regain his castle."

There was puzzlement around the table. "He's not come to any allies that I've known of," Christopher said. "In fact, Gere seemed to disappear. No one knew where he and his mother went."

"He came to me."

"And you're just mentioning that now?"

The Marshal sensed Christopher's irritation and rightfully so. If something happened on the Welsh Marches, then Christopher should be the man to know, but William hadn't told him about Gere le Marche.

"There was not any reason to at the time, Chris," he said. "Gere escaped Mount Grace with chests of silver. You see, most of the Mount Grace army was absorbed into John's royal troops using threats and promises of sharing the Mount Grace wealth. Therefore, Gere knew he was without an army. He had to pay for one and he came to me to discuss it, but secretly. He wanted my advice and I gave it to him."

"What did you tell him?"

"To find help in Ireland," he said. "I sent word to Carlow Castle, one of my holdings, and my men helped Gere raise an Irish army. Irish mercenaries are quite fearsome but Gere had a brilliant suggestion – he paid them to come to Wales and pose as Irish mine workers. It is their intention to get jobs in the mine and then raise a rebellion from within."

Christopher could see the logic in that. "John's men will have a difficult time containing something like that, if they rebel from within the ranks."

"Exactly."

"But you still should have told me."

The Marshal sighed heavily. "Why?" he said. "Chris, he knew I could not help him raise an English army, nor could you. We have enough trouble with John without the added burden of taking an army into Wales to evict royal troops from a castle. Especially me – John still thinks I am loyal to him. I cannot go about attacking a castle the man has and still keep up the illusion of loyalty. That has been my trouble from the start. Therefore, I put Gere in contact with my men in Ireland. It was all I could do."

Christopher was listening to it all very carefully. Now, what had happened at Mount Grace was making a great deal of sense to him – John's incursion and the resulting occupation. More than that, The Marshal was correct – he couldn't go charging his armies into Wales to reclaim a castle from John's army. He was walking a very fine line, publicly supporting the king yet privately working against him. Given that position, he eased back on his irritation.

"I was aware of the situation at Mount Grace but it has been very quiet," he said after a moment. "No trouble, no problems, and most importantly, no mercenaries moving in. We haven't heard tale of any foreign armies being housed there so whatever John is doing there, he is keeping it quiet. Still, I will admit that my holdings are further south so I've never had any direct dealings with Mount Grace. But that is not the case with Jax."

Attention turned to Jax, who had been sitting silently by. When he saw that the focus had shifted to him, he cleared his throat softly.

"I have six castles along the Marches and three of them within fairly close proximity to Mount Grace," he said, looking at the faces around him, including Christopher. "I have spent the past two months at my holding of Cloryn Castle, which is about nine miles due east from Mount Grace. Keep in mind that I do not live there, so my information is coming from my garrison commander. It seems that the mines of Mount Grace are working at full capacity and John is stripping a great deal of silver from them. Great convoys move out of Mount Grace and into England, presumably with the silver ore."

"Which is taken into London and smelted." Caius said what they were all thinking. "That is how John is getting his money."

"Exactly," Jax said. "It is only a matter of time before John moves mercenaries into Mount Grace and then the Welsh will be furious. We will have another uprising on our hands."

"Which we must prevent," The Marshal said with quiet firmness. "At my request, Jax has moved a couple of agents into Mount Grace, posing as miners. It is imperative that we have men on the inside and that is mostly what Jax has been doing for the past couple of months. Preparing for what is to come."

"And what is to come?" Caius asked.

The Marshal's gaze moved over the group. "Precisely this," he said. "Gere le Marche died six months ago of a fever, so his mother tells me. He had paid for eight hundred Irish mercenaries to come to Wales, docking at Chepstow and moving north. They have been camped in the Wye Valley near St. Arvans, waiting for Gere to come to them and lead them to Mount Grace."

Christopher looked at him, confused. "What do you mean waiting for Gere?" he said. "You said that Gere brought them from Ireland."

The Marshal shook his head. "This is where it becomes strange," he said. "Gere was a rather paranoid individual. He did business with only a few of my men who gathered the mercenaries on his behalf. The mercenaries were paid for and shipped to Chepstow, and that is where they are waiting. Without having ever seen Gere."

Christopher's irritation was back. "So there are eight hundred Irish mercenaries within a day's ride of Lioncross Abbey?" he said, referring to his mighty castle on the Welsh Marches.

"Even if you did not tell me about Gere le Marche, you should have told me about this."

William could see that Christopher was growing perturbed again and held up a hand to ease the man. "I have a solution, so bear with me," he said. His focus moved to Jax. "De Velt, it is no secret that you are very much against John as part of the northern warlord contingent."

Jax grunted. "I should hope that would be abundantly clear."

As the table snorted in agreement, The Marshal continued. "Gere le Marche is indeed going to lead those Irish mercenaries into the mines of Mount Grace and liberate the castle," he said. "The de Velt army will be ready to march on Mount Grace when the time comes in support of that rebellion."

Jax frowned. "But Gere le Marche is dead."

"I will have a man assume his identity."

"Who?"

The Marshal's shrewd gaze moved to the other men at the table. All of them were elite, the best that England had to offer. But William had one man in particular in mind.

"Morgan," he said. "You are a de Wolfe, from one of the original Norman families who came to these shores with the Duke of Normandy. In fact, your ancestor was none other than the man they called Warwolfe, Gaetan de Wolfe. He led an elite group of knights to these shores, men known as the *anges du guerre*, and they single-handedly helped win the Battle at Hastings those many years ago. Out of all of the men at this table, save de Lohr, your legacy is the strongest."

Morgan de Wolfe had been sitting back in the shadows until The Marshal turned his attention on him. Now, he was sitting up, sitting forward, listening to the man very carefully.

He'd had no real idea why he was part of this meeting until now.

"My lord," he said curiously, "how can I be of service?"

The Marshal leaned forward, as well, his face becoming illuminated by the cluster of dripping tapers in the center of the table.

"You will become Gere le Marche."

Morgan hadn't expected to hear that. In fact, he simply stared at the man as if waiting for more of an explanation. Or the confession of a jest. But neither were forthcoming so, after a moment, he frowned in confusion.

"I am to *become* him, my lord?" he repeated.

The Marshal nodded. "Of everything you have ever done in your life, de Wolfe, this will be a defining moment," he said. "We all have them. It is that one moment in your life that will show your worth. Either you will rise to it or you will not. You will succeed or you will fail. If you fail, you will not survive. If you cannot successfully lead this rebellion, then everything will crumble. John keeps Mount Grace and his mercenaries will sweep through England and destroy everything we hold dear. Do you understand what I am telling you so far?"

Morgan did, but he was shocked. He was sitting with some of the most seasoned men in the world, men who had served in The Levant. Men who had battled with King Richard against Saladin. They had seen and experienced death and destruction beyond belief. They'd also participated in life-or-death situations that most men could not imagine.

But what had Morgan done?

He was a de Wolfe, that was true. He had the name. He was a fine example of de Wolfe blood. He was bigger than most de Wolfe men, who tended to be on the tall and muscular side, but

Morgan took it a step further. He was taller than most of the men at the table save Christopher and Caius, who were six and seven inches over six feet, respectively. Morgan came in somewhere just shy of them, so he was very tall. But he also had the breadth as well, muscular and powerful. He had the dark de Wolfe hair and hazel eyes that looked gold in some light. Handsome was where he began. If there were women around, they usually gravitated towards him, but his wife was his career. He had served The Marshal for some years, but the last several at Richmond Castle as Caius' second in command until a larger garrison worthy of his talent became available.

But this wasn't a garrison worthy of his talent.

It was a mission that would make him… or break him.

"As you wish, my lord," he said after a brief hesitation. "Tell me what you would have me do."

William did.

CHAPTER ONE

Two months later
Mynydd Gras
Mount Grace, Wales

"THERE HE IS. *Hide!*"

The women scattered, only there weren't many places to go. They had just emerged from the chapel of Mount Grace, a massive bastion perched on a rise overlooking the River Wye. It clung to the outcropping, like a snake, following the shape of the cliffs so that the entire east side of the castle had a serpentine shape and a river view.

But it had been built that way for protection.

The Normans who built the structure had used the river's edge as part of the defense system and made the castle impenetrable on the east side. The rest of the castle had massive walls, thirty feet high in places and more than a dozen feet thick. The walls themselves housed rooms and chambers and corridors as well as trades, like the tanner and the fuel chamber for the forge situated in a small, open-air nook. The fuel chamber was full of cut wood – plenty of it – and it wasn't just for the forge. The kitchens and the castle as a whole used that giant fuel chamber, full of an entire forest of trees that had been harvested in the spring. It would be dried out through the summer, used in the autumn and winter and spring when the process would begin again.

Mount Grace was a city unto itself. Along with those walls and corridors and fuel rooms came an enormous keep that was built into the inner ward. In fact, it constituted the wall of the inner ward, with no windows or doors until the second level. The keep soared five stories into the sky, with twenty-seven chambers and a myriad of stairs, passageways, and alcoves.

But that's not where it ended.

The kitchens were enormous to feed the army it housed and there was a chapel on the second floor of the outer ward, reached by an enormous flight of mural stairs. Straight up to the carved doors that opened into the chapel overlooking the river, built with those views in mind. It seated at least twenty people, with vaults below it on the ground floor and even on the floor below that. Carved into the rock of the cliffs were more burial chambers, used in centuries past by the le Marche family.

But no one spoke of the founding family these days.

They hadn't for five years.

Yet, all of that was immaterial at the moment to Lady Amarantha de la Haye. She was well-acquainted with the walls of Mount Grace, the corridors, the keep, and the chapel, which was where she found herself at the moment. To be exact, she was emerging from the carved oak and iron doors with the iron pulls that weighed more than she did. Pushing through those doors was quite a feat for the petite young woman whose father was the commander of Mount Grace. A pious lady, she prayed twice a day, at lauds and vespers, and coming out of the chapel required a good shove with all her might.

But now, that had worked against her.

She'd barreled through those doors for all to see, including the man she *didn't* want to see. In a rush, she turned to duck back into the chapel but the heavy doors were nearly closed so she was forced to yank on them, pulling one of them open enough so she could slide back through the gap. Then she pulled the door closed but her cousin was still outside on the stoop, still exposed, so she had to throw her shoulder into the door to open it again and pull Everelda through.

They spilled back into the chapel and dragged the doors shut.

"Did he see you?" Everelda asked breathlessly.

Amarantha rushed to the nearest window, a lancet window that overlooked the outer ward, and strained to catch a glimpse.

"I do not know," she said, jumping up to get a peek. "I cannot see him. Come here and help me!"

Everelda rushed to her cousin's aid, not expecting to be forced onto her hands and knees so that Amarantha could stand on her back so she could see from the window. As Everelda grunted with her cousin's rather light weight on her back, Amarantha caught a glimpse of what she'd been looking for and she gasped.

"He's coming," she hissed as she nearly fell from her cousin's back. "Hurry! Start praying!"

She grabbed her cousin by the wrist and yanked her towards the elaborately carved altar, brought all the way from Venice and topped with a slab of orange marble. It was the only altar like it in all of Wales.

"But I have already prayed!" Everelda insisted. "I do not need to pray again."

Amarantha wasn't listening. She reached the altar and forced her cousin to her knees. Dropping beside her, she quickly crossed herself and closed her eyes, lowering her head. Everelda followed suit. It wasn't a moment or two later that the great doors to the chapel creaked open.

Creakkkkkkkkkkkk...

Amarantha continued praying, knowing it was He Who She Was Trying To Avoid. She could feel his stare on her back. She'd been trying to avoid the man for weeks, at least in her own mind, although the truth was that she'd been avoiding him for months. A local English warlord, Mount Grace's closest ally just over the Welsh border into Shropshire, whom her father was trying to marry her off to.

But Amarantha wanted nothing to do with the man.

"Quiet," she could hear her father admonish softly. "My daughter is praying. She's a good and pious lass, you know. She prays twice a day, as her mother used to. That is the mark of a fine woman."

So her father had come, too. That only made Amarantha angry. The man was trying to foist her on Sir Farran du Bonne as if she were a piece of rotten meat he was trying to toss to the wolves. He couldn't get rid of her fast enough. Well, perhaps that was not entirely true, but it certainly seemed as if her father were determined she should like Sir Farran and he should like her. The only hope now was for her to continue praying so she didn't have to talk to him.

And she prayed.

Minutes turned into an hour and one hour ran into the next. Kneeling beside her, Everelda struggled not to yawn, or groan because of her folded position, or any number of twitches and fidgets because Amarantha had no intention of coming out of her prayers anytime soon. She was going to wait out Sir Farran, who stood back with her father by the door, patiently waiting.

And waiting.

It became a standoff.

Amarantha had come to pray at dawn, the canonical hour of lauds, so her prayers were stretching into mid-morning. The nooning hour arrived and her stomach began to grumble because she hadn't broken her fast. Next to her, she heard a snore and Everelda suddenly tipped over. As the woman sprawled onto her side, Sir Farran and Amarantha's father rushed forward.

"Evey?" Hollis asked, sounding concerned. "Are you well, Child?"

Embarrassed, Everelda allowed her uncle to pull her to her feet. Because the woman's fall had snapped Amarantha from her prayers, her ruse was up. She was alert, no longer in meditation, standing up beside her cousin and brushing the dust off the woman's skirt.

"I am well, Uncle Hollis," Everelda said, chagrined. "I am sorry to have troubled you."

"No trouble at all," Farran said, his gaze only glancing over Everelda before moving swiftly to Amarantha. "My lady, I trust you are well? After such long prayers, I can imagine that you need to stretch your legs."

He meant with him. Amarantha could just tell by the expression on his face that he meant with him. It wasn't that Farran was unattractive – in fact, he was a comely man with curly, red locks and piercing blue eyes. He had a bit of a hook nose and a long jaw, but those features blended well to create a man that was generally considered handsome. He was of average height with a strong build and his ability to command men was well-known. In battle, he was formidable. His family had been in possession of Talgarth Castle, just over the border, for over a century. Farran was expected to marry well and had made no secret of his intentions with Amarantha de la Haye. Everyone thought it was a fine match.

Except Amarantha.

"Go with Sir Farran," Hollis said quickly, before Amarantha could refuse. "I will take Evey into the keep. Show Sir Farran your new horse. I am certain he would like to see it."

Amarantha resisted the urge to roll her eyes. There he was again, throwing her together with a man she had no interest in. But she smiled thinly at her father before looking to Farran.

"I would be happy to show you if you are interested," she said. "'Tis only a palfrey."

"A palfrey all the way from Arabia," Hollis said. "She will be a fine breeding mare."

Farran hadn't taken his eyes off Amarantha. "I would be honored if you would show her to me," he said. Then he extended his elbow politely. "Shall we?"

No one missed the heavy sigh from Amarantha, perhaps one of resignation, as she took the man's elbow and he led her out into the sunshine. It was a cool and breezy day, with the wind whipping up the white clouds that spread across the expanse of blue. In fact, Amarantha ended up shielding her eyes from the bright sun as they came down the stairs and into the bailey.

"Is the sun bothering you, my lady?" Farran asked. "I can just as easily find some shade to walk in."

Amarantha shook her head. "Nay," she said. "It simply seems a little bright after the darkness of the chapel."

"You were praying for quite some time."

"I know."

"How do you find things to pray for? For all of that time, I mean."

There might have been a rebuke in there, but she wasn't sure. She was sure, however, that the man knew she had been avoiding him. He wasn't unpleasant and there were times she felt guilty for hiding from him, but those moments were brief. She simply wasn't attracted to him and she didn't want to find herself the victim of a political marriage.

She'd always wanted to marry for love.

It was a fool's dream and she knew that, but Amarantha was a bit of a romantic. She wanted a big, strong knight to sweep her off her feet and carry her away to a fantastic castle where they would live on love and wine and raise a dozen children.

But that man wasn't Farran.

"I pray for many things," she said after a moment. "I pray for my father, for my mother's soul, for peace in the land. Many things."

"And that makes you happy?"

"Verily."

"Do you pray for your own happiness?" he asked, but quickly clarified. "What I mean is if you pray for a happy future. For the things you want. For a husband and children. Most young women want such things."

Amarantha shook her head. "I would never pray for such things," she said. "It is selfish to ask God for such trivial things, not when there are more important things for his attention."

"Like what?"

"Like peace," she said, looking at him. "Talgarth is a military castle and you have a big army. You have seen many battles, have you not?"

He shrugged. "Aye," he said. "But that is the nature of our world. If God did not want us to fight one another, he would not give us armies and weapons."

"Man makes armies. And weapons are made by men."

He grinned. "True enough."

"What do you fight for, if not peace?"

He scratched his red head. "I do fight for peace, but I fight for the king's right to have peace within his own country," he said. "But I also fight if I am attacked."

"Has that happened?"

He nodded. "Aye," he said. "Many times in the history of Talgarth. The Welsh consider it a Welsh castle, you know."

"Then when you repel attacks, you are fighting for the peace of Talgarth."

"When you put it that way, I suppose I am."

"*That* is the peace I pray for. So no one has to fight anymore."

He simply smiled at her. "That is an altruistic outlook and one to be commended," he said. "But the truth is that our country is in turmoil right now, mayhap more than it has ever been. I fear your prayers for peace have not been heard because God wishes for the king to triumph over his rebellious barons. There will be no peace until the king has triumphed."

It was Amarantha's turn to shrug. "So I have heard," she said. "Truthfully, I do not pay attention to the politics that go on. Men can be foolish and petty and unworthy of my attention. I would rather focus on more kind and peaceful endeavors."

"Like what?"

She cocked her head thoughtfully. "Like the children I am

going to teach."

"What children?"

"From the village," she said. "I have spoken to the priests in the village, at St. Mary the Virgin, and we have agreed that once a week I will come to the village and teach the children from the books in my father's collection."

He peered at her curiously. "What collection?"

"The books he brought back from The Levant," she said patiently. "He has chests of them. He has translated many of them from Arabic, which he learned while he was there. Did you not know that about my father? He is a very educated man."

Farran didn't really give her an answer but his expression was bordering on disapproval. "But why should you want to teach the village children about these books?"

"To teach them of another culture, another place," she said. "The world is bigger than Wales and England, Sir Farran. If we understand others, and understand their stories and lives, I believe that makes us more compassionate and understanding. And mayhap it will inspire a village child to travel to Paris or Rome and make something good of his life."

He was still eyeing her as if he didn't quite agree with her but, in the end, he simply shrugged. "Your intentions are very noble," he said. "I do not know of any fine ladies who would take the time to be generous to simple children."

"They are all God's creations," she said. Then she came to an abrupt halt and removed her hand from his elbow. "And here we are at the stables. My new horse is in the very last stall inside. Inspect her and you may tell me what you think later. Right now, I am expected in the kitchens. I have duties that cannot wait."

They were indeed in the stable yard, the smell of straw and animals filling their nostrils. Farran waited until a pair of stable servants had walked past them and out of earshot before speaking.

"I would rather accompany you on your duties," he said quietly. "It seems that every time I come to Mount Grace, you are too busy to speak with me. I promise I will be no trouble if you let me come along."

She frowned. "A man in the kitchens?" she said with great disapproval. "You must be mad."

"I've been in kitchens before."

"But not as part of your duties," she pointed out. "And not following a woman around as she goes about her business. I am afraid I cannot entertain you, Sir Farran. I have things to attend to and cannot carry on a conversation with you."

"I do not care about a conversation. I simply want to see you work."

"Why?"

He cleared his throat softly and averted his gaze. "I should think that would be quite obvious."

Amarantha wasn't going to play games with the man. They were far beyond that, but this was the first time he'd alluded to his intentions. Her first reaction was to run away – swiftly – but she held her ground. Running wasn't going to solve anything.

Perhaps an honest conversation would.

At the risk of making her father unhappy, she was going to say what needed to be said.

"Sir Farran," she said, lowering her voice. "I know that my father wishes a betrothal between us. He has made that quite obvious. He believes I should be wed."

Farran's expression flickered, perhaps with fear and a little embarrassment, as the conversation switched to something deeply personal. He wasn't a personal man by nature, which made this type of conversation very difficult for him.

"I… I think that this is a conversation I should be having with your father," he said.

She peered at him. "But it is a conversation about me," she said. "I should be involved in it, don't you think? It is *my* future we are speaking of."

"That is true, but…"

She waved him off, interrupting him. "Is this how you think a marriage should be, Sir Farran?" she said. "That your wife will have no say in anything, not even your own marriage? If that is the case, then most certainly I am not someone you would want to be married to for I will have a say in my life as well as my husband's. If I do not then that will make my husband miserable because *I* will be miserable."

Farran was actually starting to flush. "Men do not traditionally give their wives any say in certain matters," he said. "But I can understand that a woman should want an opinion on marriage and home. That is natural."

He still seemed reluctant, as if a woman with any opinion at all was an uncommon thing. It began to occur to Amarantha just what kind of marriage the man wanted – a pretty thing on his arm without a voice.

"But she should have an opinion on nothing else?" she said. "Is that really all you would want from a wife, Sir Farran? A woman to stand silently beside you? I find that very disappointing. I thought you would want more than that."

"What more is there?"

Those were key words as far as Amarantha was concerned. Slowly, she shook her head. "A partner," she said. "A friend.

Someone from whom you can seek advice. Someone you trust. Not simply a woman to bear your sons and tend your home. Any servant or mistress can do that. But a wife… she should be much more."

Farran's gaze lingered on her face for a moment before trailing down her body, all the way to her feet. "I cannot imagine more than what I already see," he finally muttered. "You have the face of an angel and the body of a goddess. Does it shock you that I should say such things? You are an exquisite creature, Lady Amarantha. Tales of your beauty abound on the border and if you must know, I do intend to have you. But I am sure that is of no surprise."

"It is not."

"In case you've not yet realized it, I have been attempting to court you but not doing a very good job. You haven't exactly been cooperative."

"And I shan't be so long as you continue to hold those views on marriage," she said. "I intend to be everything to my husband, Sir Farran. If you cannot accept that, then it is best we part as friends."

With that, she turned for the keep, leaving Farran pondering her words, her attitude. Not that he had expected less, for Lady Amarantha had always had strong views on things. He'd never seen such a headstrong female.

Nor, as he'd put it, such an exquisite one.

He watched her walk away, his focus on the sway of her hips as she moved. Truly, there was nothing like her anywhere on the border or anywhere in England, Wales, or Scotland for that matter. Lady Amarantha de la Haye was in a completely different category when compared to other women. She stood about five feet in height, with a lovely round face and big, brown eyes with a slight tilt to them. Her nose was pert and her lips were like a rosebud, all of those features framed by glossy brown hair she kept pulled away from her face. She did indeed look like an angel.

But it was her figure that had his attention.

There wasn't one man who had ever met Lady Amarantha who hadn't stared in awe at her womanly figure. She had big, full breasts, a tiny waist, and flaring hips that gave her a magnificently curvaceous figure. She wasn't flat or shapeless like some women, but full of curves and flesh that a man could lustfully lose himself in.

Truthfully, that was the allure for him. It wasn't that she was docile or obedient, because she wasn't, as she'd just demonstrated. It was that she was the finest woman he'd ever seen and he wanted to be the one to lay claim to that body. Beyond that… well, he'd have to put up with the disobedience and the need to have an "opinion". For a taste of her flesh, he was willing.

And he was willing to be patient about it.

He turned for the stables, off to inspect her new palfrey.

CHAPTER TWO

"REPEAT EVERYTHING TO me, Morgan," Christopher said. "Repeat it to me so I know there is no doubt in your mind what must occur."

They'd already been through this, several times, since that fateful meeting at The Pox those months ago. Morgan had been schooled and trained and repeatedly schooled on Mount Grace and everything about it, including the family that now held the castle. Every single detail of the House of le Marche had been seared into his brain and everything about Mount Grace in general had been fed to him until he was overflowing with it.

Now, the moment was swiftly approaching and he had to know his role.

He'd been working hard enough for it.

"My mother's name is Patience and my wife's name is Phoebe," he said, his voice low and steady as the horses plodded along a road that was swampy from recent rains. "My father was Sir Oliver le Marche, Lord Glanhen. He was born at Mount Grace, the eldest of three sons, to Sir Declan le Marche and his wife, Lady Olive. His youngest brother, Stephen, died in infancy and is buried at Mount Grace in the kitchen yard because he died in the winter and the ground was too frozen anywhere else but near the large cooking fire in the yard. His middle brother was…"

"No more lineage," Christopher grunted, cutting him off. "I've heard you go through it for the past two months and you know it well enough. Tell me about your mother and wife."

Morgan didn't hesitate. "My mother is from the House of de Hardwicke, an only child to Douglas and Maud," he said. "She married Oliver when she was seventeen years of age and I was born a year later in the spring, towards the end of April. I had a younger brother, Gregory, who died when John's troops overtook Mount Grace."

"What happened to Gregory's body?"

"I do not know," Morgan said. "We were forced to leave him behind. It was save my mother or collect my brother's body and I chose my mother."

"Excellent," Christopher said. "Do you remember the day in detail?"

"Down to the last raindrop."

"And your wife?"

"Phoebe and I met when her father came to do business at Mount Grace several years ago. He was a merchant from Ghent, the House of Destel." He paused, glancing at Christopher. "Phoebe le Marche *does* know of this scheme, correct?"

Christopher nodded patiently. "Of course she does. She was not at Mount Grace when the siege happened," he said. "So does Patience. De Velt personally explained the situation to them and they are not only agreeable, they are eager. Your arrival means a chance at regaining their home, so you will have their full cooperation."

"What of the men who gathered the Irish army for le Marche?"

"These men are all back in Ireland," Christopher said. "There is no one here to give you away. You have the name of the mercenary commander and that is all you need. That is all Gere had. He paid The Marshal's men to raise the army and was to meet them when they arrived in Wales."

Morgan sighed, looking on ahead at the soggy road and the village in the distance. It had rained the night before and the clouds still hung in the sky, obscuring visibility somewhat. They were nearing Mount Grace and he turned to see Jax riding off to their left astride a warhorse that had red eyes. *Flaming* red eyes. Or, more than likely, black eyes that only seemed as if they were flaming.

The Dark Lord could ride nothing else.

But Morgan was uneasy. He had been since this entire mission was dumped in his lap, but he kept that nervousness well-hidden. It wouldn't help him to show that uneasiness and give himself away. As far as he was told, no one would recognize that he wasn't Gere le Marche save former le Marche men and no one seemed to know how many there were. To combat this, the men that Jax had sent to the mines were under orders to seek out the le Marche men that had remained and determine their loyalties. They were under orders to kill those men who were loyal to John for fear of those men giving Morgan away. Everything was predicated on the men of Mount Grace believing Gere le Marche had returned and they'd done their best to make Morgan look as similar to le Marche as possible, down to the dark beard he now wore and the shoulder-length hair. The Marshal, who had known le Marche, had selected Morgan for this task because he bore some resemblance to the man, but it wasn't a perfect match. Close, but not perfect.

Then there was the garrison commander.

"Tell me about John's commander." Christopher spoke up as if he could read Morgan's mind. "Tell me what you know."

Morgan continued. "His name is Hollis de la Haye," he said. "The king granted him the title of Lord Craswell, and Craswell Castle to go with it, and he and his daughter live at Mount Grace."

Christopher turned to look at him. "Do you know de la Haye?"

"Nay, I've not met him."

Christopher's gaze returned to the road. "He is a staunch supporter of John," he said. "He was a lesser knight who worked his way up through John's ranks using ruthless tactics. Killing his commanders or disabling other knights, anyone he viewed as competition. He moved himself into a position of power and when John took Mount Grace, he gave the command to de la Haye."

"That is what The Marshal said," Morgan replied. "He is someone to be careful with."

"He will kill you if he discovers who you are," Christopher said bluntly. "Make no mistake, Morgan – if de la Haye discovers your assumed identity, he will kill you without hesitation. As Gere le Marche, you can destroy everything he has. He knows that. That is why once you meet the man, you must give him another name."

Morgan sighed faintly. "I am pretending to be Gere le Marche for the benefit of the mercenaries, yet when I meet Hollis, I must pretend to be someone else so he does not know I've assumed Gere's identity," he said. Then, he shook his head. "This is quite complex."

"Complex but necessary," Christopher said. "De la Haye must not know of the identity you have assumed and the mercenaries must only know you as le Marche. But most importantly, you can never be Morgan de Wolfe. That would tie you directly to Wolverhampton and Pembroke and everyone would know that The Marshal was behind this."

Morgan nodded. "I know," he said. "The Marshal was quite clear about everything. We have determined a plan of action and I am to stay to it. We will begin with the tavern next to the river, the one owned by Lady le Marche in the village of Bronllys near Mount Grace. It's called The Three Cocks and it's right on the crossroads. We can watch the comings and the goings from the castle from there."

"And then what?"

"I am to make contact with the priests at St. Mary the Virgin," Morgan continued. "They are Marshal allies and will help me with my task. In fact, I am supposed to be the cousin of one of them. That will be my identity when I meet de la Haye."

"*And?*"

"And I am to make contact with The Marshal's men who have sought employment at the mine," he said. "They have been in touch with the priests, so I'm told, so likely that contact will come through them."

"That is crucial," Christopher said. "Their objective is to rally support for Gere and to help the Irish integrate into the mining colony."

"But I must make contact with them first."

"Precisely," Christopher said. "They've been waiting south of Mount Grace for well over two months. The Marshal sent them word on behalf of Gere le Marche asking them to wait for him, but you must assess the situation at Mount Grace quickly before bringing in the Irish. That is the second part in this overall plan that must be executed flawlessly."

Morgan nodded. "I know," he said. "I understand the seriousness of it."

"Make sure you do."

"If I fail, I die. Trust me when I tell you that I do."

Christopher looked at him. "We are sending you help, Morgan," he said, his voice considerably less authoritative than it had been moments earlier. "I do not want you to think we are throwing you into the lion's den and leaving you to sink or swim by yourself. You will not be alone in this, so keep an eye out for men you know."

"Agents?"

"Indeed."

"May I know who is coming?"

"I am not entirely sure myself," Christopher said. "There are men who have been sent on ahead to infiltrate those in the mine. They will find you when it is safe. But there are still others coming to Bronllys to support you. The Marshal made the arrangements, so simply keep an eye out for men you know. That is all I can tell you."

"Then I shall be vigilant."

There wasn't much more to say after that. Christopher, Morgan, Jax, and about three hundred de Velt men had been riding east from Gloucester. Christopher was heading home, only stopping long enough to leave Morgan off at Bronllys. Jax, too, was heading north to his holdings outside of Mount Grace at the personal request of The Marshal to monitor the situation along with Christopher. Two great warlords with their eyes on a de Wolfe.

Edward de Wolfe's nephew.

That made it personal for Christopher. He and Edward, the Earl of Wolverhampton, had been friends since the days of their youth. They had served in The Levant together and for a time, Edward had served Christopher personally. Therefore, they were quite close and Christopher didn't take this mission involving Edward's nephew lightly.

He had a personal stake in it.

Morgan was walking into the lion's den.

But Christopher had observed something about Morgan over the past two months, mostly the fact that he was obedient to a fault, but also the fact that he was smarter than any man in the room but he didn't boast about it. He kept that to himself, working out a situation and coming up with a solution that almost invariably would work. That would work well in his favor, but the risk was that he would eventually become too arrogant about it and tip his hand. Christopher didn't think that would be the case, but there was something about Morgan that implied he was bigger, smarter, and far more skilled than the biggest, smartest, and most skilled man in the room. If de la Haye was as ruthless as rumor had it, Morgan would have to be careful around the man.

But he was also more than a match.

Truth be told, The Marshal wanted Morgan to befriend de la Haye, possibly to pave the way for de la Haye to trust him, but Christopher wasn't sure that was a good idea.

Too much about this mission was uncharted.

"Vigilant and cautious," Christopher said after a moment. "Morgan, I believe you are the only man who could adequately accomplish this task. The agents of William Marshal are a diverse and powerful group so I do not make that declaration lightly, but you have many factors that make you perfect for this job. You are also a de Wolfe and I believe you will prevail. I've never known a de Wolfe to fail at anything."

Morgan wasn't sure he was comforted by that. There was always a first – a first failure, in this case. He didn't want to be the one to disgrace his family, something that had been eating at him since The Marshal first proposed this mission.

"There are great expectations put upon a man with a name like mine," he admitted. "I have several male cousins and we all speak of the same thing – how we are all expected to excel in every aspect, although I will say that my Uncle Edward's youngest son seems to be the ne'er-do-well in the family. I do not think expectations for him will be so high."

Christopher looked at him. "William?"

Morgan grinned. "Aye," he said. "You've met him?"

"I have," Christopher said. "And I've heard stories. Your uncle is pulling his hair out over a lad that gambles and fights and God only knows what else. But The Marshal says he's the most genius de Wolfe of all and can't wait to get his hands on him."

Morgan laughed softly. "Unfortunately, I would agree that he is a genius," he said. "I've never seen anything like it, at least for one so young. He can fight like a fully commissioned knight, can give commands in battle that grown men will follow, and has a mind that works in great and mysterious ways."

"In other words, he's terrifying."

Morgan continued to laugh. "Indeed," he said. "He's the youngest of all of the cousins, you know. My father and his brothers had male children except for two of the kids, my cousins Meredith and Cecily, and William is the youngest of all of them. He's had to learn to be cunning and assertive against older relatives. Truthfully, you should have sent William to complete this task. He'd do it better than anyone could."

Christopher grinned at the thought of the precocious twelve-year-old boy who was as big as a grown man. "William will have his day," he said. "If he lives that long."

Morgan wasn't hard-pressed to agree. "True," he said. Then his smile faded. "I hope I live to see that day."

"You will," Christopher said confidently. He noticed they were drawing closer to the village and the clouds were beginning to lift, giving a hint at Mount Grace in the distance, and he motioned Jax forward. "We are going to leave you off to go on ahead alone very shortly. Jax, do you have anything to add that hasn't already been said?"

Jax reined his warhorse close by but not too close because of the animal's tendency to throw his big head around.

"I do," he said. "I have been listening to everything said and it is clear that de Wolfe understands the gravity of this situation."

Morgan nodded. "I do, my lord."

Jax pulled off his great helm, propping it on the horn of his saddle as he looked between Christopher and Morgan. His gaze eventually settled on Christopher.

"What you do not know is that The Marshal has given me instructions to lay siege to Mount Grace should young de Wolfe fail," he said pointedly. He watched Christopher's brow furrow in confusion. "He wants the castle at any cost, Chris. Should Morgan fail, I am instructed to march my army into Wales and take Mount Grace by any means necessary. That means The Dark Lord's tactics will be utilized against the king's troops. It means I will leave a standing army of fleshy scarecrows from Mount Grace all the way to the English border, which will send a message to John. The Marshal didn't want you involved,

Chris. Your relationship with John is strained enough without taking Mount Grace. But me… well, I can do anything I want and John will think twice before contesting it."

Christopher understood, mostly, but he was still peeved that he hadn't been privy to Jax's private orders. After a moment, he sighed heavily.

"Thank you for telling me about your plans before I had to hear about it from some passing merchant," he said. "Am I allowed to ride to your aid should it come to that?"

"Nay," Jax said flatly. "If you do that, you give John an excuse to attack Lioncross."

Christopher grunted. "He is going to do it, anyway," he muttered. "With all of the mercenaries he's bringing into England, he's going to do it at some point."

"Then let us not hasten anything. You moving into Wales to confiscate an important royal property might bring about the end sooner than you think."

Christopher couldn't disagree. His gaze trailed off to the landscape, the green and rolling hills that constituted the Welsh Marches. He hadn't been born here, but he'd taken possession of Lioncross Abbey Castle when he'd been a young man, just past his thirtieth year. In all of his years on the Marches, he'd learned to love it as if he'd been born to it. He controlled most of the mid-to-southern portion of the Marches with his mighty army and garrisons, so he was quite protective of the region.

After a moment, he simply shook his head.

"Then let us hope this scheme has the desired end result," he finally said. "Morgan is successful, Mount Grace is in the hands of The Marshal, and we can breathe a little easier knowing that John is not anchored in Wales any more than he already is."

Jax nodded faintly. He finally held up a big hand, slowing down the escort behind them, and the entire group ground to a halt.

They'd come to a crossroads.

"You head west," Christopher told Morgan. "Once you get to the village, find The Three Cocks. Be discreet. Remember that no one knows Lady le Marche's true identity, so you'll have to be careful. As far as anyone knows, you are simply the long-lost husband of Lady Phoebe, so behave accordingly. You will send reports to Jax at Cloryn Castle on a regular basis."

Morgan nodded, looking to de Velt. "I will send them at least once a month, if not more," he said. "If you do not hear from me for a couple of months, you must assume that something has happened."

Jax nodded. "Remember that The Marshal is sending men to help you," he said. Then, he paused, looking the knight over. "You are not alone, de Wolfe, but in a sense, you are *all* alone. Everything hinges on you. Stay true to your training, your instincts, and you will succeed."

"I will not fail, my lord."

There was nothing more to say. With a lingering look to Jax and then Christopher, Morgan reined his horse around and headed off west, off towards the village in the distance. Jax and Christopher watched him go, blending in with the mist now and again as it lifted from the wet, crisp fields.

"Well?" Jax said, turning to look at Christopher. "We have done all we can. He has been indoctrinated as much as he can be. The rest is up to him."

Christopher nodded, watching Morgan in the distance. "Christ, I hope he succeeds," he muttered. "I should not like to tell Edward de Wolfe that I sent his nephew off to his death.

More than that, I've been around him enough over the past couple of months to see that he has a mark of greatness about him. Truly, there is something special about him that just hasn't had a chance to fully develop yet."

Jax grunted. "Now is his time, Chris," he said, lifting an enormous arm to get the men behind him moving. "If there is greatness in him, it will emerge. As The Marshal said – this is his defining moment. We all have them. We should know in a few months if Morgan rises to his. But I will say one thing."

"What's that?"

"I am very glad I am not in his shoes."

Christopher didn't reply. Jax's comment didn't help his sense of foreboding. He didn't know why he was so worried about Morgan when he should not have been. It wasn't like he'd known the knight forever or that the man had served him. He wasn't a relative. But he was his dear friend Edward's relative and perhaps that's why he found himself angsty.

The great unknown they were all facing.

And the reclamation of Mount Grace that was going to be anything but simple.

CHAPTER THREE

The Three Cocks
Bronllys, Wales

H E COULD HEAR the singing all the way down the street.

In the village of Bronllys, Morgan was intent on memorizing everything he came across – cottages, businesses, gardens, two corrals – everything. He was supposed to know this village, as Gere le Marche, so he wandered down a couple of alleys, getting the lay of the land, before heading into the main part of town on the lookout for The Three Cocks.

As he entered the village square, he could hear singing coming from the other end of the main avenue. There was only one main street with several offshoot roads and alleys, but the main street was crowded with people mostly going about their business. A few were just standing around, chatting, paying some attention to the stranger who'd come into town astride a big, gray work horse. In truth, the horse was a very old warhorse loaned to him by Christopher, but the beast had seen better days. It just looked like a giant, weary horse.

Perfect for Morgan's purposes.

The singing was growing louder. As Morgan neared the other end of the town, one that was close to the road that led out towards Mount Grace, he could see a church off to the southeast. It was somewhat small but sturdily made, with big granite blocks and a square steeple. It was squat and tough-looking, as a structure must be on the Welsh Marches where men were free with their rebellion and battles.

The little church looked as if it were preparing for a fight.

Morgan's gaze lingered on the church, knowing that was where he needed to go in order to find the priests who were allied with The Marshal. But his focus inevitably moved towards the rather sizable tavern that was almost directly across from the churchyard, hearing the singing coming from within. Taverns and inns were required to have a sign posted to identify them by name, so Morgan fully expected to see three roosters on a board, painted on or burned on.

What he saw were three erect manhoods, all in a row.

The Three Cocks.

He tried not to grin but couldn't quite manage it. He stared at the cheeky sign for a moment, realizing that the cocks were burned in and then some kind of black paint had been used to make them more visible. If someone was looking for The Three Cocks tavern, they wouldn't be mistaken. It was abundantly clear.

"God's Bones," he muttered to himself.

He chuckled, allowing himself to enjoy the humor of the moment, before quickly suppressing the impulse. He was here on a serious matter and didn't want to walk into the establishment tied up in giggles. There was another sign for the livery, pointing down a narrow alley, and as he turned for the alleyway, he could hear the words to the song, being sung quite loudly.

"… and the wife said,
Tried and true, 'till yer balls turn blue,
I'll deny ye the touch of my lips.
But show me yer purse,
And I'll deny ye the curse,
I swear by the slap of my arse!"

Those singing the song were having a wild time, laughing and cheering as the next chorus came about. Morgan had heard the song before, a bawdy tavern song that he'd sung enough times with his own friends. He'd even heard it sung at The Pox once or twice – probably more knowing that crowd – so it wasn't anything terrible or shocking. Simply another tavern song that oddly made him feel at ease.

But he didn't want to feel too at ease.

He was here for a reason.

Taking his steed around back, he paid a skinny stable boy to water and feed the animal and bed it down for the night. He removed his baggage as the horse was led away, making sure to pick up some dirt and straw and rubbing it on himself before entering the rear of the tavern. He was dressed in a tunic and canvas breeches, looking simple enough, but he wanted to look more like he belonged with the pack that inhabited an establishment with three penises on the door. Truth be told, however, he felt positively naked. Knights of his caliber didn't go anywhere without their protection, so he was without any of his expensive armor and feeling quite uncomfortable about it.

But the sword with the wolf's head hilt was buried in the big satchel he held in one hand. That was a concession he wasn't willing to make, leaving it behind, but if anyone asked him, he was going to tell them he stole it off a dead man. Being within a two days' ride of Wolverhampton, however, he wondered if there would be men about to recognize the de Wolfe hilt. He knew he was taking a chance bringing the weapon, as it was a high-end weapon meant for a knight, but he simply couldn't part with it. He'd never been without it.

And he hoped he wouldn't need it.

Entering through the rear of the establishment, he was hit by the smell of urine. The place smelled like the streets of London where people relieved themselves and didn't think twice about it. Everything about the tavern smelled like piss, but that wasn't something that disturbed Morgan like it did some men. It was a usual smell for a usual place and as he stood at the mouth of the common room, he could see the group of singers clustered by the hearth. They'd moved on from the song about blue balls to another lively tune called Tilly Nodden.

It was a crowded place, for certain. The clientele seemed to be fairly innocuous but Morgan didn't lose himself in the crowd. He was looking for the woman who owned the place, one Patience le Marche, who was going by the name of Madam Iris. No one knew her true identity so as a serving wench came near, Morgan grasped the woman's arm and asked for Madam Iris.

The wench pointed to the kitchens.

Morgan headed in the direction indicated, finding himself in a low-ceilinged, hot and moist chamber with two big ovens. A woman with a dirty wimple on her head was shouting at a man who was taking nearly burned bread loaves from one of the ovens. When she caught a glimpse of Morgan standing in the doorway, she turned her red face in his direction.

"Out with you!" she scolded, waving her hands at him. "Get out. You'll get no service back here."

Morgan didn't move. "Are you Madam Iris?"

The woman was still waving her hands but she grabbed a broom to perhaps whack him with it. "I am," she said. "Who wants to know?"

Morgan's gaze upon her was intense. He'd been instructed to reply with one word and one word only.

"Gere."

The woman was in mid-shout but suddenly froze. Her eyes widened and, for a moment, she simply stared at him. She seemed taken aback but only for a brief second.

"Say again?" she said.

"Gere."

Wiping at her sweating face with her apron, she brushed past him. "I'll tend to you," she muttered. "Come with me."

Morgan did. The tavern was one level, not particularly wide, but it was deep. Madam Iris used the keys secured at her waist to open a heavy locked door and ushered Morgan inside. She followed him, locking the door behind her, before beckoning him to follow her down a narrow, leaning corridor until they reached a door at the end. It was locked and she used her collection of keys to open it. Only when they were safely inside, the door locked behind them, and a candle hastily lit did she turn and face him.

"He said you would come," she said, sounding quite different from the shrieking woman in the kitchen. "William Marshal has sent you."

Morgan nodded. "Aye," he said. "I am Gere le Marche."

The woman held the candle up, getting a closer look at him. "You do look a little like him," she said, her features softening.

"You have his dark hair. But you're much bigger than he was."

"Who?"

"My Gere."

That established things clearly and Morgan set his baggage on the floor. "May we speak freely?"

Madam Iris nodded eagerly. "Please," she said. "I have been waiting a very long time for this moment. Speak all you wish. There is no one to hear us."

Morgan faced her. "You know why I am here."

"I do."

"Good," he said. "Because I have many questions that need answers. For example, what you just said – that I am bigger than your son was. That very thing has been concerning me since the beginning of this task. Are there not people around here that knew him and will realize I am not him? The Marshal said your son was reclusive, but surely he did not live in a hole. How are we to account for this change in appearance?"

Madam Iris motioned him over to the table in the room and its two small chairs. She indicated for him to sit in one chair as she took the other.

"Gere's reclusiveness was partially my fault. I was reclusive, as well. I never left the castle until I was forced to after the siege. That's why no one knows who I am. Gere lived in the shadows after the siege at Mount Grace," she said quietly. "He feared for his life, feared that he would be recognized, and that he would end up the king's prisoner. As the heir to Mount Grace, he was the key to all that was valuable. He was terrified that John would somehow capture him, so he did indeed live secretively. Only a few knew him on sight and they will not betray you."

There was some logic in those words that Morgan understood. "I hope not," he said. "Even if your son lived in hiding, you live in the open. Why are you not afraid of the king?"

Madam Iris shrugged. "Because I am not the heir," she said simply. "No one pays attention to an old woman. At first, there were soldiers who recognized me and they asked me where my son was, but I told them that he was dead. I do not know if they believed me, but those questions were enough to keep Gere in hiding."

"Yet he went to see William Marshal."

"Out of sheer desperation, I assure you."

Morgan understood. Desperation could force a man to risk himself in such ways. "So he paid Marshal men to recruit an Irish army for him and retreated back here to hide," he said. "And his wife? Where is she?"

Madam Iris closed her eyes for a brief moment as if to ward off the pain that question provoked. "Dead," she said softly. "In childbirth, attempting to bring forth a new heir."

Morgan digested that for a moment. Not that the death of the wife changed the overall mission. In fact, it eliminated one less complication. But there were many others to take its place in a scheme that was full of such things.

"I am sorry for your loss," he said. "But I must ask you about the remaining le Marche men at Mount Grace. It has been five years since it was captured by John. Surely any remaining men are completely loyal to the crown by now."

Madam Iris shook her head. "You would think so, but that is not the case," she said. "My lord, we have been waiting years for this moment, to regain what was stolen from us. My dearest lad did not live to see it, which is why I sent word to William Marshal about his death. Gere's cause must not die. He was to lead the Irish into the mines where hundreds of le Marche men are waiting, used as conscripts by the king. Five long years of waiting and planning. Believe me when I tell you that they are ready to be led in battle against John's men and that terrible Hollis de la Haye."

"But they will know I am not Gere."

She shrugged. "Much can happen in five years," she said. "A man can change physically. He can grow a beard and his hair can grow longer. He can eat well and grow bigger. Some may not even remember what he looks like, for Gere traveled much and was not often at Mount Grace in his younger years. It was his father who led the army. But even if some realize you are not Gere, they will follow you regardless. With you lies our salvation."

She sounded so desperate. Morgan eyed her for a moment. "Then you think my assuming his identity will work?"

Madam Iris nodded. "It will certainly work with the Irish that Gere had paid to come," she said. "As for the men in the mines... Father Nicodemus would know better than I."

"I am to contact the priests at St. Mary the Virgin."

"*Priest*," Madam Iris clarified. "One priest. Father Nicodemus. He was my husband's personal priest. He has been in touch with the men in the mines and he knows what they are thinking. He has told them that help is coming to free them from their forced servitude. But there is something I do not understand."

"What is that?"

"When I told The Marshal of Gere's death, it was to inform him that the fight for Mount Grace was lost," she said. "But he would not accept that. I did not ask him to send someone to replace my son. That was his own idea. Why should he replace my son with you and not simply send a big army to take the castle by force?"

Morgan smiled thinly. "Madam, if you understand anything about the politics of England, then you must understand that William Marshal cannot move against John," he said. "He wants Mount Grace but he does not want John to know he is behind the quest to regain it. That is why I must assume your son's identity – for all anyone will know, Gere le Marche took back his birthright."

"But The Marshal will put an ally in charge of the castle?"

"Aye," Morgan said. "More than likely Ajax de Velt. John would think twice before trying to take the castle back from de Velt."

It all made sense, the politics of England like a giant chess game. One move brought a counter move and so on. In this case, William Marshal was going for checkmate on the Welsh Marches.

And Morgan was going to make sure it happened.

"So long as I am allowed to live out the rest of my life in my husband's castle," Madam Iris said softly. "Do you think de Velt will allow it?"

"I am sure of it."

That seemed to bring the old woman a good deal of comfort. Now that the conversation was concluded and the stakes of the situation were laid bare, she stood up from her chair.

"You must be tired and hungry," she said. "This was Gere's chamber, which is why there are so many locks, so this shall be your chamber. I would suggest you eat and rest and then tomorrow, you will go to the church and find Father Nicodemus. He will have already retired for the evening, so you will have to wait until morning."

Morgan had to admit that after such a long journey, an early night was appealing. He looked over the chamber, the comfortable bed, the overflowing wardrobe, and the table that was covered with vellum, inkwells, and quill. It occurred to him that this was the last sight of a man who should have died in the home of his birthright.

Morgan could only imagine how that must have felt. He was the eldest son, with three younger brothers, and his father's holding actually came through his mother, who had been the heiress to the Barony of Cheslyn, a fairly large piece of property south of Wolverhampton. The barony would be Morgan's when his father passed on.

Somehow, seeing the reality of where Gere le Marche had spent his final days put all of it into perspective for him. If John stole the Cheslyn barony, Morgan would do all he could to regain it… or die trying.

Like Gere did.

"Thank you for the conversation, Madam Iris," he said. "I will see the priest tomorrow and we shall move forward with Gere's plans. It is unfortunate that he did not live to see the reclamation of Mount Grace, but I will do all I can to ensure you see out your final days there."

Madam Iris put her hand on his arm, a timid touch. "Please," she said. "Will you call me Patience in private?"

"If you wish."

"May I know your true name?"

"It would be better if you did not."

"Please. I cannot call you Gere."

He hesitated a moment. "Morgan," he finally said. "My name is Morgan."

She gave his arm a brief squeeze before letting go. "Bless you, Morgan," she murmured. "You and William Marshal. May God be on our side."

With that, she pulled out her keys again, pulled the one for the chamber door off the ring, and handed it over to Morgan. She fled the room, disappearing down the darkened corridor and through the door which could be locked from the inside without a key. He heard her lock it from the outside, leaving him in a dead man's chamber, preparing for what would be a full day on the morrow.

May God be on our side.

Morgan hoped that, most fervently.

CHAPTER FOUR

St. Mary the Virgin

"...aND THE KING lived in a great cedar forest," Amarantha said dramatically to a group of wide-eyed children. "The forest was full of *simius*, who protected the king from those who wished to do him harm. He had an entire army of little creatures prepared to do his bidding. Do you remember what I told you about *simius*?"

The children, and there were about twelve of them in the sanctuary of the old church, eagerly raised their hands. Smiling, Amarantha pointed to a small boy in the front row.

"Eggert?" she said. "What can you tell me?"

The little boy was missing most of his front teeth and had blond hair that stuck up like straw, but he grinned enthusiastically. "They come from far away," he said. "They have hair on their bodies and they live in trees. Ancient people had them as pets."

Amarantha turned the book in her hands around so the children could see the illustrations in the margins of *simius*, or monkeys, something she was teaching them about on this day.

Monkeys that were climbing trees, shooting bows and arrows, dining with rabbits, and generally making mischief on all the margins of the exquisite manuscript.

And the children loved every inch of it.

The book was from Hollis' cache of manuscripts that he'd collected over the years. As a young knight on crusade, his collection started when he'd raided the compound of a wealthy merchant who was supplying money and arms to the Muslim armies. Hollis had been with a group of several Christian knights who had broken into the compound, killed the servants and anyone else who got in their way, and absconded with what they could carry. In Hollis' case, it was manuscripts and treatises.

His love of such things began there.

It didn't matter how Hollis obtained things for his collection, only that he did. He broke into monasteries and while traveling home from The Levant, he broke into villas of the wealthy in Rome and along the coast. If there were manuscripts or bound books, he would take them, so much so that by the time he arrived in England, he had several donkeys traveling with him who were carrying his burdens. He treated his ill-gotten gains better than most people treated beloved members of their family, but the result was the largest collection of books, manuscripts, and treatises on the Marches if not the whole of England.

And Amarantha had grown up with all of it.

Her father had taught her to read at an early age and by the time most well-bred young women were just learning something about poetry and literature, Amarantha could recite many tales verbatim. The particular book that Amarantha had on this day was an ancient story from the sands beyond The Levant, in an ancient land of two rivers, where magical temples rose out of the golden landscape that had once housed gods. It was the story of a traveler and his friend on a hunt for a king, who lived in a cedar forest that was protected by monkeys. The manuscript was lavishly painted and the village children were enthralled with the pictures. But Amarantha was teaching them with a purpose – they were learning to spell ten words on this day, one of them being *simius*.

Several children were already scratching it out in the dirt of the sanctuary. One little boy was even drawing the monkeys, mimicking what he'd seen in the book. All the while, Amarantha continued to read from the pages while a small, older man in well-worn woolen robes hovered about, listening to the lesson, helping the children with their spelling. It was true that these were all village children – offspring of smithies and merchants and the like – and needing to know how to spell *simius* wasn't exactly something they could use in their everyday life. But it was all part of teaching them Latin aside from what was in the bible, and how to write, and that there were people beyond the shores of England. That was much more than many children of the nobility were taught and the only reason the priest allowed it was because he felt it was important to teach the children compassion and understanding that way.

Even peasant children.

Fortunately, it was an excitable and eager group. They had sticks and were writing their letters in the dirt as Amarantha read aloud to them. The little boy drawing the monkeys began drawing trees and flowers, too. He was talented. Amarantha stopped reading long enough to praise his skill, scolding another child as he tried to erase it all out of jealousy. A fight nearly broke out but she managed to defuse it by telling the children to write a passage from the book in the dirt.

Omnes fratres mei.

All men are my brothers.

That quieted them down as they began to carefully write the letters. Father Nicodemus stopped pacing at that point, leaning over the children to watch their work.

"It is improving, is it not?" Amarantha asked him. When he looked at her curiously, she indicated the scribbles in the dirt. "Their writing. It is improving."

Father Nicodemus nodded. "Verily, my lady," he said. "The children are learning quickly but they could not do it without your patience and your father's books. You will again thank him for his generosity."

Amarantha smiled. "He is happy to do it," she said. "He feels that teaching these children stories about monkeys and men in faraway lands will make them want to join armies and fight these men. I do not tell him that we teach them to show compassion instead."

Father Nicodemus smiled faintly. "Even though that very book says that all men are brothers?"

"Brothers in arms, my father thinks."

Father Nicodemus snorted softly. "Such is the mind of a fighting man," he said. "We are teaching these children tolerance and he thinks we are teaching them *in*tolerance."

"That sums up the situation nicely."

"What will happen when he discovers the truth?"

Amarantha shrugged. "I will tell him that I have no intention of teaching children hatred," she said. "My father and I do not share the same views on things. Surely you have realized that."

Father Nicodemus nodded. "Indeed, some time ago," he said. "I have known Hollis de la Haye since he came into possession of Mount Grace. He is not a man of great patience or understanding. I am surprised that he tolerates your opinions."

Amarantha sighed faintly, looking back to the children. "He will tolerate me as long as he thinks he can make an advantageous marriage," she said. "After that, I will be my husband's problem and he will wipe his hands of me."

"Sir Farran?"

Amarantha rolled her eyes at something the entire village of Bronllys was aware of. "I am sure my father would be very happy about that," she said. "Farran is a nice man, but I do not want to marry him. I do not want to marry anyone right now."

"It is your duty to marry, my lady," Father Nicodemus reminded her. "All finely bred young women must marry and have as many children as possible. Be fruitful and multiply, says God. Marriage pleases Him."

Amarantha looked at him, then. "You sound like my father."

"Your father is right."

Amarantha geared up to scold the priest with whom she was good friends, but she couldn't quite muster the outrage. He was right and they both knew it. Father Nicodemus was like the annoying but lovable older brother she never had, a platonic relationship that involved the realm of a love of books and good horses and nothing more. Father Nicodemus was a man who had sworn off material wealth, but the truth was that he'd been born into a noble family so he understood the finer things in life.

Even if he wasn't able to experience them personally.

"He is," she said after a moment, sounding resigned. "And I

should like to marry, someday, but just not at this moment."

"Why not?"

"Because I like my life the way it is," she said. "I wish to keep teaching the children. If I marry, then I must manage my husband's home and have my own children. I will have no time for my charity."

Father Nicodemus had a glimmer of a smile on his lips. "I am certain Sir Farran will wait for you," he said. "He seems quite smitten with you."

"How would you know that?"

"Because he is at Mount Grace weekly. I am not daft."

Amarantha frowned at him but she couldn't quite sustain it, so she turned away before he saw her grin. "Nay, you are not daft," she said. "But you are intrusive. May I continue with my lessons?"

She heard the priest snort. "By all means."

As Amarantha glanced at him, a smirk on her lips, Father Nicodemus broke out in a grin and, clasping his hands behind his back, began to meander around again and inspect the spelling of the pupils as Amarantha resumed reading from the book. As Father Nicodemus bent over the boy with the straw-like hair, he noticed a figure entering the church. It was hours from the next mass so he turned to see who had come.

All he could see was an enormous, dark shadow back by the entry.

Curious, he moved in that direction.

The drone of Amarantha's voice faded as he moved towards the doors, which were partially open. The day was bright outside, and white light streamed in through the gap, but the interior of the church was cool and dim in the recesses away from the altar.

He approached the figure.

"I am Father Nicodemus," he said, purposely introducing himself so the dark figure might think twice if he'd come to rob him. "May I be of assistance, my lord?"

The figure didn't move, but when it spoke, the voice was deep and rumbling.

"Madam Iris has sent me," he said, "I have come seeking you, Father Nicodemus."

"Oh?" Father Nicodemus said. "For what purpose?"

"Gere."

"What did you say?"

"*Gere.*"

He dragged the word out, pointedly, and suddenly Father Nicodemus realized what he meant. Like Patience, he knew that word. He knew what it meant and, frankly, he could feel a wave of shock roll through him as the man spoke it quietly. He hadn't expected to hear that name anytime soon.

Gere.

That was the most underground, secretive word he knew.

But perhaps he was reading too much into it. Gere could mean something else – a location, a phrase… anything. He'd sided against King John long before Hollis de la Haye took command of Mount Grace, but even more so after that because he'd been Oliver le Marche's friend as well as his priest. He knew Oliver and Patience and their sons, Gere and Gregory. Oliver and Gregory had perished when John's troops overran Mount Grace, but it was only by a sheer miracle that Gere and Patience had escaped. Father Nicodemus had been very much on Gere's side as he'd worked to reclaim his castle.

He knew all about it.

He knew that Gere had kept himself hidden away, terrified

that John's men would find him and imprison him. Father Nicodemus himself had carried messages to William Marshal's men from Gere, all of it related to raising an army of Irish mercenaries who were supposed to pose as miners. When Gere had died, Father Nicodemus had been fearful that the dream of regaining Mount Grace had died, too, but Patience refused to submit. It was Patience who had sent a missive to William Marshal asking for more help in the wake of Gere's death.

Now, William Marshal had sent it.

But Father Nicodemus had to be sure.

"Are you looking for someone, my son?" he asked. "Is that a man's name?"

The shadowy figure stepped closer, into the dim light, and Father Nicodemus was faced with an enormous man with hazel eyes, dark hair, and a growth of beard around his jaw.

His gaze was intense.

"William Marshal has sent me," he rumbled. "If you are not the man I am supposed to make contact with, then you are breathing your last because I will kill you where you stand."

Father Nicodemus took a step back, putting up a hand in both surrender and silence.

"I am who you seek," he whispered. "But speak quietly. You do not know in whose presence you are and it would not do for her to hear you."

The man's focus lingered on him for a moment before looking to the woman several feet away and the children crowded around her. Morgan quickly understood the implication.

"Who is that?" he asked.

Father Nicodemus turned to look at Amarantha, who was waving one arm like the wing of a bird. "Hollis de la Haye's daughter," he muttered. "That is Lady Amarantha. Now, tell me your name. Your *real* name."

The hazel gaze moved back to him. "Morgan," he said after a moment. "That is all you need to know. For all intents and purposes, I *am* Gere. You understand that."

"I do."

"You have information I seek."

"When the lady has gone, I will tell you everything," Father Nicodemus said. "Go back into the shadow and pretend you are praying. I will hurry her away."

As Morgan wandered over to a pillar that supported the roof and leaned against it, lowering his head and closing his eyes, Father Nicodemus went to the entry door and peered up at the sky before closing it. Then he returned to Amarantha, who was having the children write the Latin word for *bird* in the dirt.

Everyone was scribbling quite happily in the hard-packed earth of the sanctuary, which made an excellent slate. There was some giggling and chatter going on but, for the most part, they were serious and willing students. They would make excellent members of society as adults, learning of the world outside of their own as they were.

Father Nicodemus stood beside Amarantha, watching the group.

"The hour is later than I thought," he said casually. "I believe it is time to come to a close for the day. We will resume the lesson next week."

Amarantha looked somewhat surprised. "It is?" she said. "I did not think I'd been here even an hour."

"Time moves swiftly when you are enjoying yourself."

She grinned in agreement. "True enough," she said. "But Kenan told me he would return for me in an hour. Is he not returned yet?"

She was speaking of her father's knight and captain of Mount Grace's army, Sir Kenan de Poyer. Kenan was the man who made sure all of Mount Grace ran smoothly to Hollis' liking and a more punctual man did not exist. Given that Father Nicodemus knew this, he couldn't very well throw the lady out of the church before her escort arrived.

He smiled weakly.

"Nay," he said. "You may continue until de Poyer arrives. I have tasks to attend to, but I will be nearby should you need me."

Amarantha nodded, returning her focus to the children, as the entry door was pushed open again. Father Nicodemus turned to see if Hollis' knight had arrived, but he only saw two figures enter. Men by the size and dress of them, but he didn't notice more than that. His attention shifted to Morgan, slumped in the shadows. As he moved across the sanctuary towards Morgan to catch the man's attention, the two men who had entered the church intercepted him.

"Are you the priest?" one of them asked.

Impatiently, Father Nicodemus nodded. "I am," he said. "What do you wish?"

"Your coin. And anything else of value."

Father Nicodemus caught the flash of a wicked-looking dagger. Oddly, he wasn't afraid. This kind of thing happened from time to time and he was usually able to talk the would-be robbers out of their heinous intentions. The village of Bronllys was a crossroads between England and Wales so they often had transient men in the village, looking for food or something to steal. He thought ironically that he'd been suspicious of Morgan when the man had first entered, but he'd been wrong.

It was the men he hadn't been suspicious of who were the threat.

"We are a poor parish, my son," he said, lifting his hands to show that he was unarmed. "We have nothing of value here."

The man with the dagger tossed back the hood of his cloak, revealing a missing eye and dark, bushy eyebrows. His companion began to move towards the altar, a skinny man with red hair, as the one-eyed man thrust the dagger in Father Nicodemus' face.

"You won't mind if we look for ourselves, will you?" he said. Unfortunately, he caught sight of Amarantha and the children, who were now realizing something was wrong, and his eyes narrowed. "See there? A fine lady is here. She'll have coin on her."

"That lady has knights with her."

That gave the one-eyed man pause, but only for a moment. Grabbing Father Nicodemus by the neck, he yanked the man towards Amarantha while his companion began to ransack the area around the altar.

Amarantha had been watching the scene unfold with increasing concern. In all the years she'd been visiting St. Mary the Virgin, she'd never once seen any act of violence, unusual considering Bronllys could sometimes be lawless. As the man with the dagger roughly shoved Father Nicodemus towards her, she quickly shut her father's book and tucked it under her arm, hoping the man wouldn't care about something like that. The truth was that it was quite valuable and quite fragile and even if the man took it from her, he probably wouldn't know what he had.

But she hated to lose it.

"Come, children," she hissed at the group. "Quickly – run

away. Run home!"

The children, sensing danger, dropped their sticks and began to scatter. Fortunately, the robbers didn't give the children a second glance and all of them were able to flee unharmed. The robber with the dagger seemed to be far more interested in Amarantha, who was backing away even as the man approached. When he got close enough, he let go of the priest, who fell to his knees, and reached out to grab Amarantha by the arm.

He yanked hard.

"Where's your coin purse, Lady?" he demanded.

The book that Amarantha had been trying to protect flew out of her hands and tumbled to the ground. "Let me go," she hissed, trying to pull away. "Let me go or you shall be severely punished!"

The robber grinned lewdly, dragging his one-eyed gaze up and down her body. Clad in a mustard-yellow garment with a tasseled belt around her impossibly slender waist, there was no mistaking her stunning figure.

"You're a luscious bit of baggage," he said. "I may not stop at your coin purse. What's your name?"

Amarantha continued to struggle with him. "That is none of your affair," she said. "You'll release me if you know what's good for you."

"Release her," Father Nicodemus said as he lurched to his feet. "She has nothing of value. I will show you where I keep the gold, though we do not have much. Let her go and you are welcome to what we have."

It was clear that the robber's focus was now fixed on the exquisite lady in his grasp. He snorted rudely.

"I may have found something more valuable than gold," he

said. "Look at the hills of Venus on this one. Have you ever seen anything so beautiful?"

He was referring to her breasts, which were quite large and pert, most definitely an outstanding feature. The more she tried to pull away, the more he tried to pull her close.

"Be friendly, Lady," he said. "Be friendly and I may go easy on the priest. If you want the man safe, you'll stop fighting me."

He smelled of ale, putrid and stale. Amarantha was terrified that the man was going to try and violate her somehow and she tried desperately to pull away from him. All he did was laugh low in his throat and hold up the dagger between them, his message obvious. Amarantha ended up backing herself into a wall, preparing to kick the man since she couldn't seem to loosen his grip, when something odd happened.

The shadow over by the pillar began to move.

One moment, the shadow had been across the sanctuary and in the next, he was on top of the robber, grabbing the wrist of the hand that held the dagger and using that same dagger to slit the one-eyed man's throat.

Blood splashed onto Amarantha, who gasped in surprise and horror, as the one-eyed man's companion came running over from where he'd been rifling through an alcove. He, too, had a dagger, though a small one, and the man from the shadows easily turned that dagger on the man and he fell dead, a hilt protruding from his chest.

In only a few seconds, the situation was firmly, if not violently, resolved.

Amarantha stood there with blood on her dress and hands, shocked at what had happened. She barely had time to push stray hair from her eyes when the man from the shadows was next to her.

"Are you well, my lady? Did he hurt you?"

Amarantha turned to the man but realized she was looking at his chest. She had to crane her neck back to look him in the face.

And what a face it was.

The man had eyes that were more gold than they were hazel, with a straight nose and square jaw that was embraced by several days' worth of stubble. He was positively enormous, with fists that were as big in circumference as her head. In a world full of pale, average-sized men, the man from the shadows stood out as something much bigger and better than heaven should allow.

He was magnificent.

"I… I'm well," she stammered, feeling like a fool that she'd taken so long to respond. "Thanks to you, I am unharmed. You have my gratitude, my lord."

The man's golden-eyed gaze lingered on her for a moment before looking to her stained dress.

"I am sorry for the mess," he said. "It could not be helped."

Amarantha tore her gaze off him long enough to look down at herself. "My life is a small price to pay for a stain of blood, I assure you," she said, returning her focus to him. "I am not concerned and certainly you should not be, either. You saved my life."

The man's golden eyes glimmered slightly. "If I was of assistance to you, then I am glad to help," he said. "Are you sure you are well? Would you like to sit down? Mayhap Father Nicodemus has some sacramental wine he'll share with you. You've had a fright."

He seemed very concerned, which set Amarantha's heart beating faster than it already was. For a woman who didn't pay much attention to men and certainly didn't want to get married, that was an unusual state for her.

Thump, thump. Thump, thump, THUMP.

The feminine side of her, the one who was just the least bit giddy, saw an opportunity.

God, how foolish I am…

"I am sure I will recover," she said. But as soon as she said it, she put her hand to her forehead and weaved a little. "God's Bones, I suppose I could sit down for a moment. I feel a little… weak."

As she'd hoped, the shadow man was suddenly next to her, putting a massive arm around her waist while the other held her hands to keep her upright.

"Come," he said. "Sit down. Father Nicodemus? A chair, please."

Feeling like a silly, giddy wretch, Amarantha leaned against him and let him carefully lead her in pursuit of Father Nicodemus, who was running to the rear of the church in his quest to find a chair, hissing instructions to a few startled acolytes who had witnessed the attempted robbery. But Amarantha didn't notice. She was completely focused on the shadow man, so powerful that she could feel it in everything about him. He was warm and firm and she liked that very much.

To be held in arms like this was like nothing she'd ever experienced before.

"Truly, I'll be well again quickly," she said. "I do not even know the name of the man who saved my life."

The shadow man hesitated for a moment. "We've not been properly introduced," he said. "It would be rude and forward of me to give you my name."

"I am Amarantha de la Haye," she said without delay. "My

father is Hollis de la Haye, the garrison commander at Mount Grace. There, now we are introduced. What is your name, please?"

He sighed faintly; she could hear it. "My name is Morgan, my lady," he said. "And it is a great pleasure to meet you in spite of the circumstances."

They reached the rear of the sanctuary where Father Nicodemus had a small chair pulled out. Morgan guided her right into the chair, making sure she was steady before letting her go.

That was a sad moment for Amarantha as he released her.

"Morgan," she said, rolling his name over her tongue. "What is your family name?"

"I have no family, my lady. Simply Morgan will do."

She didn't push. "Are you traveling through Bronllys, Morgan?"

"For now," he said. "I have business in the area. And I saw you with your book – were you teaching the children?"

He was deftly deflecting the focus off of him and Amarantha went with it. "Aye," she said. "I come once a week and teach them to read and write. My father has a vast library of books on many different subjects. Do you like to read books, Morgan?"

He nodded. "Indeed," he said. "I had a master, once, who considered himself quite a collector of literature. As a child, I hated being forced to read, but once I became a man, I realized there was nothing finer when it came to expanding the mind."

Amarantha smiled, displaying a spectacular grin with a big dimple in her right cheek. "That is exactly the way I feel," she said. "But only scholars and priests feel that way, so your profession must be either of those. Yet… yet you fight with great skill. Are you a knight?"

A smile tugged at Morgan's lips. "One does not have to be a

knight to ably disarm two fools," he said. "Most men in England have some manner of training with a sword and dagger. I've heard that women have some training, too. Have *you* had such training, my lady?"

Amarantha laughed as she was, once again, successfully diverted off of him as a subject. "The only training I have had are things that most young women are trained on," she said. "I can sew better than any man or challenge him with my painting skills, I suppose."

"Do you paint?"

"Very well, thank you."

Morgan's smile grew. "Then you are a woman of many talents," he said. "I am honored to have made your acquaintance."

Amarantha was smiling openly at him now. "And I, yours," she said. "Will you please come to Mount Grace? I know my father should like to thank you for saving my life. Will you come tonight? You will be our honored guest at the evening's meal."

Morgan couldn't seem to take his eyes off her, swept up by her charm and her sweet voice. The woman was all shades of mesmerizing. However, accepting an invitation to dine with her was, at face value, probably not the smartest thing to do.

Or perhaps it was.

"It would be my honor, my lady," he said after a moment. "May we also include Father Nicodemus? I have a feeling he could use good food and drink tonight, too. He's had a fright, as well."

Amarantha's focus moved to the priest, who was just accepting a cup of wine from one of the acolytes he'd hissed orders to while hunting for the chair. She could see that his hands were still shaking.

"Of course," she said. "He was rather valiant, too. Will you come tonight, Father?"

"That would be appreciated," Father Nicodemus said, turning the wooden cup of ruby liquid over to Amarantha. "I've not seen your father in a few weeks, so it will be good to see him again."

Amarantha took the cup. "I am certain he would like to visit with you also," she said. "Then it is settled. The both of you will come to Mount Grace when the sun sets. I will make sure we have a good meal this night."

As she sipped the wine, Father Nicodemus turned to Morgan, giving the man a look that suggested he'd gone mad by accepting the invitation to Hollis de la Haye's lair, but Amarantha didn't see the expression on the priest's face because she was too busy looking at Morgan. The man seemed to have her entire attention. Morgan smiled politely in return, knowing that the priest wasn't at all happy about his invitation to Mount Grace.

But Morgan had a plan.

As he mulled over what an invitation to Mount Grace could mean in the grander scheme of things, a couple of men and several boys entered the church from the priest's entrance, moving into the sanctuary to clear away the bodies. When Father Nicodemus had demanded the chair, he'd also sent for help to dispose of the bodies. There would be no delay on that. The gravediggers from the parish were shuffling around in the sanctuary, putting the bodies of the robbers into litters and hauling them away while the remaining acolytes tried to cover the blood in the hard-packed earth of the sanctuary floor.

"I cannot remember the last time I had a truly fine meal," Morgan said. "It is appreciated almost as much as the good conversation. You said that you liked to paint?"

Amarantha had been trying to peer around them to watch the gory happenings, but his question had her distracted. "Paint?" she repeated. "Aye, I do."

"What do you like to paint?"

"Flowers and birds. I think I would do very well illustrating a book."

"You would do very well writing a book," Father Nicodemus said, a glimmer of mirth in his eyes. "You have a great imagination. I have heard you tell the children great stories, pretending to read from your father's books when that was not what was written on the pages. Mayhap you should write a book of your own."

Amarantha scoffed. "A book written by a woman?" she said. "I may be contrary to many of my father's opinions, but that is not one of them. A woman should not write a book."

"Why not?"

"Who on earth would read it?"

"Me," Morgan said, a smile playing on his lips. "I would like to hear some of these great stories."

Amarantha smiled modestly, a pink mottle on her cheeks. "But if you knew a woman had written a story, would that not matter to you?"

"I do not care if a dog writes the story. A good story is a good story."

Amarantha's smile grew and she averted her gaze, embarrassed yet rather coy. It was a charming gesture, not missed by Morgan, and certainly not missed by Father Nicodemus when he looked at Morgan's face as Morgan looked at Amarantha. It took him a moment to realize that Morgan found the lady quite attractive.

No wonder he accepted the invitation to feast.

He should have guessed it.

Loudly, he cleared his throat softly.

"Mayhap you should gather your things," he said, urging the man away. "The lady's escort will be here soon."

And you do not want to be seen, at least not yet.

Morgan managed to tear his gaze away from Amarantha, taking the hint. He was already taking quite a chance as it was. With a slight bow to the lady who was still behaving somewhat coy, he returned to the shadows, out of sight and pretending to busy himself with any possessions he might have with him. The truth was that he had nothing, but he'd already been too forward with Hollis de la Haye's daughter and he probably shouldn't have been. He knew that Father Nicodemus was going to give him an earful about it and, if William Marshal had seen it, he might have done the same thing. But Morgan didn't do anything without a purpose.

And he had one.

Still...

All objectives of the mission aside, the lady had his full attention.

Morgan peered around the pillar where Amarantha was standing up, talking to Father Nicodemus as she once again inspected the bloodstains on her garment. He found himself inspecting the woman. She was petite, but she had the body of a goddess. A ripe, full, luscious goddess. In a world where it was considered fashionable to conceal one's natural curves, Amarantha couldn't have concealed her curves had she tried. She had full, delicious breasts, a tiny waist, and flaring hips that gave him heart palpitations simply to gaze upon her. If that wasn't enough, she had the face of an angel – long, dark hair, delicate features, and wide, dark eyes with flaring lashes.

Truly, he'd never seen finer.

But she was Hollis de la Haye's daughter. That put a damper on everything, a dousing of icy water to cool his hot blood. All he'd heard about Hollis was how ruthless the man was, but he had a daughter who was perfect. Literally perfect. How did God allow a man like that to have such magnificent offspring? More than that, could he use the daughter to ingratiate himself to the father? It seemed that he was already well on his way.

William Marshal had ordered him to get acquainted with Hollis… so he would.

Through the daughter.

As he stood there, peering around the pillar and eyeing both the lady and the priest, the entry doors lurched open again and a knight appeared. A heavily armed knight, in fact. Morgan's attention shifted from Amarantha and Father Nicodemus to the killing machine that had just entered. The man and a few cohorts made their way over to Amarantha, who gasped when she saw them.

"Kenan!" she said. "Where have you been? I was attacked and you were nowhere to be found!"

Sir Kenan de Poyer, the man loaded down with weapons, frowned. "Attacked?" he repeated. "Who attacked you?"

Before Amarantha could answer, Father Nicodemus pointed to the blood that the acolytes were still attempting to bury. "Two men tried to rob us," he said steadily. "It did not end well for them."

De Poyer was looking at the ground with some horror. "What happened?" he demanded. Then he abruptly turned to the priest. "I have told you to keep those doors barred while Lady Amarantha is here. I have told you this for your own safety. If something happens to Lady Amarantha, Lord Hollis will burn this church over your head. Do you understand?"

"Perfectly," Father Nicodemus said steadily. "And I have told *you* that this is a church. We do not lock anyone out. Anyone who enters may do so with welcome."

Kenan sighed heavily. He and the priest had the same argument time and time again. Kenan was a decent man, and a logical one, but his entire being was rooted in warfare. He knew the nature of men and it was not good, but the priest didn't seem to agree with him.

"Then you tempt fate and you toy with Lady Amarantha's very life," he said with frustration. "This proves my point."

"If you are that worried, you should leave soldiers to guard her."

"I would not have to if you would only bar the door."

"I am not barring the door."

Kenan's jaw ticked. "I will tell Lord Hollis about this," he said. "He will have something to say about it."

"*I* will tell him," Amarantha insisted. "And nothing happened because we were saved by a man who had come to pray. I have invited him to sup with us so that my father may thank him properly."

She was looking over at the pillar where Morgan had gone, only the man wasn't there. She even scampered over to the pillar and walked around it, coming up empty. She looked at Father Nicodemus questioningly.

"Did you see him leave?" she asked.

Father Nicodemus hadn't, but he'd been focused on Kenan. There would have been opportunity for Morgan to slip out unnoticed. "Nay," he said. "But I am certain you will see him tonight. I do not imagine the man would fail to show himself for an invitation to dine."

Truth be told, Amarantha was disappointed. She had hoped to see the man again before she left for home, but that was not to be. Only the thought of seeing him later that evening kept her spirits from sinking completely.

"I suppose," she said, noticing the book where it had fallen and going to retrieve it. She picked it up carefully, brushing off the dirt. "I will see you tonight, Father. Until that time, will you do something for me? Will you make sure the children are well? They were very frightened when they ran away. I would not like it if they were hurt in their haste to escape."

Father Nicodemus nodded. "I will," he said. "Go with Kenan now. I will see you later."

Amarantha did. She handed the book over to Kenan and collected her cloak, slinging it over her shoulders and heading out into the bright afternoon sunshine. Father Nicodemus watched Kenan lumber out after her, shutting the door behind him. Once the door was closed and he was alone in the sanctuary, he began looking around.

"Morgan?" he called out quietly. "Morgan, are you here?"

"I am."

The voice came from the priest's entrance to the sanctuary, in back of the altar. Father Nicodemus turned to see Morgan enter.

"Where did you go?" he asked.

Morgan threw a thumb in the general direction of the churchyard. "Out," he said. "I may not take issue with becoming acquainted with de la Haye's daughter, but I draw the line at one of his knights. At least for now."

Father Nicodemus took a few steps in his direction, studying the man's features. There was something edgy about the way he spoke that led him to think there was something more behind his statement than simple caution.

"Afraid you might be recognized?" he asked.

Morgan looked at him. "What makes you say that?"

Father Nicodemus' eyebrows lifted. "I have seen a great many knights in my time," he said. "The way you killed those two robbers tells me that you are highly trained. I could see it in the way you moved, in the skill you displayed. And I know you have come from William Marshal who has only the most elite of men serve him."

Morgan smiled humorlessly, averting his gaze. "You are observant."

"Will you not tell me your family name?"

"Is it important?"

"If you die, it is. I should like to tell your family how brave you were."

Morgan chuckled softly. "I have only just arrived," he said. "Already, I am dead?"

Father Nicodemus shook his head. "Nay," he said. "But let us be realistic. Death happens even with the best of intentions. As a knight, you know that."

"True."

"Tell me your family name."

Morgan sighed heavily. "You must not speak it if I do. You understand that my life would be in your hands."

"It already is."

That was the truth. Conceding the point, Morgan reluctantly told the man what he wanted to know. "De Wolfe."

That drew a reaction. "Wolverhampton?"

"My uncle."

Father Nicodemus had only known him by Morgan until

that moment, but now… now, the man's breeding and lineage had come to bear and the priest knew that it was no ordinary knight who stood before him. Not only was he a William Marshal man, but he was from the House of de Wolfe.

The house was legendary.

"Thank you for confiding in me," he finally said. "I shall take your secret to my grave."

Morgan's gaze lingered on him, the weight from those golden eyes almost heavier than he could bear.

"You'd better," he muttered.

Father Nicodemus didn't take the threat lightly. In fact, he was quite determined to protect Morgan at all costs.

But that brought about the subject at hand.

"Then tell me why you accepted the invitation to Mount Grace," he said, almost pleadingly. "We are intent to ensure your mission is fulfilled, Morgan, but going into the belly of the beast is not exactly a recipe for good health. Why did you do it?"

Morgan lifted his eyebrows. "Because The Marshal ordered me to become acquainted with Hollis de la Haye," he said. "Earn his trust is what I was told. If I do, it will make it much easier to move in and out of Mount Grace."

"And have contact with those who will follow you into rebellion."

"Exactly."

"But what about the Irish?"

"You know about them?"

"There is not much I do not know."

Morgan cocked his head. "I am to rendezvous with them after I scout the situation here at Bronllys and at Mount Grace," he said. "They will go to de la Haye and ask for work in the mines. Would you be prepared to vouch for them?"

Father Nicodemus nodded. "Aye," he said. "In fact, Gere had already asked that of me before he died. I will tell Hollis that the men are trustworthy. Let me meet the leader and I will tell Hollis that the man is my cousin. That should get them into the mines."

"Good," Morgan said. "If I earn Hollis' trust, that will make it much easier for me to contact the Irish as well. I will be able to move more freely."

"As what?" Father Nicodemus said. "What do you intend to pose as?"

Morgan lifted his shoulders. "I am not entirely sure," he said. "There are some plans that cannot be made until you are in the midst of the situation. I was charged with coming here to pose as Gere le Marche. I was told to earn de la Haye's trust somehow because that will make it easier for me to infiltrate Mount Grace. But based on what happened today, I am thinking that mayhap I should offer my services as a knight. Mayhap that is the way I shall become part of Mount Grace."

Father Nicodemus nodded. "It seems the best way to me," he said. "You saved Lady Amarantha and her father will be indebted to you. Ask him for a position at his side."

"I will."

"But what name will you use?"

"Lady Amarantha already knows my name is Morgan," he said. "But, clearly, I cannot use de Wolfe or le Marche. Nor can I use my mother's family name of le Mon because that is well associated with Richard the Lionheart."

"Do you have another family name to use? Something obscure?"

Morgan shook his head, but quickly began to nod as a

thought occurred to him. "My father's family has the blood of Mercian kings in their lineage, so it would not be a lie to call myself Morgan of Mercia."

"Excellent idea," Father Nicodemus said. "That is an old and distinguished line, but you had better come up with a background. Where you fostered and all that."

Morgan nodded. "I will," he said. "I can come up with any one of a dozen lies to cover that."

Just when it seemed all was settled, Father Nicodemus snorted. "You are Morgan de Wolfe posing as Gere le Marche, and now you are posing as someone else yet again," he said. "I hope you can remember who you are when this is finished."

Morgan gave him a lopsided grin. "As I said, missions of this sort cannot be perfectly planned," he said. "One must learn to improvise as the situation dictates in order to complete the task at hand."

"Very true," Father Nicodemus said. "But now that I know you are a de Wolfe, that will help me keep you from harm. If I see men who might know the house of de Wolfe or if anyone comes asking, I will tell you. Thank you for entrusting me with your secret."

Morgan sighed faintly, as if he still weren't entirely sure it had been a good idea. But it was done. "It was probably better that you did not know, but that cannot be helped now," he said. Then, his gaze grew intense. "To your grave, Priest. Take it all to your grave."

Father Nicodemus nodded. "For the man who will finally gain back Oliver le Marche's castle?" he said. "I would burn for you if it would save your life."

Morgan's expression tightened. "Let's hope it doesn't come to that."

A sentiment echoed by them both. Considering what they were facing, something like that wasn't out of the realm of possibility if their subterfuge was discovered.

CHAPTER FIVE

"A MMIE?" EVERELDA SAID dreamily. "Tell me of him again."

It was sunset at Mount Grace Castle. The sun was nestled in the western sky, casting brilliant rays of light, fingers that reached into the darkening sky to pull down the cowl of night.

Amarantha was standing at the lancet window of her bedchamber, looking out over the purple and gray landscape as torches were lit all across the compound. The great hall was not in her line of sight, but she could see smoke rising from the rooftop. There were people down below, servants and soldiers, moving about their duties before night fell completely. She couldn't see the gatehouse from her chamber but she hoped her mysterious savior had arrived.

She was quite anxious to get to the hall.

"I have already told you everything that happened," she said, turning away from the window. "He is tall and very handsome, with dark hair and eyes of dark gold that glimmered. His name is Morgan. That is all I know."

Everelda was lying on Amarantha's bed, a large and comfortable piece of furniture and probably one of the more expensive possessions at Mount Grace. Hollis spared no expense when it came to his daughter. Everelda was propped up on a pillow, watching her pet raven walk all over the bed and try to steal any pieces of thread or fabric it could get its beak on.

"Morgan," Everelda repeated the name, rolling it over her tongue. "That is a Welsh name. Do you suppose he is Welsh?"

Amarantha went to her mirror for the tenth time in as many minutes, inspecting her reflection yet again to make sure she was presentable. Normally, she didn't give her appearance much consideration but tonight, she was.

She had a reason.

"He did not sound Welsh," she said after a moment. "He spoke quite properly, as if he were raised in England."

"Will you discover more about him tonight?"

"That is the plan."

Everelda's big raven hopped off the bed and began waddling on the floor, looking for something to steal. Violet the Raven was always looking for something to steal. But she passed too near the edge of the bed and an orange paw shot out from underneath the bed, batting at her.

The chase was on.

Amarantha's cat, named Palu after an ancient goddess, was slightly smaller than the raven, but it didn't deter the bold, orange tabby from pursuing the bird. The bird, however, wasn't threatened and continued to waddle around as the cat trailed after it, batting at it and then darting off when the raven would turn and screech. It was a daily battle that held great entertainment value because Palu couldn't actually hunt Violet and the bird knew it.

Violet ended up chasing Palu back under the bed.

"I heard Uncle Hollis say that Farran was going to be here tonight," Everelda said, turning her attention away from the battling pets. "I suspect he will not approve of you paying attention to this man, even if the man did save your life."

Amarantha knew that. She'd been trying to push that very idea out of her mind ever since she'd returned to Mount Grace, but Everelda was quite correct. Farran would be in attendance this night because he was here almost every night. She'd known that all along. Perhaps she was hoping the man would break a leg and be unable to attend, but she knew that, even now, he was somewhere on the grounds.

Waiting.

Watching.

"As is Kenan," she sighed, turning away from the mirror. "You know that Farran and Kenan do not get on with each other."

"Because Kenan has been sweet on you for years."

Amarantha held up a hand to silence her. "I do not care," she said flatly. "Kenan is my father's knight. He is a nice man and I like him as such, but he's no better than Farran in my mind. I like them equally – as pleasant men and nothing more, only Papa thinks he can make a smart marriage with Farran. If Farran were not around, it might be Kenan. Or someone else. My father only has marriage in mind for me and it grows wearisome."

Everelda sat up on the bed. "You should not complain over something that other women might want."

"What do you mean?"

"Me, for instance?" Everelda said. "I would not mind being courted by a man or two, but nay – when they see you, all other women cease to exist. I do not have a chance. Why can't Uncle

Hollis make a match for me, too?"

There was some bitterness in that statement and Amarantha's gaze moved over her cousin, child of her father's sister. She was a year younger than Amarantha's twenty years and one, a pretty girl with pale coloring and big, green eyes. But she was small, without much meat on her bones as her father put it, and she wore clothes that always, inevitably, looked too large for her.

Then Amarantha looked down at herself.

She was wearing a pale purple silk with a dark purple surcoat that laced up the front. That meant her tiny waist was emphasized and her full breasts were well on display. She turned to look at herself in the mirror again, seeing her curvy shape, remembering the time when she was younger and how embarrassed she was by her developing body. She'd sprouted breasts at about ten years of age and a waistline at about twelve. By fourteen, she had what she considered big hips, something that had greatly embarrassed her. She'd been fostering at Warwick Castle at the time and she remembered the girls whispering about her and the men staring at her. *Good childbearing hips* was what the knights would snicker at.

Truly, she'd always been ashamed of that.

She never wore fanciful clothing, at least not like some of the women wore. Women at court were known to wear daring necklines and, she'd heard once, fabric that one could see through. But Amarantha wasn't an exhibitionist like that, at least not intentionally. She wore simple but well-made clothing, with fine fabrics and simple but elegant accessories. Her father had stopped buying her jewelry long ago because she never wore any, afraid of looking too ostentatious or obvious.

Therefore, Everelda's words hurt.

"It is not as if I try," she said. "I do not try to stand out or attract men. It simply… happens."

Everelda held her hands up in front of her chest, mimicking the shape of breasts. "Because of these," she said frankly. "You cannot help it, I know, but it is still difficult for me when I see a handsome man and he looks right at you."

Amarantha was starting to become annoyed. "You do not need to keep speaking of it," she said. "I do not know why you are bringing that up now. I have an evening ahead of me with a special guest and I do not want to hear your complaints."

"I'm not complaining."

"Then stop making me feel beastly."

Everelda could see that she'd offended her cousin. Violet the Raven jumped onto the bed beside her, making clicking noises as she waddled onto her mistress' lap. Everelda petted the bird, eyeing Amarantha as the woman fussed with a ribbon in her hair.

"I did not mean to make you feel beastly," she said. "You are the most beautiful woman I have ever seen. You look like your mother, God rest her soul. You do not look like the rest of the de la Haye family. We are all homely and like to complain about it."

She was trying to defuse the situation with some humor, which worked. Amarantha smiled weakly.

"You are *not* homely," she said. "That is what I keep trying to tell you. But please… please stop talking like I deliberately try to entice men away from you. It only makes me feel bad."

"I am sorry. I will not do it again."

"And you will help me as hostess tonight? Mayhap entertain Sir Farran?"

Everelda knew what she meant. "You mean keep his attention while you speak with your Morgan?"

"He is not my Morgan but, aye, that is what I mean."

"I will do my best."

Amarantha turned to her cousin and smiled. The young women grinned at each other for a few moments before Everelda set her raven on the ground and stood up.

"Then let us make sure the hall is prepared," she said, holding out her hand. "Let us make this a night to remember."

Amarantha took her hand, leaving Violet to fly to the lancet window and evade Palu for the night, and they headed down to the keep entry and the inner bailey, bathed in moonlight, beyond.

The stage was set.

CHAPTER SIX

HOLLIS DE LA Haye was a tall man with a crown of bushy, white hair, the result of thick auburn hair that had gone gray at an early age. He wasn't particularly muscular, but simply a big man with big hands and a booming voice.

And he was loyal to King John to the bone.

The de la Haye family held Craswell Castle to the north, near Chester, and they had always been vastly loyal to the crown of England. Hollis' father, Harker, and his father before him had all fought for the English kings. Though they weren't well-known in the politics of England and, in fact, tried to stay clear of the extreme politics that always enveloped the English crown, they were still loyal to any king who sat upon the throne. It was, in truth, a rather mindless loyalty. If the king demanded it, they would obey.

That was what Hollis did with John.

He obeyed.

In this case, that loyalty had won him a premier outpost in Mount Grace. John gave him a cut of the product from the mine, so Hollis was a heavy-handed overseer. He drove those who worked in the mines with an iron fist, so much so that the death rate was higher than it should have been. Men were not allowed to leave their task. Once a miner, always a miner. He'd worked many a man to death that way.

Something he kept from his only child.

As far as Amarantha was concerned, her father was a stern but fair task master because no one had ever told her differently. No one had the courage to. She lived in a fantasy world of Hollis' creation because he wanted his daughter to think well of him. Everyone who had any contact with her, and that was tightly controlled by Hollis, only said pleasant things. They filled Amarantha's head with visions of her strong and virtuous father, though the truth was that Amarantha had seen her father behave in a manner that was less than virtuous several times.

She wasn't as naïve as her father wanted her to be.

Even tonight, Hollis made sure he was in control of things. Thanks to Kenan, he knew that his daughter had invited the man who saved her life to sup and he was not displeased. He was eager to thank the man. But he was also eager to put his fist into Father Nicodemus' eye for allowing his daughter into a dangerous situation.

He had, therefore, been lingering at the gatehouse, watching people come and go as evening fell. There were a few travelers who requested lodgings for the night and since it was customary to agree, he'd had his men show them where they could bed down. If it was an important guest, he would direct them to the keep where his daughter would find them a bed, but if it was no one of importance, the stables and unused outbuildings were good enough.

Kenan came to stand with him at one point, directing his

soldiers to make sure the gates were secured for the night, but not before Farran slipped in on a stallion the color of the sunset. The fiery stallion snapped and threw its head around, a powerful beast and the envy of any man who saw him. Farran was in the habit of having horses and homes and possessions that impressed others, which was half the reason he was so determined to marry Amarantha.

Yet another possession to be admired.

He dismounted the beast just inside the bailey and muzzled it, handing it over to a nervous groom. As the horse was led away, Farran greeted Hollis with a smile but that smile faded when it came to Kenan. He was polite but not friendly. There was competition there and had been for years, so a polite word was all he could manage, which amused Hollis greatly. He loved to see the competition between the two dominant knights. Once or twice, he'd even broken up a fight. He suspected there may have been other fights he'd not been witness to, but neither man would admit it.

It was nearing the time that the feast would begin and the gates were about to close when Father Nicodemus finally showed himself, riding on an old palfrey that Hollis himself had given the man. Alongside him was a very big man astride an old, swayback warmblood, hardly a fine horse although he might have once been, years ago. They came into the bailey alight with torches and Father Nicodemus headed straight for Hollis even as men moved to collect their horses.

"My lord," Father Nicodemus said, lifting a hand to Hollis as he threw his leg over the horse's back and slid to the ground. "I hope this night finds you well. Thank you for the invitation to dine with you."

Hollis cocked an eyebrow at the short, spry priest. "The

evening finds me very well," he said. "But it also finds me very concerned about what happened this afternoon with my daughter. I understand you allowed her to be put in danger."

The conversation had already gone to that terrible event. Not that Father Nicodemus had really expected otherwise, but he'd hoped there would have been a few more pleasantries before he had to explain himself. He had no doubt that this was only the warm-up to the main event, for Hollis de la Haye was a man with much to say, especially when it came to his daughter and her safety.

"My lord," he said frankly, eyeing Kenan because he knew that Kenan had made the event in the church seem as horrible as possible. "As I explained to de Poyer, St. Mary the Virgin is a church. We cannot and do not lock doors. We do not lock people out of the church. The church is there for a reason and that is to welcome everyone."

Hollis pursed his lips irritably. "Even robbers who would harm my child?"

Father Nicodemus wasn't going to concede the point. "There was no way I could have anticipated such a thing," he said, holding up a hand before Hollis could counter. "But I will say that some of the blame is yours. You should leave de Poyer at the church while your daughter is teaching and he would deter any threat. Or mayhap you should send a dozen soldiers with her to protect her. You cannot place the blame solely on me when your men leave her off and simply disappear. Are they not supposed to protect her?"

Hollis didn't have an argument to that because the man was right. Whenever Amarantha went to town, orders were for soldiers to remain with her, but over the months, they had been lax about it. The church was safe and nothing ever happened, and even though Kenan argued with Father Nicodemus about locking the entry door, he'd never really demanded that it be done. In fact, Kenan had taken to leaving Amarantha off, going about his business, and then returning for her. He'd grown too casual about it. Therefore, in a sense, it really *was* his fault.

Hollis looked at Kenan.

"Why didn't *you* stay?" he said. "Why do you always leave her off and return to the castle?"

The fingers of blame were pointing furiously and Kenan's eyes widened when he realized he was now shouldering all of the guilt for the lady's near-assault. "Because we had some trouble in the mine and my attention was required elsewhere, my lord," he said steadily. "By your order, I might add."

The blame was now back on Hollis, who didn't like that in the least. His face screwed up with great annoyance and he waved everyone off.

"A ridiculous conversation," he said. "I will not continue on this subject but I will say that from now on, de Poyer will not leave my daughter alone. He will remain at the church as long as she is there."

Pleased he'd caused some trouble between Hollis and his knight, Father Nicodemus smiled. "An excellent decision, my lord," he said. "But before we close this subject, I should like to introduce you to an old friend. He is the man who saved your daughter's life."

All focus turned to Morgan, who had been standing a few feet behind Father Nicodemus and watching Hollis intently. That was the man at the heart of everything and Morgan was grateful for a few moments to observe the man in a candid moment. When the attention turned to him, he didn't hesitate – he moved forward, facing Hollis without fear. Father Nicodemus put his hand on Morgan's shoulder.

"This is Morgan of Mercia," he said. "Morgan comes from a very old and distinguished family and he was visiting me when your daughter was attacked. Had it not been for Morgan, the situation might have been much more unpleasant. We owe him our thanks."

Hollis stepped closer to him, looking him over curiously. Morgan could see that he had the same color eyes as his daughter did – dark, but with a hint of brick red to them. They were unique eyes. After a moment, Hollis nodded his head as if approving of what he saw.

"Morgan of Mercia," he repeated. "You have my deepest gratitude for what you did. I understand you killed both men."

Morgan nodded. "I did, my lord," he said. "There was no choice. Your daughter's life was at stake."

Hollis' eyes widened. "Was it as bad as that?"

"They were both armed, my lord. I could not take the chance."

Hollis seemed very relieved. "A wise choice," he said. "You are a knight?"

"Aye, my lord."

"Where do you serve?"

"Can we discuss this inside?" Father Nicodemus interrupted. "I am famished and I know Morgan is, as well. He has been traveling all day. Let us continue this in the great hall."

Attention was successfully diverted as Hollis immediately turned away, issuing orders to Kenan, who headed back to the gatehouse. Farran, who had stood silently through the exchange, went with Hollis as Morgan and Father Nicodemus hung back, just far enough back so their conversation couldn't be heard.

But they followed.

"Quickly," Father Nicodemus hissed. "Where do you serve?"

Morgan kept his eyes on Hollis. "I am not going to tell him the truth," he muttered. "I suspected this question would come up and I will tell him Thetford Castle. That's a de Winter property and de Winters are loyal to John. They also happen to be close friends with my uncle, so they will vouch for me if it comes to it."

It seemed logical enough. "Where did you foster?" Father Nicodemus pressed. "You had better come up with an answer."

Morgan nodded. "I told you I would," he said. "Whatever I say, simply confirm it. Also, you introduced me as an old friend. How do we know one another?"

"Our fathers were friends."

"Good enough."

They continued on into the hall without any further con-versation, passing into the inner ward, which was just as enormous as the outer ward. The great hall was straight ahead, a stone building with a steeply pitched roof and sparks shooting from the chimney into the night sky. Entering the hall was like walking into a wall of heat. It was quite warm as they followed Hollis and Farran to the dais.

"Sit," Hollis said, indicating a seat directly across from him. Then he started shouting for wine before taking a seat himself. "I will confess that I have a weakness for fine wine which is why I table my own. I have vineyards in Vezelay, something I inherited through my mother's family. It is the best wine in all of France."

On cue, cups and pitchers of deep, garnet-colored liquid were set upon the table. Morgan found himself looking at an enormous cup, filled to the rim with wine. He collected it, trying not to spill it, and drank deeply.

It was delicious.

"Magnificent, my lord," he said. "Congratulations that your fruit of the vine is better than any I have sampled. I taste Sessile oak with a hint of apple."

Hollis puffed up with pride. "You are a man who knows your wine."

"I have had my share, my lord."

Hollis took a long drink himself, smacking his lips with satisfaction. "Then you have sampled much?"

"As much as any man, I suppose."

"Have you traveled, then?"

Morgan could see that Hollis was starting to probe him and he was prepared. He glanced at Father Nicodemus to see if the man was realizing Hollis' intentions and could see from his expression that he did, indeed. Morgan had thought they would have some time to run inane conversation around the table before delving into anything personal, but that was evidently not to be.

Hollis wanted to know about the man who saved his daughter's life.

"Nay," he said, taking another drink of wine. "I've never been one with a longing to travel. My family is from Norfolk and I served at Thetford Castle for years. In fact, I am on business for the garrison commander and that is the only reason I am traveling. That is how I ended up on the Marches."

Hollis peered at him curiously. "What business?"

Morgan was thinking quickly. "The garrison commander, a man named Summerlin, is missing a brother," he said. "Rumor has it that the brother traveled to Aberystwyth, so I followed the trail there. No one has seen nor heard of him, although I had some old salt in a local tavern tell me that he saw a man of that description abducted by the Scottish pirates that roam those waters. However, someone else said they saw the man heading southeast with a merchant caravan, towards Gloucester, so I was trying to pick up the trail when I stopped at Bronllys to see Father Nicodemus. That is how I happened to be in the church when your daughter was present."

Hollis grunted at the perfectly believable story. "Thank God that you were," he muttered, pouring himself more wine. "My daughter told me that you were highly skilled. You have impressed her."

"I was only doing as I was trained, my lord. I was glad to help."

Hollis grinned, glancing at Farran, who had thus far remained completely silent since the introduction of Morgan of Mercia. "We have a modest man among us," he said. "I do not think I've ever seen you so modest, de Bonne. There is something to be said about a humble man."

Farran lifted a red eyebrow, his gaze fixed on Morgan. "Mayhap," he said, clearly not pleased that Hollis was taunting him. "Thetford is de Winter property, is it not, Sir Morgan?"

Morgan nodded. "It is, my lord."

Hollis waved his hand between them. "I've not properly introduced you two, Sir Morgan, but this is Sir Farran de Bonne of Talgarth Castle and he should be particularly thankful that you prevented something terrible from happening to my daughter. He has intentions towards her."

It was a clumsy way of explaining Farran's presence, and his interest in Mount Grace in general, but Morgan pretended to be quite subservient to the man.

"My lord," he greeted with respect. "It is an honor to know you."

Farran nodded faintly, acknowledging the polite response, but his gaze was still riveted to Morgan in a most intense way. "Have you lived in Norfolk all your life?" he asked.

Morgan nodded. "Indeed, my lord," he said. "My family has always been in service to de Winter."

"I've never been to Norfolk."

"It is wet. Very wet."

"Is de Winter still in support of the king?"

They were treading into dangerous political territory, but Morgan had expected that. Knights and men of power were always interested in politics. Much of Morgan's education and training had been in the political arena because his uncle, the Earl of Wolverhampton, was an important political player in the government of England and that was part of what made Morgan valuable to William Marshal.

He knew how to play the game.

"De Winter is always in support of the king, my lord," he said, sounding as if he were mildly scolding the man. "The House of de Winter has never been against the king, no matter who sits upon the throne. Even now, as warlords turn against John, de Winter holds fast to the crown."

Farran had perhaps deserved the mild rebuke to question the stalwart House of de Winter, so he simply nodded his head. Hollis, however, was more interested in that part of the conversation.

"Norfolk is full of John's supporters," he said. "Roger Bigod, the Earl of Norfolk, has hardly left John's side for many years."

Morgan nodded. "That is quite true, my lord," he said. "De Winter is Norfolk's war machine. Between Norwich Castle,

Narborough Castle, and Thetford Castle, de Winter keeps thousands of troops. With the trouble the king has been having, those armies have been called forth with regularity except de Winter refuses to ally with the mercenaries John has been bringing over from France. De Winter will fight with other English warlords, but not the mercenaries."

Hollis nodded his approval. "I do not blame the man," he said. "But John has had a time of it with rebellious barons. God's Bones, we are surrounded by them even here."

"My lord?"

Hollis was in the middle of a big swallow of wine. "They're all along the Marches," he said, licking his lips. "De Velt has six castles all within a two days' ride of Mount Grace. There is de Shera to the north and that bastard de Lohr to the south. And here I am with this jewel of a castle, with rebelling barons to the east and hateful Welsh to the west. It is a difficult position."

"You have me, my lord," Farran reminded him, sounding offended. "I have a thousand men to lend support to you and the king. Mayhap it is not as much as de Lohr's thousands or the terrifying de Velt war monster, but I've never lost a battle."

Hollis knew he'd pushed Farran a bit this night and he put his hand on the man's shoulder. "You are an excellent ally, de Bonne," he said. "Why do you think I would be happy to have my daughter marry you? We would make an unbreakable familial alliance, you and I."

Farran was soothed somewhat, accepting more wine from a passing servant, but his attention was quickly back on Morgan.

"And you, Sir Morgan?" he said. "Do you have a familial alliance?"

"My lord?"

"Are you married?"

Morgan didn't hesitate. "Aye."

That seemed to give Farran a good deal of relief. His body language changed almost immediately. "I hope it is a good marriage," he said. "Do you have sons?"

Morgan shook his head. "Nay," he said. "In time, every man hopes for sons to carry on his name."

Farran nodded firmly, becoming less guarded and more animated. "My sentiment exactly," he said. "In time, I too hope to have sons. A man should have as many as possible."

"Agreed."

"In fact…" Something caught Farran's attention and he turned in full towards the hall entry. "Here comes the young lady whose life you saved today. If I've not thanked you for that, I will do so. You have my gratitude."

That was about as much attention to Morgan as he could give. Something far more interesting had his focus and Morgan turned to see Amarantha and another young woman heading in their direction.

What he saw took his breath away.

Wearing a purple silk gown that clung to her indecently, Amarantha smiled weakly as she approached the dais to a host of men looking at her. Her dark hair was braided and she wore a circlet of gold around her head, an utterly exquisite picture. Morgan couldn't take his eyes off her as she came towards him.

"Sir Morgan," she greeted. "I am so sorry I am late. Did my father properly introduce himself?"

Morgan stood up, towering over her as he smiled politely. "Your father has been most hospitable," he said. "So has Sir Farran. We have been having a very interesting conversation but now that you are here, the conversation is better already."

Amarantha's smile turned genuine at the kind compliment.

She indicated the young woman standing next to her. "This is my cousin, Lady Everelda," she said. "May we sit next to you?"

Morgan nodded, pulling out a chair for her while a servant pulled out one for Everelda. Morgan smiled pleasantly at Everelda, a lass with a pale beauty, but Everelda didn't seem very inclined to be friendly. She wouldn't even meet his eyes.

Not that Morgan cared. He was fully focused on Amarantha as she sat down next to him. He was the first one to give her a cup as Farran reached across the table to pour her a measure of wine.

"Your father was telling me of his vineyards in Burgundy," he said. "I have told him that his wine is the best I have ever tasted."

Amarantha collected her full cup. "It is very good," she said. "But last year, he purchased wine from Navarre that was very sweet. I liked that much better."

"Have you been to Navarre, then?" he asked.

She nodded. "Once," she said. "It was the same trip that we visited the vineyards in Vezelay, where my father's vineyards are. They have belonged to his mother's family for centuries. Family legend says that the vines were brought from Ancient Rome."

Morgan looked at the wine. "No wonder I feel like donning gladiator's garb and fighting in an ancient arena."

Amarantha laughed softly. "It sounds like a terrible and bloody business," she said. "My father has books that tell of the gladiatorial games. Clearly, you are an educated man if you know of them."

"Sir Morgan was telling us that he serves in Norfolk," Hollis said. "He serves de Winter. That is why he was so able to protect you. De Winter only has the very best men serve him."

Amarantha looked at Morgan, impressed. "I knew you were a skilled knight when I saw you dispatch those men," she said. "I am very glad you were there to help me, Sir Morgan. I shall never forget it."

He dipped his head modestly. "As I told your father, I was glad to help."

"When are you returning home, Sir Morgan?" Farran asked, interrupting their conversation. "You said you were searching for your garrison commander's brother? Surely you must be in a hurry to head home."

Morgan could see that the man was all but showing him the door. He thought he'd defused that situation by telling Farran that he was married, but clearly that wasn't the case. Jealousy burned in the man's eyes as Amarantha paid attention to him and the last thing Morgan wanted to do was become *persona non grata* at the castle. But on the other hand, it wasn't as if he could actually leave.

This was where he needed to be.

"I am afraid I cannot return just yet, Sir Farran," he said. "I do not have word of my garrison commander's brother, one way or the other, so I still have some investigating to do before I can return home."

"Then you are staying in town?"

"At The Three Cocks."

"Nonsense," Hollis said. "You must stay here while you conduct your search. I will lend men to your cause should you require it."

That wasn't an offer Morgan had expected, but it was more than perfect. He glanced at Father Nicodemus, who was surprisingly neutral about it. Before he could accept or decline, Amarantha lay her soft hand on his arm.

"Please stay," she pleaded. "We have no way of repaying you for saving my life other than this meal, so please let us provide you with shelter and food while you are conducting your search. I would feel so much better if you would accept our hospitality. It is small compensation for what you have done, but it is as much as we can offer. Will you stay?"

There was no way Morgan could refuse. *Would* refuse. Farran or no Farran. Gazing into Amarantha's face, he tried very hard not to seem too eager or too grateful. He was also acutely aware of Farran glaring at him from the other side of the table, so he looked straight at the man.

"With your permission, my lord," he said. "I would not feel comfortable if you did not approve."

That was an unexpected twist, catching Farran off guard because, truly, Morgan didn't need his permission. But he was acknowledging Farran's claim, which was quite gracious of him. Before he could reply, however, Amarantha removed her hand from Morgan's arm and scowled at both her father and Farran.

"You do not *need* Sir Farran's permission," she said, focusing on her father. "What have you told him that he should think to ask permission of Farran?"

Hollis was trying not to appear intimidated by his angry daughter as the mercurial dinner conversation took another swing in an unexpected direction. "I told him that I was happy to have you marry Farran," he said. "I did not say you were going to. Only that I would be happy to see you wed to him."

Amarantha was mortified. "I see," she said, jaw ticking. "So you would tell this stranger, a man we do not even know, that you wish for me to marry Farran? How could you, Father? That is not something to discuss with a stranger!"

Hollis held up a hand. "And this is not an appropriate subject to argue about for all to hear," he said. "I did not mean to upset you, Amarantha. It was merely a comment and nothing more."

"I must apologize," Morgan said, looking between Farran and Amarantha. "I was stupid to assume anything at all, but based on what your father said, I thought… I can see that I was wrong. Please forgive me, my lady. I thought it was the right thing to do."

"It was," Farran said, standing up. "You were quite right to ask me, but clearly the lady has other ideas. That being the case, I see where I stand so I will bid you a good evening. Thank you for protecting the lady today, Sir Morgan. If I can ever return the favor, you will let me know."

With that, he headed away from the table, running straight into Kenan as the man came to join the group. Kenan looked at him curiously but Farran simply kept walking. Hollis leaned over the table towards his daughter.

"Get him back here," he told her. "You did not need to scold the man like that and embarrass him. Tell him to return."

Amarantha shook her head. "I will not," she said. "Papa, you've ruined this meal already and I wanted it to be nice and pleasant for our guests. If you want Farran back, *you* go after him. I will not do it."

With a frown, Hollis slammed his cup of wine down and stood up, storming after Farran as the man marched from the hall.

Morgan sighed heavily.

"I did not mean to offend anyone," he said. "Your father made it clear that you were meant for Sir Farran and I did not realize the feeling wasn't mutual."

Amarantha turned to him, forcing a smile. "My father is

desperate to marry me off," she said. "Sir Farran is a nice man and I find him pleasant, but I do not wish to marry anyone right now."

As Morgan nodded, unwilling to pursue that line of conversation, Father Nicodemus spoke up. "The lady and I had the same conversation earlier today," he said. "I have told her that it is the duty of all young ladies to marry and produce children. She does not seem to agree."

The food began to come, great trenchers with boiled pork and beans and peas being placed in front of the diners. Amarantha was served first and she collected her spoon.

"I did not say that I disagreed with you," she said as she began to break up the pork. "I simply said I do not wish to marry right now."

Morgan had an enormous portion in front of him and he began picking apart the chunk of pork with his knife. "There is no crime in that," he said. "Though desperate fathers and nosy priests might think otherwise."

"And what do you think, Sir Morgan?"

He glanced at her. "I think that marriage should be a happy occasion," he said. "My parents are quite fond of each other and always have been. The example set for me is a happy marriage."

"Are you married?"

Morgan hesitated this time, but because he'd already told Hollis and Farran that he was, he had to continue the lie.

But something inside him was very reluctant to tell her.

"Aye," he said simply.

The expression on Amarantha's face visibly shifted; he could see it. The light went out of her eyes and she returned her attention to her food, continuing to pick at it.

"I hope it is a good marriage," she said, pretending that she meant it. "Do you have children?"

"Nay."

He didn't elaborate and she didn't press. It was like all of the warmth had gone right out of the conversation in those few exchanges. What had started out quite promising was now stagnating in ruin. The conversation threatened to die completely.

Truth be told, Morgan was still trying to figure out why she seemed so disappointed that he was married. It gave him the strangest sense of hope that this glorious creature, a woman among women, could actually find him attractive. Perhaps she was even interested in him.

Could it be true?

But, God… what a dangerous thought.

"Lady Everelda," he said, changing subjects because the one they were on was uncomfortable at best. "Why are you not teaching at the church, also? It seems like a fine task for well-bred young women. Surely you have much knowledge to teach."

Everelda's head snapped up from her trencher, surprised she was being brought into the conversation. "I do not teach, my lord," she said. "I do not do much of anything."

Morgan shoveled pork and beans into his mouth, almost a type of nervous eating. Anything to get his mind off of Amarantha and the idea that she found him attractive.

"I'm not certain I believe that," he said. "You seem like a well-educated young woman."

Everelda looked at Amarantha with some uncertainty before answering. "I fostered for many years," she said. "I suppose I am as educated as the next noblewoman."

"Where did you foster?"

"Oakhampton Castle, my lord."

Morgan swallowed the bite in his mouth and shoveled in more. "In Devon?" he said. "That is quite far from Mount Grace."

Before she could answer, Amarantha suddenly lifted her head. "Where did you foster, Sir Morgan?"

He looked at her, meeting those dark eyes with the long lashes and feeling a jolt go through him. Something warm and electric and completely unexpected. "In Kent," he said. "Chilham Castle. Have you heard of it?"

Amarantha shook her head. "Nay," she said. "That is far from Norfolk."

"Not too far."

"Did you meet your wife at Chilham?"

Morgan could see simply by looking in her eyes that she wasn't going to let the subject of his wife go. He didn't even have a damned wife and here he was, making one up to a woman he found utterly captivating.

He desperately wanted off the subject.

"Nay," he said. "Did you foster at Oakhampton, too?"

He was switching the subject back on her, making it clear, more or less, that he didn't wish to discuss his phantom wife. Amarantha's gaze lingered on him for a moment, receiving his message, before shaking her head.

"Nay," she said. "I fostered at St. Austell in Cornwall and also at Warwick Castle."

"Two castles?"

"I hated St. Austell," she said, focusing on her food. "It was damp and isolated. The only reason I went there was because the lord is a friend of my father's, but I wrote my father and begged him to let me go to a bigger castle that wasn't so far away. So, he sent me to Warwick."

Morgan was alternately focusing on his meal and her. "Warwick was one of the great cities in Mercia," he said. "Warwick was a fortified settlement long before the Normans came."

Amarantha looked at him. "You know much about Mercia."

"I should. It is my family's history."

"And you have always been called Morgan of Mercia?"

He nodded. "For my branch of the family, aye," he said, thinking quickly as he went along because he'd always been a smooth liar, a trait he didn't draw upon too often because it offended his honest senses. But in this case, it was necessary. "My family is rather large, so the surname de Mercia or of Mercia defines my father and his brothers."

"But you do have a family name?"

"De Stafford."

Amarantha nodded, returning her focus to her trencher. Morgan breathed a sigh of relief because he felt as if he'd been flying by the seat of his pants through the entire conversation. Wolverhampton was in Staffordshire, which is how he came up with de Stafford. Staffordshire was within what used to be the Kingdom of Mercia, so in a sense, he really wasn't lying. His family really was part of that legacy.

But it was a fine technicality.

Amarantha seemed to have run out of questions and Morgan dared to glance at Father Nicodemus, whose expression also suggested relief that Morgan had deftly navigated those tricky waters. When Amarantha began speaking to Kenan across the table, Morgan turned to Father Nicodemus.

"You should excuse yourself early and find my contact," he muttered. "I must know the loyalties of those left behind when

John took the castle. That is imperative."

Father Nicodemus took a big bite of bread and butter, mostly to muffle his voice. "I know," he said. "I will depart shortly for that purpose. Do you really intend to accept Hollis' invitation to stay here?"

"I think I should."

"I think you should, too."

"I'll return to The Three Cocks for the night and then return in the morning," Morgan said, lifting a cup to both conceal his lips and mute his words. "I must tell Patience of the situation."

"Sir Morgan?" Amarantha distracted him from the priest. "I fear you have not been properly introduced to Sir Kenan de Poyer. He is my father's captain."

Morgan found himself looking at the dark-haired, dark-eyed knight who was big, burly, and perhaps the slightest bit homely.

"My lord," he greeted. "I saw you when I entered the gates but there was no opportunity for introductions."

Kenan wasn't quite over being scolded by Hollis in front of everyone when the priest and Morgan had first arrived. He looked straight at Father Nicodemus.

"That is because the priest made sure that I was to blame for the entire incident with Lady Amarantha today," he said, watching Father Nicodemus shrug. Annoyed, he returned his attention to Morgan. "You impressed the lady with your skill. We are all grateful you were there in a time of need."

"As am I," Morgan said. Then he cocked his head curiously. "I ran into a man a few years ago named Keller de Poyer. He serves Pembroke, I think. A relative?"

Kenan cleared his throat softly as he poured himself some

wine. "He is," he said. "Where did you see him?"

Morgan shook his head. "I do not remember," he said. "I think it was on a trip I took with my liege to London. As I recall, a big man with dark eyes. I think he looked like you."

"He should," Kenan said. "He is my brother."

The way he said it suggested that he did not wish to speak on it. Truth be told, Morgan knew Keller de Poyer fairly well, as the man served William Marshal and was loyal to the bone. He didn't know de Poyer had a brother and suspected that perhaps their different loyalties might be the reason for Kenan's seeming bitterness. One brother serving a hated king, one serving the rebellion. That wasn't unusual these days with John tearing up the country.

Therefore, he let the subject drop.

"I see," he said. "How long have you served at Mount Grace?"

It was a swift change in subject, one Kenan readily followed. "I fostered here," he said. "I ended up serving Lord Hollis at Craswell Castle, but I have always had a soft spot for Mount Grace."

That was something Morgan hadn't expected to hear. He assumed de Poyer had never been to Mount Grace prior to John wresting it away from le Marche, but that clearly wasn't the case. Morgan could feel his blood run cold because that realization, if true, changed everything.

Kenan de Poyer would know Gere le Marche on sight.

Damnation.

Why hadn't Father Nicodemus told him about de Poyer?

"Then you know this place well," he said, trying desperately to sound casual.

But Kenan nodded his head.

"Well enough," he said. "I was here for only a few years before duty took me elsewhere, but when Lord Hollis assumed control, it was quite fortuitous that I was able to come with him."

The more Morgan thought on it, the more shocked he became. De Poyer could be the fly in the ointment that ruined everything, blowing his cover. They had worried about le Marche men in the mines making it known that he was not Gere le Marche, but it never occurred to any of them that they would have to worry about a previous pledge.

A man close to Hollis de la Haye.

Morgan struggled to keep the conversation relaxed.

"From what I've seen, it's an idyllic place," he said. "It must have made you happy to return."

Kenan nodded. "It was home to me when I first came to foster," he said. "I was sad to leave it and glad to return. Some men are attached to people or a family or a cause. I seem to be attached to a place."

Morgan smiled faintly, though the pleasantness was all an act. "You speak with great fondness," he said. "That is the way I feel about Thetford, where I serve. It was home to me from the beginning."

"Thetford?" Kenan repeated. "Isn't that in Norfolk?"

"Aye."

"You are a long way from Norfolk."

Morgan downed the last of his wine. "As I told your lord, I am on an errand for my liege," he said. "I am trying to locate the man's brother and I have followed his trail to Bronllys. I will be here for a few days to see if I can locate anyone who has seen him."

"Papa invited him to stay at Mount Grace," Amarantha,

who had been largely silent through the conversation, spoke up. But then, she abruptly stood up, pulling Everelda with her. "In fact, we must go and prepare a chamber for him. Will you entertain our guest until Papa returns, Kenan?"

Kenan nodded as Amarantha fled the hall without another word, pulling her cousin with her. Morgan didn't dare watch her go, fearful that Kenan would assume that the gesture meant he was interested in her and, at the moment, Morgan was almost in over his head with the situation. He was in the presence of a man who knew Gere le Marche on sight and that, fundamentally, changed everything. He had to get Father Nicodemus alone and discover why the priest didn't tell him of Kenan's history at Mount Grace.

He was desperate to get out of there.

"I feel as if our host and hostess have left us," Morgan said, looking at Father Nicodemus. "Was it something I said?"

It was meant to be a jest and Father Nicodemus smiled weakly. "It seems as if there is a good deal going on around us," he said. Then he put a hand on Morgan's arm. "Mayhap this is not a good evening for socializing. I fear we may be more of a burden to the situation because they will feel they need to tend to us. Mayhap we should come back another time."

He was reading Morgan's mind, who was already standing up from his seat. "My thoughts exactly," he said. "We should leave."

Kenan stood up, as well. "Please do not go," he said. "This evening was meant to show you our thanks for what you did for Lady Amarantha. I am sorry you are left with me, but I will try to be a proper host."

Morgan wasn't unkind about it. "Mount Grace has shown great hospitality," he said. "The food was excellent, as was the wine, but I think it is best if we depart. The truth is that I have been traveling all day and am quite weary to the point of exhaustion, so I really must beg my leave. If you will tell Lord Hollis that I shall return on the morrow to accept his invitation to stay at Mount Grace, I would be grateful."

Kenan nodded. "I will, of course," he said. "Are you sure you will not stay? They will think I have chased you away."

Morgan forced a smile. "You have done nothing of the kind," he said. "I will make sure Lord Hollis and his daughter understand that when I return tomorrow."

Kenan didn't have much more to say to that so he simply nodded his head. Without another glance to the man, Morgan headed from the hall with Father Nicodemus on his heels. The evening had been most informative, the kind of information Morgan needed, but it wasn't the information he'd expected.

Strategies might have to be changed.

It wasn't welcome information in the least.

Exiting the stale, warm hall, the men crossed the inner ward with its halo of torches on the walls, heading to the outer bailey and not speaking a word between them. It simply wasn't safe, given the subject matter they both intended to speak of. Morgan wanted answers and Father Nicodemus knew what questions would be coming his way.

The silence between them was ripe with tension.

The gatehouse was sealed up for the night, but the appearance of Morgan and Father Nicodemus had the grooms bringing out their horses from the stables and the gates being opened. Several armed soldiers were at the ready when the gate cracked open enough to allow Morgan and Father Nicodemus through, prepared to fight off anyone who might try to rush the gates. But there was no one lying in wait and the pair headed down the road swiftly as the great gates closed behind them, groaning and creaking beneath the brilliant night sky. Only when Morgan was certain they were far enough away did he rein his horse to a walk, turning to the priest astride the hairy palfrey.

"You didn't tell me about de Poyer," he hissed. "If the man fostered at Mount Grace, surely he must know Gere le Marche on sight!"

Father Nicodemus took a deep breath. "Had I known, I would have told you," he said. "De Poyer and I have never been close, certainly not close enough to discuss subjects like fostering or where he has served his entire life. This is the first I am hearing about it."

Morgan rolled his eyes. "God's Bones," he muttered. "You were Oliver le Marche's priest, were you not?"

Father Nicodemus nodded. "I was, but only for a few years before John stole Mount Grace away. De Poyer must have fostered there well before I arrived."

"And you never knew?"

"Never."

"It never came up in any conversation? Not even with Lady Amarantha?"

"Why would it?" Father Nicodemus said, raising his voice in frustration. "Morgan, had I known, I surely would have told you, but Kenan de Poyer and I do not exactly see eye to eye. I do not ask about him and I do not speak of him, and it has simply never come up in any rumor, discussion, or confession I've ever heard. I did not know of his association with Mount Grace, I swear it."

Morgan sighed heavily. "I find it incredible that you did not know, but I will give you the benefit of the doubt," he said unhappily. "Rather than panic about it, let us think this through logically – if de Poyer fostered here, it had to be many years ago because the man has seen at least forty years. He is not young."

"Nay, he is not."

"That means he had to foster here at least twenty-five or more years ago."

"That stands to reason."

"Gere le Marche was only twenty years and eight when he died."

Father Nicodemus was coming to see what he was driving at. "Then even if he knew Gere, he would only know him as a child."

"My thoughts exactly."

"Unless he saw him during the battle for Mount Grace five years ago."

Morgan waved him off. "Even if he did, how close did he get?" he said. "He would have seen him at a distance. Remember that Gere evaded capture and escaped. But why wouldn't Lady Patience have told you about de Poyer?"

"Mayhap she does not even know," Father Nicodemus said. "De Poyer is not one of those knights who haunts taverns. He does not even come to mass. All he ever does is stay up at Mount Grace. Even if he did go to The Three Cocks, if he fostered at Mount Grace twenty-five years ago, Patience might not even know the man at all."

So many possibilities had Morgan's head swimming as much as that strong burgundy wine did. He grunted with frustration.

"That is a question we are going to find an answer to because if Kenan de Poyer knows Gere le Marche on sight, that… that will be a problem." He ran a hand over his face, trying to think logically on the problem. "The key lies with Patience."

"Then we'd better find out before you return there on the morrow."

Morgan couldn't agree more.

CHAPTER SEVEN

"YOU'RE GOING *WHERE*?"

The somewhat shocked question came from Everelda. It was just after dawn on a bright morning after the disastrous supper the night before that saw Farran fleeing in a rage, Hollis furious because of it, and the guest of honor slipping out because of the discord.

Amarantha wanted to set everything right.

"I said that I am going into Bronllys," she said. "I fear we chased off Sir Morgan last night with our bad behavior and I must apologize to the man."

Everelda frowned as Violet strutted into Amarantha's chamber behind her, looking for a cat to tease. "But why must you seek him?" she asked. "You invited him to sup. He had a good meal. You spoke to him and everyone thanked him, so why must you seek him again?"

Standing in front of her polished bronze mirror, Amarantha was inspecting her reflection closely. She had selected her dress carefully, a purple silk with gold thread.

And it clung to every curve.

"Because," she said simply.

"Because *why*?"

Amarantha knew the answer and she felt horrible about it. But not horrible enough to change her plans. Morgan of Mercia was the most handsome man she'd ever seen and there was something about him that drew her like a moth to a flame. From the top of his dark head to the bottom of his enormous feet, he drew her in as if she had no will of her own, dragging at her, sucking the willpower right out of her. All she wanted to do was stare at him.

She couldn't get him out of her mind.

"I told you why," she snapped softly. "To apologize for what happened last night. I am ashamed that things happened the way they did. I cannot have the man thinking we are a bunch of ill-bred fools."

Everelda knew that was somewhat the truth, but she suspected there was much more behind it. "He's married, Ammie," she said softly. "Why should you pursue a married man?"

Amarantha's head snapped to her, dark eyes flashing. "I am *not* pursuing him," she said. "I would never do that. He has a wife and that bond is sacred. But… oh, I do not know. I know he is married but that does not stop me from wanting to see him again if mayhap only to make a new friend. I know it seems pathetic, but there was something about him I cannot seem to push from my mind."

The last few sentences came out as a confused plea in a sense. Something was stirring in Amarantha's heart and mind, something she couldn't control. She'd never met a man who had captured her attention the way Morgan of Mercia had.

Even if he was married.

"Then I'll go with you," Everelda said, sighing in resignation. "You must not go alone. I will send for Kenan."

"Nay," Amarantha snapped. "I do not want Kenan along, nor anyone else. Evey, you know they all have designs on me, like I'm some ripe fruit ready for the picking. You saw how they reacted around Sir Morgan last night, as if he were some interloper into their territory. All because the man saved my life. Farran is still furious about it."

Everelda watched her turn back to the mirror and fix a pin in her braided hair. "Where is he?"

Amarantha sighed. "In the knight's quarters," she said. "He and Papa were arguing all night, evidently. I heard some of the servants speaking on it. Farran thinks I am bold and without manners and should be married immediately and Papa told him he will not be forced into anything. I suspect I will see Farran at some point today and if he finds out I've gone into town to see Sir Morgan, the man will more than likely either follow me or challenge Sir Morgan to a fight. He's mad, I say. Absolutely mad."

Everelda came up behind her and tucked a stray piece of hair from the back of her head into the golden net she wore on her hair.

"He is mad for you," she said frankly. "He has always been mad for you. We hide from him, try to stay away from him, but still he comes back. He is going to break your father down, Ammie, and then what will you do? You will be forced to marry a man who only wants to keep you as a possession."

Amarantha knew that but she wasn't sure what she could do about it. "I would hope it's more than that," she said. "I would hope he is interested in what I think. I would hope we would find humor in life together were we to marry."

"Then you are not opposed to it?"

Amarantha stared at her reflection in the mirror. "I am not certain what choice I have," she said. "That is what is so terrible about being a woman. We have very little choice in life. If my father wants me to marry Farran, no matter how I fight him, I must still marry Farran. And I simply do not want to."

Everelda put her arm around Amarantha's shoulders, giving her a squeeze. They were both resigned to what life had to offer because Hollis held the same power with Everelda. With her mother and father dead, Hollis was her guardian. She would have to marry the man he dictated, too.

"Come along," Amarantha said, patting her hand and moving to find her cloak and purse. "Let us head into Bronllys and find Sir Morgan. Father Nicodemus should know where he is, so we shall go to St. Mary the Virgin first. Go down to the stables now and have the groom saddle two palfreys. We can leave through the postern gate and take the trail down to the river."

Everelda headed for the door. "I will meet you in the stables."

"I'll be there."

Everelda slipped out as Amarantha slung her cloak over her shoulders. As she fastened it, her thoughts drifted to the big man she hadn't spent nearly enough time with last night. She had to admit that her enthusiasm to speak to him dampened after he told her that he was married and she further had to admit that she'd fled the hall as a result, but she'd come to grips with his marital status. To say she was disappointed was an understatement, but what she told Everelda was true – if she could make a friendly acquaintance of the man, then that was the best she could hope for. She would never cross the line and try to seduce him, but if a friend was the best she could have…

well, she'd take it.

It was better than nothing.

Grabbing her purse, she fastened it to her belt and slipped from her chamber, heading down to the stables. The trick from this point on would be to evade Kenan and, even worse, her father. She wasn't allowed to travel without an escort but as she'd told Everelda, she simply didn't want one this time. She would ride into town, find Morgan and apologize, and then return to the castle before anyone missed her.

At least, that was the hope.

CHAPTER EIGHT

"D E POYER? THE name sounds familiar. Why do you ask?"

It was early morning at The Three Cocks and the smell of baking bread was so strong that it was enough to make one sneeze. The scent of yeast was in the air, permeating the walls, as Morgan and Father Nicodemus stood in the kitchens with Patience. They'd just asked her a question that had to wait all night to be asked and when they'd presented it, Patience simply looked confused.

"Did Lord Oliver have a pledge or a squire by the name of Kenan de Poyer years ago?" Father Nicodemus asked. "I do not remember such a man during my years with your husband, so he must have been before my time. Do you recall?"

Patience pushed her bushy white hair out of her red face, thinking on the question. "De Poyer," she said again, mulling it over. "Before your time, you say? We had many boys and young men who came to foster in our home."

Father Nicodemus looked at Morgan, silent frustration echoed in his expression. Morgan tried not to become impatient with the woman they'd interrupted making bread at this early hour.

"He has dark hair and dark eyes," he said. "His face may have had eruptions in his youth because his skin is riddled with marks. It would have been, mayhap, fifteen years ago? Mayhap even twenty."

She pondered that a moment as a servant behind her removed bread loaves from the oven, dropping one on the ground. Patience snapped at her before returning her attention to Morgan and Father Nicodemus.

"Skin with eruptions, you say?" she said thoughtfully. "There was a lad, as I recall, who had terrible skin on his cheeks and chin. The boys used to call him Roasty because his skin was red enough that it looked as if it were cooked. I think his name was Kenneth or Keegan."

"Kenan," Morgan said with great relief. "Kenan de Poyer."

The light of recognition came to Patience's eyes. "Aye, I remember him," she said. "He was shunned by the other lads so he helped in the kitchens. He could not have been more than ten years of age. He left us when he was nearly twelve because his father wanted him to train at Kenilworth."

Kenilworth was the premier training ground of knights in England, which meant Kenan had been trained as an elite warrior. Somehow, that made him more dangerous than before and Morgan was careful as he continued.

"Was he close to Lord Oliver?" he asked. "Do you remember anything specific about him?"

More bread needed to come out of the oven so Patience began to help the servant in removing the bread before it burned. Morgan and Father Nicodemus followed her as she moved around the kitchens.

"I remember that Oliver sent him to the kitchens to protect

him from the other boys," she said. "Boys can be cruel at that age. As I recall, Kenan was quiet and efficient. He did his duties when asked. We had no trouble with him."

"Who was his father?"

Patience slid several loaves off of a board onto a table. "As I recall, his family was from Devon," she said. "I do not remember more than that, as Oliver was the one who accepted pledges, but I remember that Kenan was a good lad. Helpful. But… alone. I do not recall he ever had any friends."

"Was he close to your sons? To Gere?"

Patience shook her head. "God's Bones, nay," she said, shoving more raw bread into the oven to bake. "Gere was only an infant when Kenan was at Mount Grace. They never knew each other."

That was all Morgan wanted to hear. Relieved, he looked at the priest, who also seemed greatly relieved. That meant the man didn't know Gere le Marche on sight, meaning Morgan wasn't going to have to worry about that aspect of an already increasingly difficult task.

Thank God.

As for Kenan himself, it was interesting background information without much substance. Kenan was a loner who was helpful and then he went to train at Kenilworth. It didn't tell them much, but at least they knew a little about him.

What they didn't know, however, were his loyalties.

They could only assume he was loyal to John because of his service to Hollis, so that seemed to be the only logical conclusion. How dedicated was anyone's guess – there were those loyal to the king because they were told to, or had to be, and there were those loyal to him because they wanted to be. Not that it mattered in Kenan's case because he was Hollis' knight and he would do what Hollis told him, but Morgan had a feeling he was going to watch his step even more closely around Kenan.

Something told him to be vigilant.

As they turned to leave the kitchens, Patience stopped them.

"The Irish," she asked softly, making sure she wasn't heard. "Are they coming still?"

Morgan nodded. "Still."

"Where are they?"

"Near St. Arvans, waiting."

"That's not too terribly far," Patience said. "When are you going to meet them?"

Morgan offered her an encouraging smile. "Soon," he said. "But there are some things I must take care of first."

She didn't seem fond of that answer. "They have been paid already," she said. "They will not wait forever. You must act swiftly."

Morgan held up a hand to ease her. "I will act as soon as I can," he said. "I must have more information before I contact them and that is what I am gathering now. You have been most helpful in that regard."

Morgan didn't wait around for more questions or demands but rather headed out of the kitchens with Father Nicodemus at a rather clipped pace. They moved into the common room of the tavern, which was just coming alive as the new day dawned. Like most taverns, patrons slept all around the common room and were usually charged a pence or two for it, so one of Patience's serving wenches was going around, shaking sleeping men and demanding payment. Once, she got slapped, but she punched the man in the head and sent him to the ground. As Morgan watched, she took his purse, counted out three pennies, and went on to the next man.

As Morgan was coming to see, The Three Cocks was an interesting place.

"Patience does not seem to be living up to her name," Father Nicodemus muttered.

Morgan looked at him curiously. "What do you mean?"

"She is growing impatient."

Morgan grunted. "It will do her no good," he said. "I will not run off to the Irish without anything to tell them. Only a fool would act before he had all of the facts."

Father Nicodemus knew that but he wondered if Patience was going to give them trouble. He'd been seeing the anxiety building in her the past few months, ever since Gere had died and she'd sent to The Marshal for help. She wanted the help but she didn't seem content to wait for it.

He hoped it wasn't going to be a problem.

"What are you going to do this morning?" he asked Morgan, shifting the subject.

Morgan scratched his head wearily. "Probably sleep for a few hours," he said. "I did not get a wink of sleep last night worrying over the situation with Kenan, but now that I know he never knew Gere le Marche, I can rest easy. At least for this morning."

"You told Kenan that you were going to return to Mount Grace this morning," Father Nicodemus reminded him. "Do you still intend to go?"

Morgan nodded. "Indeed," he said. "I will sleep for a few hours, gather my things, and go to the castle. I must make contact with The Marshal's men in the mines before I can head off to find the Irish who, I am sure, are becoming increasingly impatient. They must be. They arrived in Wales more than two months ago and they've been sitting around, waiting."

Father Nicodemus lifted his eyebrows in agreement. "I hope they've not returned to Ireland."

"The Marshal sent word to them to wait, so I would assume not," Morgan said. "But they will not wait forever."

Father Nicodemus nodded quickly. "How are the men in the mine to contact you?"

"That is a good question," Morgan said. "The Marshal told me he sent men to the mine to determine if there was enough support for a rebellion, so I must assume that the men know someone is coming to Mount Grace, posing as Gere le Marche. I know many of The Marshal's agents, and they know me, so I would assume when we recognize each other, we will know."

The priest held up a hand. "Let me make it easier for you," he said. "I go to the mines on occasion. I know the men up there and I can tell you that there is great support for a rebellion. Let me see if I can find The Marshal's men and I will direct them to you."

"But how will you know them?"

"How long have they been in the mines?"

"Four, possibly six months."

"Then I shall ask about new men."

"But you cannot ask them if they serve The Marshal. If they do, they'll assume you're there to betray them to Hollis."

Father Nicodemus paused. "Mayhap you are right," he said. "But I can ask some of the seasoned miners, men I know who are loyal to le Marche, and they will tell me if The Marshal's men are among them. Morgan, you must realize that a rebellion has been rising for quite some time. The men are ready. If The Marshal's men are among them, promising them assistance, they will know about it."

That made sense but Morgan was reluctant to agree to the priest acting as an agent. That was his task, not the priest's. Still… he needed the help.

"Very well," he said. "You can move more easily among the miners than I ever could, so I will trust you to this task. I think it would be wise for me to wait here until you return. If I go to Mount Grace, you will have to find me there and I would rather not have Hollis and his men see us conversing. It is true that we are supposed to know one another, but I do not want to do anything that might bring them any suspicion at all."

Father Nicodemus understood. "Then wait here," he said. "I will return as quickly as I can. It is morning and the miners are just getting started with their daily tasks, so I will discover what I can."

Morgan tilted his head in the direction of the door. "Then go," he said. "I will be out of sight, back in the chambers that Gere used to occupy."

Father Nicodemus headed out, but not before there was more slapping in the common room, this time with the serving wench beating a man around the head and neck until he handed over a few pence for having spent the night laying on the floor. The priest frowned at the aggressive money collector, but it made Morgan grin. The slapping of old men by frustrated women struck him as humorous. He was just about to turn back for the kitchens and procure a meal before retreating to his chambers when he caught sight of a couple of men entering the tavern as Father Nicodemus exited.

It took him all of a split second to recognize the men.

You will not be alone in this, so keep an eye out for men you know, The Marshal had said.

Help had arrived.

CB

THEIR EYES MET and instant acknowledgement was in the air.

All Morgan had to do was discreetly motion the two men to follow him and the trio headed down a corridor where the series of locked doors awaited. Morgan had the keys that Patience had given him, so he quickly unlocked one door and ushered the men in. Not a word was spoken as he locked the door and proceeded to the second door at the end of another corridor, unlocking that door and indicating for the men to enter.

They did.

Morgan followed them into the chamber, shut the door, and locked it before finally facing the pair, who were clad in heavy cloaks, their features partially obscured by the hoods. But those hoods and cloaks began to come off and Morgan found himself looking at two of William Marshal's most seasoned and trusted agents. Powerful didn't even begin to encompass all they were. If the Executioner Knights had an inner circle, then these men were in the middle of it.

Bric MacRohan and Alexander de Sherrington were gazing back at him.

"Is this all the greeting we are to receive?" Alexander asked. "Christ, Morgan, you might offer us a cup of wine or a bit of bread. We've come a very long way to make sure you do not foul up this mission. So you could show your gratitude, at the very least."

He was jesting and Morgan knew it. Breaking into a grin, he reached out his hand in greeting. Alexander, a man otherwise known as Sherry to his friends, possessed black hair, black eyes, and big, white teeth surrounded by a black beard. He flashed that big grin at Morgan and took his outstretched hand, laughing softly. Bric, on the other hand, was the exact opposite of Alexander in coloring, with hair so blond that it was almost white and blue eyes so pale and pure that they were silver. As Alexander and Morgan shook hands, Bric tossed his cloak onto the bed and fell down on top of it.

"Christ," he muttered in his heavy Irish brogue. "Bring me some food and I will sleep for the rest of the day. When I awaken, you can tell us everything that has happened."

Morgan watched the man as he sprawled across his small bed. "I will bring you food, but sleep will have to wait," he said. "I have been to the belly of the beast and I must give you a report."

Bric's pale eyes opened and fixed on him. "You've been to the mines?"

Morgan shook his head. "Nay," he said. "But I was invited to Mount Grace last night to sup with Hollis de la Haye himself. The man has a daughter and… wait a moment. Let me find some food and I'll hurry back. I'll tell you everything when I return."

With that, he unlocked the door and rushed out, leaving his comrades behind. Morgan made it into the kitchens where Patience was pulling more bread out of the oven and had a serving wench put together a fairly large meal of fresh bread loaves, butter, boiled apples and cinnamon, warmed over beef and gravy from the night before, porridge, and warm wine mixed with boiled fruit juice. He took it back with him on a big tray, going through the locks and relocking doors, only to find Bric snoring on his bed and Alexander sitting in a chair, his head against the wall.

Alexander lifted his head when Morgan came back in and

Bric stirred, but it was clear that both men were exhausted. Morgan set the tray down, tapping Bric on the leg to rouse him. When the man struggled to sit up, Morgan handed him a cup of warmed wine. Bric took it gratefully.

"Did you travel all night?" Morgan asked.

Bric gulped the wine. "We have not slept for two days and nights," he said. "We hurried to come, unsure of what we would find and unsure of what is transpiring."

"Then I will not keep you long," Morgan said. "I have made contact with Patience le Marche, who owns this tavern, and a priest from St. Mary the Virgin who used to be Oliver le Marche's personal priest. He is very much in support of a rebellion to regain Mount Grace and has been instrumental in helping me discover what I can about the current situation."

Bric had moved over to the small table where he and Alexander were stuffing their faces with hot bread and butter.

"And what have you discovered?" Alexander asked, mouth full.

Morgan pulled up a stool next to the table and sat heavily. "Yesterday, when I went to the church to contact the priest, there was a lady inside the sanctuary teaching some of the local village children," he said. "The lady, as it turned out, was the daughter of Hollis de la Haye. Naturally, I remained in the shadows, but as I lingered there, outlaws came to the church and tried to rob the lady. I was forced to kill them both in her defense and that action garnered me an invitation to sup at Mount Grace."

Alexander and Bric, in spite of their weariness, were listening closely. "Excellent," Alexander said. If there was a mission to be undertaken, he was usually in command of it, so it was usual that he was on hand when important missions were happening. "You were supposed to make contact with Hollis."

"And I did," Morgan said. "The priest and I came up with a cover – my name is Morgan of Mercia and our families share a long friendship. That was enough to invite Hollis' instant trust in me, at least so far, and he has invited me to lodge at the castle during my stay in Bronllys."

"What do you mean 'during your stay'?" Alexander asked.

Morgan fixed on him. "I had to come up with a story as to why I am actually here," he said. "My backstory is that I serve de Winter at Thetford. My garrison commander's brother has gone missing and I am following the man's trail, a trail that has led me to Bronllys."

"Brilliant," Bric muttered, rubbing his eyes. "You can remain here nearly indefinitely, all under the guise of searching for this missing brother."

"That's what I thought," Morgan said. "If it comes to the point where I have overstayed my welcome, I can always ask Hollis if he will accept my fealty. By that time, I hope to make myself completely indispensable so that he cannot refuse me."

There was approval in the air. Bric and Alexander understood the situation and what had transpired so far.

So far, so good.

But one thing hadn't escaped either Bric or Alexander.

"You are Morgan pretending to be Gere now pretending to be Morgan of Mercia," Bric said as if piecing together a great puzzle. "That is rather convoluted."

Morgan grinned. "I had little choice," he said. "I'm Gere for the Irish and the lads in the mine and Morgan of Mercia for Hollis and his daughter. It's not as if I could tell de la Haye that I'm Gere le Marche."

"Or Morgan de Wolfe, nephew of a rebelling warlord," Bric said.

"Exactly."

"Even so, you have done well," Alexander said. "Now, you will introduce us to Lady le Marche so that she may employ us around the tavern. We are here to keep an eye on you and to help you if needed, but The Marshal also thought that Bric should go with you when you contact the Irish mercenaries. It might help to have another Irishman at your side. It might invite trust."

Morgan nodded. "Agreed," he said. "Even now, the priest has gone to the mines to contract the men that The Marshal sent. Do you know who they are?"

Alexander shook his head. "Not me," he said. "That has been kept secretive, for obvious reasons. But I am assured we will know them when we see them."

"That is what I was told," Morgan said. "They are to meet me here at some point, so until I speak with them, I cannot seek out the Irish. Not yet. The rebellion must be coordinated from all parties, so I must speak to The Marshal's men first."

"Agreed," Alexander said. He glanced at Bric. "Bric thought that we might find jobs in the mine, but I think we'll be more valuable here. Miners only hear certain things, isolated as they are, but here in town, we'll have a larger picture of what is happening, I think."

"And working in the tavern will make you privy to the gossip of men," Morgan said. "I agree that you are better served here. Besides… Bric doesn't look like a miner."

They grinned at the big, Irish knight who looked like a mythological god from old. If anyone did *not* look like a miner, it was Bric MacRohan. The man couldn't stand out more if he tried.

"Then it is settled," Alexander said. "We will stay here. Let us gain a few hours' sleep, introduce us to Lady Patience, and we will be at your disposal."

Morgan nodded. "She goes by Madam Iris here," he said. "No one knows otherwise."

"Understood."

Morgan sighed, looking around the room, feeling his fatigue from a restless night. Now that he'd briefed Alexander and Bric, he could fall back to his schedule for the day.

"Truth be told, I could use a few hours of sleep myself," he said, standing wearily from the stool. "Let me pull a couple of beds in here and we'll use this chamber as our base. It belonged to Gere le Marche and, as we know, the man was a bit of a recluse."

"I was wondering about the locked doors," Bric muttered.

"Evidently, he kept himself locked up," Morgan said. "Sherry, help me with the beds. I do not think Bric is going to move off that one."

To prove the point, Bric lay back down, half a loaf of warm bread in his hand, chewing with his eyes closed. Alexander lifted a disapproving eyebrow at the man as he followed Morgan out into the tavern in the hunt for more beds. They managed to find two in other rooms, the only beds in the room, but that couldn't be helped. Let travelers sleep on the floor.

The knights wanted the beds.

Morgan was still undressing when snoring of such magnitude filled the chamber that he swore the walls were rattling. Bric was bad, but Alexander was worse. However, being too tired to care, Morgan fell into the smallest bed in the chamber, one his enormous frame hardly fit on, but it was enough. He wasn't in a position to be picky.

As the morning around them deepened, his snores ended up being the loudest of all.

CHAPTER NINE

"ARE YOU SURE this is where he said that he was staying?" Everelda sounded incredulous. Truth be told, Amarantha was a little incredulous herself. Both women were standing in front of a large, run-down establishment with a sign nailed above the door that had three phallic symbols burned into it.

The Three Cocks.

Amarantha sighed faintly.

"That's what he said," she replied reluctantly. "If you do not want to go inside with me, I understand."

Everelda looped her elbow around Amarantha's. "You're not going in there alone," she said. "If you must go, then I shall go with you. Proceed."

Fighting off a grin, and perhaps a measure of trepidation, Amarantha entered the smelly, low-ceilinged tavern. It was dark inside in spite of the time of day, which was later than Amarantha had planned. Difficulty getting out of Mount Grace unnoticed had seen them come to Bronllys close to midday. Though some of the tables had oil lamps that gave off a slight amount of light, there was more light coming in through the window at the front of the establishment, enough so that they could see the room fairly well.

There was a table right in front of the window, in fact, and Amarantha headed directly for it, sitting in a rickety chair and pushing Everelda into the other one, which happened to have something wet and chunky on the seat. Everelda groaned when she realized she'd more than likely sat in vomit, but she stayed down, hating every minute of this little venture already. But Amarantha wasn't looking at her miserable cousin.

She was looking at the room.

People were eating at this nooning hour and the entire place smelled heavily of freshly baked bread. When a droopy-eyed serving wench approached the table, Amarantha ordered a meal for herself and Everelda. The wench wandered away, leaving the women to remove their gloves and settle in as the fire in the hearth gained in intensity. But they kept their cloaks on, hoods on, trying to hide a little from the room at large or at least be as inconspicuous as possible. Nothing screamed danger like two lone women in a tavern where men were relieving themselves in the corner while still others lay sleeping on the floor.

"This is a terrible place, Ammie," Everelda hissed. "Did you truly have to come here? Could you not have simply sent the man a missive?"

Amarantha watched one man walk right up to the hearth, drop his breeches, and piss straight into the flame. Disgusted, she turned her head.

"Nay," she said flatly. "There is no guarantee he would have even received a missive. It would have been careless to send one and I do not wish to be careless. Hopefully, he will make an appearance soon and we can be done with this… this *place.*"

Everelda sighed heavily, pulling her cloak more tightly about her slender shoulders and looking out of the window to the street beyond. The mist from the morning had lifted and green fields could be seen beyond the road. However, she seemed to be riveted to something outside, something that had her stiffening as she watched it move closer to the door. When the panel flew open and three armed, loud men entered, she quickly lowered her head.

"I want to leave," she hissed. "*Now*, Ammie. This is not a safe place!"

Amarantha's back was to the door so she had to turn her head slightly to see what had Everelda so upset. She, too, could see the armed soldiers entering, looking around for an unoccupied table and finding one on the opposite side of the hearth. They were crass and rough, pushing men out of the way, claiming a table and demanding food. Amarantha stopped looking at them and pulled her hood down even further.

"Just a moment longer," she said softly. "As soon as Sir Morgan makes an appearance and I have apologized, we shall leave. I promise."

"But I am afraid!"

"I know," Amarantha said soothingly. "Just a moment longer to see if Sir Morgan shows himself. *Please*."

Everelda simply lowered her head, making sure her face was covered, as the soldiers at the other table received drink and bread from an equally rough serving wench. Meanwhile, the droopy-eyed servant had returned to Amarantha and Everelda with bread, butter, hot wine, and a slab of eggs baked with cheese and what turned out to be pieces of pork.

The women turned their backs to the room and began eating, realizing the food was very good. They ate until they could hold no more and finished off the wine. It took some time to accomplish it all and they were coming to think that Morgan might never make that appearance. The only things happening in the common room were more customers coming in from the outside and the soldiers near the hearth growing louder and louder. Amarantha was coming to think that it was time to leave when she caught movement out of the corners of her eyes.

There was a doorway on the south side of the common room that led to a dark corridor. Morgan emerged from that doorway and went straight into the kitchens. Bolstered by his abrupt appearance, Amarantha strained to catch a glimpse of what was going on back there, hearing his voice but not his words. Her heart was pounding in her chest at the mere sight of him when Morgan suddenly emerged from the kitchens with an older woman in tow. As the woman headed off to another part of the tavern, Morgan was heading back to the corridor.

Amarantha knew that if she didn't catch his attention, he would pass her by.

"My lord?" she suddenly said, standing up to attract his attention. "Sir Morgan?"

Morgan was about to go into the corridor when he heard his name and saw the ethereal vision of Lady Amarantha standing near the window. At first, he thought that he was dreaming. Surely the woman wouldn't have come to this place! But the more he stared at her, the more he realized that she was indeed real. She was here. Startled, not to mention greatly puzzled, Morgan headed in her direction.

"Lady Amarantha?" he said, incredulous. "God's Bones, what are you doing here? Where is your father?"

"At Mount Grace," she said, her focus riveted to the man like there was nothing else in the entire world to look at. "He does not know I am here, but I had to come. I had to see you after the debacle last night."

Morgan frowned. "What debacle?"

Amarantha seemed ill at ease as she spoke. "My father leaving the meal so rudely," she said. "Sir Farran leaving the meal. Everyone leaving the meal and leaving you alone with Kenan. Truly, I had to apologize to you. We are not a bunch of animals, I swear it. I should have never left you alone and I am deeply sorry."

Morgan's eyes twinkled at her, seeing that she was both nervous and apologetic, and sincerely so. Honestly, he'd never given the evening another thought other than to think of her, but he could see that the situation had upset her and, like a well-bred lady, she had come to make amends to a guest who had been poorly treated, at least in her opinion.

And he couldn't have been happier to see her.

"I *was* deeply offended," he said, teasing her to see how she would react. "I came back and cried myself to sleep."

Amarantha looked at him in horror only to realize that he was jesting. Truth be told, it relieved her a great deal to see he was willing to joke about such a breach of etiquette. It said something for the man's character.

He was willing to forgive.

But she wasn't beyond jesting with him return.

"Did you?" she said, feigning sympathy. "I am so sorry. You poor man."

"Aye, it *was* awful."

"Will you ever recover?"

His lips twitched with a smile. "It is doubtful," he said. "I only know of one way."

"What is that?"

"If you will let me sit with you while you finish your meal."

It was clear from the debris on the table that they'd already eaten, but Amarantha indicated for him to sit, anyway. Any opportunity with him she would take. He grabbed a chair at a nearby table and planted himself between the two women, his focus completely on Amarantha.

"I feel much better already," he said. "But I do have a question."

"What is that?"

"What is your father going to do when he realizes you are missing?"

Guiltily, Amarantha looked at Everelda, who simply lifted her eyebrows as if to suggest she'd been saying the same thing all along.

"Send men to find me, I suppose," she said. "But I could not let you think we were a bunch of savages. I had to apologize."

A lazy smile creased his lips. "You did not have to, not in the least," he said. "But the fact that you are here, and have risked your life to come, tells me you are a woman of character. And I am deeply honored that you should be so concerned for my good opinion."

Amarantha's cheeks flushed a bright red at the gentle compliment. "It was my obligation and my pleasure," she said, struggling not to avert her gaze because he was smiling so openly at her. "I hope we at least fed you well before you were forced to flee."

"I've never had finer," he said. "You have an excellent cook."

Amarantha smiled, relaxing as the conversation turned pleasant. "Thank you," she said. "She is from France. My father says the best food and drink in the world come from France."

But Morgan turned up his nose. "The French use parts of the animal's bodies that I do not care to eat," he said. "Brains, stomachs, kidneys, livers. When they serve those things, I feel like a vulture feeding on carrion."

He said it rather dramatically and Amarantha and Everelda giggled. "Kidneys are quite tasty," Amarantha said. "You do not like them?"

Morgan shook his head. "Believe it or not, you are looking at a man with a surprisingly finicky appetite," he said. "When I was young, all I would eat was porridge and chicken."

"And now?"

He chuckled. "I have learned to like other things," he said. "Chicken, beef, pork, quail, eggs. My repertoire has expanded."

"But that is all you like?"

He nodded. "Unfortunately for me," he said. "I would rather starve than eat some of the things that are presented on fine tables."

"Ah," Amarantha said. "Then you are an ungrateful guest."

"That is *not* so."

She lifted her eyebrows. "What if I had served you eels? Would you have refused to eat them?"

He started to shake his head but just ended up laughing. "If I ever return to Mount Grace, please do not serve me eels," he said, pretending to plead. "I would not dream of offending you, but a trencher full of eels just might force my hand."

Amarantha watched him as he smiled. He had a glorious smile that changed the shape of his entire face. "I will not, I swear it," she said. "But what do you mean 'if you return to Mount Grace? You promised us that you would come and stay while you conducted your sad business in Bronllys. Have you forgotten your promise?"

He shook his head. "Not at all," he said. "In fact, I was just preparing to go to the castle even now. If you and your cousin are ready to leave, I can escort you personally. It would be my honor."

It was a kind way of saying she needed to get out of that seedy tavern and return home before something dreadful happened. As much as Amarantha wanted to stay and talk to him, she knew there would be time later when he came to Mount Grace.

She would make good use of that time.

"Very well," she said. "We accept. In fact, I think *we* need to escort *you* to the castle so you can see that we really do have good manners. I would hate you leaving Mount Grace thinking otherwise."

"I would never think otherwise."

He was smiling warmly at her, causing her heart to leap in all directions. Something in the way he looked at her set her all aflutter.

But perhaps it was all in her mind.

He'd told her that he was married. She had known that since last night, a bit of information that caused her to flee the hall like an idiot. She knew the man had a wife and probably children, too. He was a kind, polite, and attractive man and he was only being polite to her with his warm smile. She *knew* that.

… didn't she?

But, God, she was becoming smitten with him.

"I was wondering something, Sir Morgan."

Everelda suddenly entered the conversation. She hadn't spoken a word last night and, today, remained largely silent, so her voice startled Amarantha out of her daydreams about Morgan of Mercia. She looked at Everelda but the woman was looking at Morgan, who dipped his head politely.

"Speak, my lady," he said. "What is troubling you?"

Everelda shook her head. "Nothing is troubling me," she said. "That is, nothing serious. I was simply wondering about your wife. Have you been gone a long time? Won't she be missing you?"

If Amarantha could have reached Everelda under the table, she would have kicked her as hard as she could. Amarantha didn't want to hear about his wife, but Everelda clearly thought differently. Perhaps she was reminding Amarantha that the man was, in fact, already married, and truth be told, Amarantha needed that reminder. She was so swept away by the man that she didn't *want* to remember.

But she needed to.

Morgan, however, didn't seem to mind the question. He scratched his head before replying.

"Can you keep a secret, ladies?"

Amarantha and Everelda looked at each other curiously before returning their focus to him and nodding solemnly.

"Of course, Sir Morgan," Amarantha said seriously. "We can absolutely keep a secret."

Morgan looked at her. "It is very important that no one know," he said. "In fact, it is vital."

"Are you sure you want to tell us?"

Morgan nodded. Then he scratched his head again, a nervous gesture. "I am *not* married," he said quietly, as if it were some great revelation. "I only told your father and Sir Farran that because Sir Farran was looking at me as if he wanted to run me through. He is quite possessive of you, Lady Amarantha, and I did not wish to tangle with him, so for his peace of mind, I told him I was married. I did not want to be perceived as a threat. But you must never let him or your father know that because they will think me a liar."

Amarantha's mouth popped open in surprise. "You... you're *not* married?"

He shook his head, his eyes glimmering. "Nay."

When Amarantha realized that he was serious, she couldn't describe the burst of hope she felt. But along with it came a burst of anger.

"You do not need to do anything to soothe Farran," she said, clipped. "He does not own me. God knows that he has tried to woo me, but I am not interested in being another possession of a man who has many fine possessions. That is all he wants me for."

Morgan lifted his eyebrows. "Are you certain?"

"Of course I am," she snapped softly. There was disgust in her tone. "He simply wants a prize on his arm. There is no feeling involved, only what *he* wants, and I do not want to marry a man who is so bloody selfish."

Strong words from such a delicate-looking lady, but in those words, Morgan could see her strength. She may have looked like a goddess, a fragile being that needed tending, but he was coming to see that she wasn't. Any lass brave enough to elude her father and slip out to a tavern, unescorted, was either very stupid or very courageous.

Morgan was coming to see that it was the latter.

Truthfully, he wasn't exactly sure why he told her the truth about his marital status. It would have been much easier to keep up the pretense, but he couldn't seem to manage it. He wanted her to know that he was unattached and, God help him, it was quite dangerous to even think those thoughts much less enable them. By telling her the truth, he was enabling everything. He was telling her that he was free.

She was free.

His common sense was being sorely beat upon by his attraction to the lady.

"I think all men are inherently selfish, my lady," he said after a moment, trying to distract himself from musings that seemed to linger on her heavily. "But I am sure Sir Farran is a good man. I do not think your father would advocate for him if he were not. He wants to see that you are happy and protected."

Something in Amarantha's eyes dimmed as he spoke and she lowered her gaze. "I am certain he wishes for me to be protected," she said, omitting the acknowledgment that her father wanted her to be happy. "Now, we were to head back to Mount Grace. Will you come with us?"

She was changing the subject off of Farran and Morgan complied, but it wasn't a subject they would get off completely. He knew there would be more to come at some point. The lady was verging on a betrothal that she was clearly unhappy about and, truth be told, Morgan wasn't so sure he didn't care about it, either. It didn't concern him in the least, yet he couldn't seem to help it.

"Aye, I will," he said, forcing himself to focus on something else. "Let me collect my things and I will return shortly. You will not move from this table, ladies. Is that understood?"

With the loud soldiers over by the hearth, laughing and snorting and making crude jokes, both Amarantha and Everelda nodded seriously. Morgan eyed the table of fighting men before standing up and making his way over to the corridor. Down the hall to the locked door he went, but by the time he was preparing to unlock the door, he could hear hissing behind him. He turned to see Patience scurrying towards him.

"That woman," she hissed as she came near. "Those women you are with. I know them."

Morgan nodded. "I would think you would," he said. "I have been invited to stay at Mount Grace because I protected de la Haye's daughter yesterday and they are returning the favor."

Patience's jaw ticked. "That's Lady Amarantha," she said. "The other woman is her cousin. I have seen them in town with Mount Grace soldiers over the years."

"You've never had contact with them?"

Patience shook her head. "Nay," she grumbled. "Any contact I would have would involve a dagger to the little bitch's belly. For what her father did to my family, she deserves nothing else."

A warning bell went off in Morgan's head. He hadn't seen this side of Patience before but he wasn't surprised. The woman had lost everything to John and, subsequently, Hollis. But now Amarantha was involved, an innocent victim of her father's ambition and Patience's venom, and he didn't like the fact that Patience wanted to kill her.

Not simply kill… *murder*.

"That would not be wise," he said, trying not to sound too stern. "You have been living in anonymity since the fall of Mount Grace and although I understand your desire for vengeance, killing Hollis' daughter would only bring his wrath down on you. You would not survive it and, in fact, I could only imagine he would make sure you suffered in the most painful way possible."

"I do not care," Patience said, her eyes flashing. "It would be worth it."

"But Mount Grace would remain with Hollis," Morgan pointed out. "If you die, then all that is left of the House of le

Marche dies. Hollis and the king will be the victors forever. Is that really what you want? To be so reckless when we are so close?"

That gave Patience pause, but she was still angry. Old anger from years of pain and suffering was difficult to overcome.

"Then take her a hostage," she muttered. "Take her and hold her and demand that Hollis leave Mount Grace or we will send him his daughter's fingers, one by one, until there are no more fingers left. If he refuses still, we will send him her toes and so on. Do you not know how to use leverage, Gere?"

Morgan wasn't entirely sure she was calling him Gere because that was his assumed identity or if she really thought, for a moment, that he was her dead son. There was a hint of madness in her eyes that he hadn't seen before and the fact that she was advocating extremely brutal negotiating tactics was suspect.

He didn't like it.

The last thing he needed was for the woman to fall into the abyss of insanity.

"It will not work," he said evenly. "Men like Hollis de la Haye will not be coerced. Their pride and loyalty to the king is worth more than a daughter and, in the end, you'd have a fingerless and toeless woman on your hands who, in the grand scheme of things, is an innocent."

Patience looked at him in outrage. "How can you say that?"

"Because it's true," Morgan said, pulling out the key for the door. "She did not order the attack on Mount Grace, nor did she participate in the slaughter of your family. If you harm her, you are not punishing Hollis. You are only harming an innocent woman, so I would suggest you leave her out of this mess. We must stay the course, my lady. Agreed?"

Patience didn't want to agree. "I have waited years for this moment," she said, her anger building. "You did not see your husband and son killed before your very eyes. You did not experience the grief. Of course you can be patient about the situation, but I cannot. The Marshal promised me help and you are not giving it."

Morgan could see that there was going to be a problem unless he defused this quickly. Nothing he was saying was causing her to see reason. It was an unexpected complication that needed to be resolved or there would be real problems.

Probably sooner than he realized.

"I only just arrived yesterday," he said, more firmly than he had intended to. "You must give me time. We have a plan. It will work, but you must have faith. Abducting Hollis de la Haye's daughter will not achieve victory. It will destroy everything Gere has worked for."

Patience, in the throes of fury, slapped him across the face, hard. "Do not utter my son's name," she growled. "You are not worthy to speak it. He did all he could to regain his legacy until God took him and sent you instead. There are almost a thousand Irish mercenaries waiting to be released against Mount Grace. Imagine how much easier their task would be with a hostage – a de la Haye hostage!"

Morgan's jaw was ticking faintly, grossly unhappy that she had slapped him. Had Patience been a man, she would be bleeding out on the floor by now, but because she was a woman… well, it was a good thing she was a woman. Morgan had never raised a hand to a woman and never would.

But that didn't cool his rising anger.

"It would be stupid to have a hostage," he said flatly. "Do not behave stupidly. Stop thinking with your heart and think with your mind. I am telling you that a hostage would do no good, so we will not speak of it anymore. I am certain your son would agree with me and if you slap me again for speaking of him, know that you will not like my reaction. My hand is bigger and stronger than yours. Do we understand one another?"

Patience may have been enraged, but she wasn't foolish. She had no way of knowing Morgan's big hand was an empty threat, but she was wise enough to back off. She muttered something and turned away as Morgan went through the unlocked door and bolted it behind him. No more words were spoken.

But that didn't mean the subject was at rest.

Quite the opposite.

Patience turned her attention to the common room, coming out of the corridor and standing at the mouth of it, watching the two small women at the table over near the window. To her, she saw the key to everything in Hollis de la Haye's daughter even if Morgan didn't. She didn't agree that taking her hostage wouldn't solve all of her problems. At the very least, it would deprive Hollis of his daughter as Hollis had deprived her of a husband and son.

Morgan was wrong.

Amarantha de la Haye *was* the key.

But Morgan didn't think so. He was focused on his mission, on creating a rebellion to regain Mount Grace, when all he had to do was take one little woman hostage and blackmail her father.

That was the best possible solution.

Gere had worked tirelessly to gain enough manpower to regain Mount Grace, a burden that Morgan had assumed. While Patience appreciated William Marshal and his men in the quest to regain Mount Grace, for them it was all about politics. He who controlled Mount Grace controlled a great deal, so there was no altruism involved.

Only politics.

But for Patience, this was her husband's home. It was where both of her sons had been born. She'd lost everything and now she was the sole survivor of an old but bereft house. Madam Iris had been born out of necessity and desperation, but Patience le Marche had never died. She was still there, demanding justice for those who had been stolen from her. Just when she thought it was in sight, the very man sent to help seemed to be reluctant to find a swift and logical solution.

Patience wasn't patient anymore.

Morgan didn't have the passion that she had. He didn't care as much as she did. This was simply a directive to him, given to him by William Marshal and there was nothing inherent in him that was desperate to gain the castle back. He had no stake in it and it showed. But she did. She was going to get her castle back and she was going to use Hollis de la Haye's daughter to do it.

She had a plan.

CHAPTER TEN

"DO YOU THINK I have time to use the privy?" Everelda asked.

Amarantha looked at her cousin with exasperation. "*Now?*"

Everelda had to relieve herself at the most inopportune times. Since she'd been a child, there was no holding back if she had to piss, so Amarantha knew, even as she asked, what the answer would be.

Now.

She grunted with annoyance.

"I do not even know where it is," she said, looking around timidly. "Moreover, Morgan told us to stay here. He'll join us shortly."

Everelda frowned. "That may be, but I will still have to use the privy," she said. "It will only take a few moments. Do you suppose it's outside?"

Amarantha knew there would be no stopping her. "Probably," she said. "Ask one of the serving wenches. Ask them if it is safe for you. Do you want me to go with you?"

Everelda shook her head. "Nay," she said. "If Sir Morgan

returns and finds us both gone, he may become angry."

Amarantha shook her head slowly. "If he returns and finds you gone, he will be angry regardless," she said. "Hurry, now. If you've got to go, then go."

Everelda was on her feet, looking for the nearest serving wench. She spied one just coming out of the kitchens and rushed off to intercept her. Amarantha watched the brief conversation and the wench pointed out to the rear of the tavern, back where the livery yard was. She watched Everelda disappear into the kitchens, heading to the yard in the rear. More than likely, it was simply a pit in the ground, which both disgusted Amarantha and made her want to laugh. Everelda was very picky about her privacy.

But her humor would have to wait. Morgan had told them not to leave the table and they'd already disobeyed somewhat, so she sat fast, hood pulled up around her head and facing the window rather than the room. She could hear people behind her, eating and talking, and still more people were entering simply to drink. The only taverns or inns that Amarantha had ever been in were those with her father, and they had been quite luxurious as far as establishments go. The Three Cocks wasn't even close to what she was used to, so she was anxious to leave.

The moments ticked away slowly.

"My lady?"

The voice came from behind. Startled, Amarantha turned to see an old woman with a wild frizz of white hair behind her. It occurred to her that she'd seen the woman around the tavern. In fact, she'd see her with Morgan.

She smiled politely.

"Aye?" she said. "May I be of service?"

The old woman nodded. "I think so," she said. "Your companion was just sent to the privy out back. I think she needs your help."

Amarantha was immediately on her feet. "Where is she?"

The old woman gestured for her to follow. "Come with me," she said. "I will take you to her."

Amarantha didn't hesitate. "Is she well?" she said. "She did not seem ill when she left me."

The old woman continued to walk quickly back into the kitchens, which were vacant for the most part. "This way," she said, not directly answering her question. "I sent her in here."

They took a turn and passed through a larder, cramped and low-ceilinged, and into a chamber beyond. Amarantha thought nothing of it when the old woman stepped aside and allowed her to pass through first. She ended up in a chamber that had straw on the bottom, solid stone walls, and a door that led to the stable yard beyond.

The door to the yard was closed, but Amarantha still didn't think anything of the situation. She turned towards the old woman to ask her where Everelda was but she didn't quite get that far. Something heavy and solid hit her on the side of the head, so hard that stars burst before her eyes. She began to fall and tried to catch herself on something, but that ended when a second blow knocked her out completely.

After that, there was only darkness.

CHAPTER ELEVEN

MORGAN HAD JUST finished shoving a tunic into his satchel when he happened to catch a glimpse of Patience driving an old wagon out of the stable yard. There were tiny windows in his chamber for ventilation, one facing the stable yard and one facing the alleyway to the south, and he watched Patience drive the wagon, filled with straw, down the alleyway and disappear.

But he never gave it another thought.

People moved in and out of the stable yard at all hours, as he'd seen since his arrival, so there was nothing strange about the owner of the tavern heading out in a wagon. More than likely to get supplies, he was certain, and then he noted a merchant riding into the stable yard on an exceptionally fine warmblood that he found himself admiring as he finished securing a second satchel. He only had two.

On the other beds, Bric and Alexander were stirring.

"Christ," Bric muttered in a brogue so thick that it was difficult to understand him. "What time is it?"

Morgan glanced up from his task. "Just after the nooning hour."

Bric rubbed his eyes before looking over at Morgan with his bags on his small bed. "Where are you going?"

Morgan sat down on the bed to tighten up the ties of his right boot. "While you have been getting your beauty sleep, I have been making plans to go to Mount Grace," he said. "As fortune would have it, Lady Amarantha de la Haye came to this very tavern a short time ago and now I am going to escort her and her cousin back to the castle."

By this time, Alexander was awake, sitting up wearily. "Why did she come here?" he asked, groggy.

Morgan smirked. "Believe it or not, to apologize to me," he said. "Last night's feast was a bit irregular because the man who very much wishes to marry Lady Amarantha became offended and stormed off, followed by her father and eventually by the lady herself. I was left alone at the table with the priest and a knight named Kenan de Poyer. Do either of you know Keller de Poyer of Nether Castle?"

Alexander yawned. "In Powys?"

"I believe so."

Alexander nodded. "Aye, I know him," he said. "He mostly stays to Wales and the Marches, but he was The Marshal's garrison commander at Pembroke Castle for years. He's not really an agent, but he supports anything we do. And he's loyal to The Marshal until the end of all things. He is a good man."

Morgan hadn't been part of the Executioner Knights for years as Alexander and Bric had been, so he didn't know some of the men as well as they did.

"As it turns out, Kenan de Poyer, commander of Mount Grace, is Keller's brother," he said. "I do not know any more than that, but I sense there is bad blood between them."

Alexander grunted. "Is it any wonder?" he said. "Keller

serves The Marshal and his brother serves the king. They are not the only family touched by such politics."

"True," Morgan said. "In any case, Kenan fostered at Mount Grace, information that caught me by surprise, because I was concerned that if he'd spent some time there, he would know Gere le Marche on sight."

That bit of news had both Bric and Alexander registering concern. "And does he know Gere?" Alexander asked.

Morgan shook his head. "He does not," he said. "He was at Mount Grace when Gere was an infant, so there is no way he would recognize the grown man. We do not have to worry over that."

It was good news. "That is a relief," Alexander said. "What now?"

Morgan stood up from the bed and grabbed his bags. "I go to Mount Grace and you two find work around this fine establishment," he said. "I just saw Lady Patience ride out of here, so when she returns, tell her who you are and she will give you something to do. Meanwhile, I am escorting Lady Amarantha and her cousin back to the castle, but I will return once I have spoken with The Marshal's men in the mines. Father Nicodemus is supposed to set up a meeting with them."

"Have them meet you here," Alexander said. "I would like to talk to them, too."

Morgan headed for the door. "I'm told that the miners aren't allowed to leave the miners' encampment, but if they can leave it, I'll suggest we meet here," he said. "I will keep you advised."

Bric was suddenly behind him and Morgan paused by the door, looking at the big Irishman. "Where are you going?" he asked.

Bric gestured to the door. "Out to find the privy," he said. "And I intend to look around a little."

"Not too much," Morgan said. "The last I saw, there were several de Cleveley soldiers in the common room, so we do not want to attract attention."

"That's Anchorsholme Castle."

"It is. And they are loyal to John, so avoid them."

Bric merely nodded. Morgan unlocked the door and Bric follow him to the second locked door, finally emerging into the dark corridor that led out to the common room. They proceeded to the doorway that opened up into the tavern that was now filling up as the weather outside began to cloud over.

There was a smell of rain in the air; both Morgan and Bric inhaled it as it wafted in through the open windows. As Bric headed to the rear of the tavern in search of the privy, Morgan's attention moved to the table by the window.

It was empty.

He'd told the women to wait there, but they hadn't. He wasn't particularly concerned about it, simply annoyed. He went over to the table and slung his bags on it, thinking that the women might have gone to the privy themselves. The soldiers were still at their table, still mostly keeping to themselves, so it wasn't like they'd run off with the women. In fact, the room seemed calm for the most part, with people talking and laughing, eating and drinking, and the serving wenches moving among the tables and chairs.

It looked like any normal afternoon.

Morgan took a seat to wait.

He'd no sooner sat down than he saw Everelda coming in through the rear door. She had her cloak pulled tightly around her, scurrying over to the table where Morgan was sitting and plopping into a chair.

"Filthy," she said unhappily. "Everything is utterly filthy out there. Do you know that the privy is in the stable?"

Morgan fought off a grin at her outrage. "I found that out this morning."

Everelda shook her head. "Disgusting," she said. "It's a stool with a hole cut out of it over a hole in the ground. And there's a dog lingering about, waiting to sniff your…"

She abruptly stopped and turned away, embarrassed by what she was going to say. But Morgan knew exactly what she was going to say and he laughed low in his throat.

"It hardly sounds like a suitable place for a lady," he said. "I wonder what story your cousin will have when she returns from her visit."

Everelda look at him curiously. "What visit?"

"Where you were."

Understanding registered. "Ah," Everelda said. "Is that where she went?"

"I would assume so. She was not here when I arrived."

Everelda shrugged. "We did have quite a bit of watered wine," she admitted. "I will try to entertain you until she returns."

"I am certain you will do a good job."

Everelda fought off an embarrassed smile, eyeing the knight and seeing what had her cousin so fascinated. He was most definitely something to look at and he was charming, too.

She cleared her throat softly.

"Are you *truly* not married, Sir Morgan?" she asked.

He looked at her. "I am truly not married."

Everelda hesitated. "Are you looking for a wife?"

It was a bold question and Morgan wondered if she was

asking on behalf of Amarantha. Undoubtedly, anything he said would get back to her. He thought it was a rather good opportunity to express his interest, as reckless as it was. *You're on a mission*, he reminded himself. Romance had no place in his line of work.

He knew that.

But he still couldn't help himself.

"That is not my focus, no," he said. "But if one falls in my lap, I would not be unhappy."

Everelda studied him for a moment. "Like Amarantha?"

He grinned, a nervous gesture. "I have only just met her," he said. "It is a little soon to be asking that question."

"Do you think she's pretty?"

"I have never seen a more beautiful woman."

"She is smart, too. She is educated."

"I know. She teaches at the church."

Everelda didn't say anything for a moment, but it was clear that her mind was working. After a sufficient pause of mulling over the situation, she leaned forward and lowered her voice.

"You were correct when you said Sir Farran would have run you through if he thought you were interested in her," she said quietly. "Amarantha has had other interested suitors in the past but, somehow, they all disappeared. We thought they simply gave up or decided she wasn't what they were looking for, but I heard Uncle Hollis say once that Farran eliminated any competition. I do not know exactly what that means, but it cannot be good."

The warm expression faded from Morgan's face. "Nay, it cannot."

"If you are at all interested in courting my cousin, then you'd better not tell Sir Farran."

The point was taken. Morgan caught sight of Bric as he headed back into the tavern and turned down the darkened corridor. Bric had returned from the privy but it occurred to him that Amarantha had not. He looked over his shoulder at the door leading out into the livery yard.

"What do you suppose is keeping your cousin?" he said. "There is a hint of rain in the air and we should head back to Mount Grace before the weather turns."

Everelda didn't like the idea of traveling in the rain. "Shall I go and find her?"

Morgan stood up. "We'll go together," he said. "If she is in an indelicate… situation, I am certain she would not want me to see her, so you can forge ahead. I'll follow for protection."

Everelda's brow furrowed. "In a stable yard?"

"You'd be surprised what lurks in a stable yard."

Everelda simply shrugged and headed out the way she'd come in, through the rear of the tavern and out into the livery yard beyond. There were men standing over near an old fence where a trench had been dug and they were pissing into the trench. Everelda continued into the livery itself, which had two stalls that were set aside as a privy, presumably for women who required some privacy.

Morgan was right behind Everelda until she entered the smelly livery and poked her head in to find her cousin. He watched a drunk man teeter out of the tavern and head over to the trench, waiting patiently for Everelda and Amarantha to come walking out of the stable until Everelda emerged alone.

He looked at her with some concern. "What's wrong?" he said. "Why did she not come with you?"

Everelda shook her head. "She's not there."

Morgan let that sink in for a moment before entering the

livery himself and noting that, other than the horses and a cow inside, it was empty of humans. Curious, he came out and started looking around the stable yard.

"Where could she have gone?" he wondered aloud. "Did she say anything to you about going anywhere in the village? I noticed there are a few merchant stalls. Could she have gone there?"

Everelda didn't think so but she followed him out of the livery yard and into the main road. The village was a busy one, being the crossroads of a few major roadways from the west and also the east, but the bad weather was starting to roll in and they could see the stalls starting to close up for the day.

Morgan made his way over to the nearest stall, a merchant who sold all types of fabrics. They were stacked everywhere, the stall small and cramped, but Morgan stepped in to look around. The merchant, who was pulling in goods he'd had sitting outside, noticed the enormous man.

"Can I help you, my lord?" he said in a thick Welsh accent. "I am closing shop, but if you wish to see something, I will show you."

Morgan shook his head. "I'm looking for a woman."

"Aren't we all, my lord?"

Morgan flashed a grin. "I do not mean in that way," he said. "I am missing a young lady. She is about so tall with long, dark hair and a beautiful face. I believe she was wearing purple."

He was holding his hand about chest high to indicate Amarantha's height. But the man shook his head.

"I've not see her," he said. "Some wives need a tether, my lord. Mayhap she is across the street. He sells perfume over there."

Morgan thanked the man and crossed the square with

Everelda skipping after him. Fat droplets of rain were beginning to fall, indicative of the storm that would soon be upon them. The perfume merchant was almost completely closed but he, too, hadn't seen a woman of Amarantha's description. He suggested a man who sold leather goods down the way, so Morgan and Everelda went down there to inquire.

No luck.

A half-hour later and still no Amarantha, Morgan was beginning to get a very bad feeling.

⋈

SHE COULD SMELL hay.

The scent of hay was heavy in Amarantha's nostrils, the first thing she was aware of as she came out of the dark and into the light. Moderate light, anyway. It was as if the light were filtered somehow. More than that, she was moving. She was in something that was moving, bouncing roughly, and that included her head.

It felt as if it weighed a thousand pounds.

Becoming more aware, Amarantha tried to move but she couldn't seem to do it. It took her a moment to realize that her arms were restrained. Her legs seemed to be free, but her arms were tied. *She* was tied. She managed to lift her head, seeing that there was a binding of some sort across her chest. Wincing as she looked upward, there was a cover over her, canvas she thought. And the hay – it was very strong.

It was all around her.

Amarantha truly had no idea what was happening. The last thing she remembered was following the woman with the white hair in search of Everelda. Was Evey around somewhere, too? Was she in the same predicament? Amarantha didn't want to call out for fear of putting them both in harm's way more than they already were, so she kept silent, feeling every bump of the wagon as it struggled over the road.

But what on earth was she doing here?

Amarantha's head was throbbing and it was difficult for her to keep her eyes open because the light hurt them, but she struggled to think clearly. Somehow, someway, she had ended up in the bed of this wagon, covered up by canvas and hay, so it was evident that someone was out to do her harm.

… but *who?*

The first thing she thought of was Farran. The man had never been threatening towards her in any fashion, but he was a man who was used to getting what he wanted and what he wanted was her. Perhaps he'd finally had enough of her resistance and had decided to take what he felt was his. Perhaps they were heading off to a priest at this very moment.

She simply didn't know.

The wagon continued to lurch over the road and Amarantha lay there, her mind racing, and struggling not to become ill. She felt terrible as it was and the movement of the wagon wasn't helping.

On and on it went.

She had no idea how long.

It was difficult not to feel fear. She wasn't a fearful person by nature, but in this situation, it was only natural to be frightened. But she didn't like the feeling so she tried to focus more on her curiosity about the situation than her fear. A hysterical woman wouldn't be able to help herself and she most definitely needed to help herself.

Whatever the situation was.

And she waited.

God help her.

CHAPTER TWELVE

Mount Grace Castle

EVERELDA WAS SOBBING dramatically.

"We only w-went because A-Ammie wanted to apologize t-to Sir Morgan," she wept. "S-She wanted to go but I did not. I told her not to go, but she did anyway!"

"She wanted to go? *Why*?"

"B-Because last evening's feast did not go well. She did not want S-Sir Morgan to t-think we were all ill-bred!"

Hollis was listening to his niece sob, snot, and choke her way through a story about how she and Amarantha ended up in Bronllys and now Amarantha was missing. Hollis had already spanked Everelda once, hence the hysterical weeping, but now his anger at their actions was being overtaken by utter horror.

His daughter had gone missing.

"You two deliberately left the castle without an escort," he said, barely keeping control of his spanking hand. "You stubborn, foolish women left and now see what has happened? Amarantha is gone!"

Everelda let out another squeal of hysterics as Morgan

spoke up. "We looked for her until the storm came," he said. "Even then, we continued to look, but it became clear that she was nowhere to be found. I would have continued searching, but I could not let Lady Everelda return to Mount Grace alone, so I have come with her to ask you for more men to search the town."

Thunder rolled overhead and a bright flash of lightning spilled in through the lancet windows of the great hall. It was full of soldiers on this night, men finding shelter out of the elements, but they didn't have any idea what was going on at the dais as the men surrounded a weeping Everelda.

One of those men was Farran.

He'd come to the castle, as he always did, for the evening meal so that he could once again sit with the object of his desire and once again try to speak to her, to charm her and woo her. It was an awkward dance they did almost every night, but on this night, he'd walked into a disaster.

His intended was missing.

And he knew why.

"Search all you will," he said, his gaze darting between Hollis and Morgan. "You will not find her, for she is not there."

Hollis, Morgan, and Kenan looked at him with concern and distress. "What do you mean?" Hollis said. "How do you know this?"

Farran's jaw was ticking faintly. "I know exactly what has happened," he said, looking straight at Hollis. "She is not missing as much as she has run away. Slipping away into the village was only part of the story. She intended to do this all along. Your daughter has run away."

Hollis' eyebrows flew up. "Run away?" he repeated, shocked. "Where would she go?"

"Anywhere that was far away from me," Farran said, his face beginning to turn red with rage and embarrassment. "I told you that you should not have given her a choice in the matter. You should have simply told her she was going to marry me and that would have been the end of it. Now she has done something foolish and I do not deal with foolish women. This is the last insult, Hollis. I will not be humiliated yet again."

Hollis' eyes narrowed. "What is that supposed to mean?"

"Consider my suit of your daughter rescinded."

Hollis looked at the man with utter contempt. "My daughter is missing and all you can think about is your humiliation?" he growled. "How dare you say such things about her? She is *not* foolish. Mayhap I was wrong to think you would have been a good husband to her if you think that she is capable of such foolish behavior."

"She didn't run away!" Everelda said in a new round of sobs. "We never even discussed Sir Farran. This has nothing to do with him. Someone has taken her!"

"My lord, time is of the essence," Morgan said, finding himself hoping that Farran would indeed walk out. He could see that Amarantha was right about him – only thinking of himself even in this critical situation. "You must gather the men to search for her. It is possible she has not been abducted but is injured somewhere. We must look for her now, before it is too late."

Farran whirled on him. "And you," he hissed. "Why do you care about her at all? Go back to Thetford and back to your wife. You have caused nothing but trouble since you arrived."

Morgan eyed the man who was shorter than he was and weighed about sixty pounds less. If it became a physical confrontation, it wouldn't be a fair fight because Morgan had the advantage and he would most definitely use it. The more he heard from Farran, the more he didn't like him.

"I prevented trouble, if you recall," he said steadily. "Point fingers where you wish, but do not point them at me. I have only helped the woman when she needed it, evidently unlike you. Rather than help, you think the worst."

Farran tensed up, grievously insulted by a man who had only been polite to him until this moment. It was more than his pride could take. But Hollis put up a hand between them, stopping what could have been a serious fight before it got started.

"Enough," he said quietly. "Farran, if you feel as if you cannot lend a hand to search for my daughter, then leave and do not come back. Sir Morgan, I appreciate your help in the search. Kenan, rouse five hundred men. Prepare them to head into Bronllys within the hour."

Kenan nodded and headed off while Farran was still glaring daggers at Morgan. Everelda was still weeping and Hollis finally went to her and patted her on the head to comfort her, but she would not be comforted. She ran off sobbing.

Morgan watched her go.

"If it makes any difference at all, once I found your daughter and Lady Everelda in The Three Cocks, I was preparing to escort them back to the castle right away," he said. "While I think it is admirable that your daughter wished to apologize to me for the deterioration of the feast last night, I do not think it was wise for her to leave the castle without an escort and I told her so. But I believe her motives were altruistic."

Hollis sighed heavily. "Altruistic motives that have put her in grave danger," he said. There was genuine worry in his face. "She's stubborn, my daughter. She has always done what she pleases, but she has never been foolish about it. Until now."

Morgan could see that the man was quite distressed. "I am sorry she felt the need to apologize to me," he said. "Truly, I was not offended by the evening's feast. It was a fine meal and I had the privilege of speaking with you and Sir Farran and Sir Kenan. I thought it was quite a good evening, after all, so her apology was unnecessary. I will help you search for her and I will not rest until we find her."

Hollis looked at him, clearly appreciative. "You have my thanks," he said sincerely. But then he caught Farran out of the corners of his eyes and glared at the man. "Are you still here?"

Farran's mottled cheeks flushed bright red and he whirled on his heel, marching off across the hall. Hollis and Morgan watched him disappear into the rain outside.

"Idiot," Hollis muttered. "I do not know what I ever saw in the man that I should pledge him to my daughter. 'Tis a pity you are married, Sir Morgan. You seem like a man of compassion and understanding. Those are important qualities in a husband that I should like my daughter to benefit from. A man like you would know how to handle her."

Morgan saw an opportunity at that moment to bond even closer to Hollis. He felt as if he were already laying an excellent foundation, but that soft utterance had him thinking.

Perhaps it was time for him to make another strategic move where Hollis was concerned.

"My lord, the truth is that I am not married," he said. "I only said that because Sir Farran was quite territorial over your daughter. I did not want to become a target for his animosity, so I told him I was married to ease his mind. It worked, for a little while, but now that he believes I have caused all of the world's ills, I see no reason to continue the charade."

Hollis looked at him with some surprise. "You're *not* married?"

"Nay, my lord. I have never been married."

Hollis blinked as if the information both surprised him and gave him an idea. "What do you think of my daughter?" he asked hopefully.

"I think she is a beautiful, intelligent, and compassionate woman."

"Would you consider courting her?"

"What about Sir Farran?"

Hollis rolled his eyes. "We will not speak his name any longer," he said. "He just showed me what kind of man he truly was and I do not want that kind of man for my daughter. But you…"

He grinned knowingly. Morgan simply lifted his eyebrows and looked away but, inside, he was fairly dancing a jig. Perfectly strategic in the course of his mission, but it was more than that.

He really was interested in Amarantha.

Was it dangerous? Absolutely. Everything about this task was dangerous. But he was doing what William Marshal told him to do – get close to Hollis de la Haye. Earn the man's trust. Did that include marrying the man's daughter? Of course not.

But the opportunity was here.

Morgan found that he wanted the man's daughter above all else. She was the real prize in all of this. But he would complete his mission and he would perform flawlessly, and he would take the castle from Hollis and return it to Patience under William Marshal's control.

He wasn't sure where that left Hollis but, at the moment, he didn't much care. Hollis wasn't his concern.

Amarantha was.

He had to find her.

CHAPTER THIRTEEN

AMARANTHA HAD LOST track of time. She didn't know if it was day or night. The injury to her head had her wanting to sleep and she'd drifted off after initially waking up, only to wake up again now because the wagon had stopped.

Everything was silent.

One thing she noticed, however, was that the straw around her and covering her was heavy. It was also damp – she could smell it. Clearly, there had been rain and now she was covered with an oiled canvas and damp straw.

She lay there without moving, listening. She could hear birds and the wind whistling gently, but no voices. No people. Fear, however, kept her still and silent. If Everelda was nearby, she wouldn't call out to her for fear of repercussions. Truth be told, she was somewhat paralyzed by the terror that now had her in its grip. She was no longer curious about her situation, simply terrified. She had no idea what was going on, or who had abducted her, or why. Therefore, it was safer to simply wait it out.

Until someone grabbed her ankle and yanked.

Startled, Amarantha yelped as there was a second tug on her ankle, pulling her to the edge of the wagon bed. The damp canvas was tossed back and wet straw fell on her face, into her hair. Another yank and she was half-hanging off the end of the wagon with her skirts up around her knees. She struggled to sit up and but she couldn't pull her skirts down because her hands were still bound. Someone grabbed her by the arm and tossed her right onto the ground.

On her bum on the wet earth, Amarantha tried to shake the hair out of her eyes. It was dawn and the sky was the color of steel, cold and gray, with a hint of sunlight behind the clouds. Her gaze moved to the person who had pulled her so brutally from the wagon and she was both confused and shocked to see the old woman with the wild white hair from The Three Cocks standing in front of her.

Astonishment filled her.

"What is the meaning of this?" Amarantha asked, her voice trembling. "Why am I here?"

The old woman didn't look nearly as polite and kindly as she had back at The Three Cocks. Her brow was furrowed, her jaw set and hard. She rested her fists on her rounded hips as she glared down at Amarantha.

"I did," she said. "You are Hollis de la Haye's daughter, are you not?"

Amarantha nodded before she really stopped to think about the implications of that question or the results her answer would have. "Aye," she said. "Who are you? Why have you brought me here?"

The old woman cocked her head as if debating whether or not to answer the question. Then she snorted bitterly.

"I do not know why I am being kind to you," she said. "I do

not know why I am even speaking with you. Your father was not kind to my family. He murdered my husband and younger son with, I am sure, no conversation involved. He wanted them dead and he killed them."

Amarantha was confused. "*My* father?" she said. "He killed your family?"

"He did."

"But when? *When* did he do this terrible thing?"

"At the siege of Mount Grace."

"When was that?"

The question didn't please the old woman. None of the questions were pleasing her. Lashing out a hand, she slapped Amarantha across the face. As Amarantha gasped and recoiled, the old woman seethed.

"Do not ask such a stupid question," she said. "Do you take me for a fool?"

Amarantha didn't want to be slapped again, but she truly had no idea what the woman was speaking of. "I do not know of any siege," she said, leaning away from the old woman as far as she could go. "When was there a siege?"

The old woman put her hands on her hips again. "When King John stole the castle from my husband," she said. "It was five years ago last month."

Amarantha was still leaning far back in case the old woman decided to slap her again. "Five years ago I was at Warwick Castle," she said. "Four years ago, my father sent word to me to join him at Mount Grace, so I came. He said that John had taken possession of the castle and he was made garrison commander, but that is all he told me, I swear it. When I came to Mount Grace, they were building… something. I think walls. I thought they were strengthening the walls, but parts of them looked damaged."

"From the siege," the old woman said. "John wanted Mount Grace for the silver production, so he came to my husband's home under the guise of friendship and ended up starting a revolution from within. His army attacked the Mount Grace army and the royal troops were many. It was only a matter of time before they gained control of the castle, and my husband and youngest son were killed in the battle."

Amarantha listened with mounting apprehension. Her father always had been so incredibly careful about keeping information from her. That had been true since she had been old enough to understand the spoken word. No one spoke ill of Hollis and no one told his daughter the extent of her father's activities. Amarantha had never much cared about that until now.

Now, her lack of awareness had put her in a very bad position.

"My lady," she said steadily. "I was never involved in my father's business. In fact, he has always made a great effort not to tell me anything. I suppose when I think back to the first time I came to Mount Grace, the castle did look as if it had been worn. As if it had been neglected or beaten. Since my father told me that the king had come into possession of it, it did not occur to me that he had taken it by force. But I can see that it should have occurred to me. Was it a terrible battle?"

The old woman sighed faintly, starting to lose some of the rage in her expression. "Terrible enough," she said, her voice dull with the memory. "The king had come in friendship, but the truth was that he'd come to steal what belonged to us."

"And my father was part of the siege?"

The old woman nodded. "Part of it," she said. "He came a

day or two after it started. I remember very clearly seeing his army arrive with their crimson tunics. Someone said it was Craswell Castle."

"That is my father's castle."

The old woman grunted. "After he came, there was no longer any hope," she said. "He was part of the siege, indeed. Mount Grace fell within the next two days. My eldest son and I escaped, but my youngest son and my husband were killed."

Amarantha was starting to see that this woman had lost a great deal. The anger was still there, still in her body language, but her manner had cooled.

Pain had seen to that.

"May I know your name, my lady?" Amarantha asked softly.

The woman scratched her head and looked away. "I am Lady le Marche," she said. "Patience le Marche. My husband was Oliver le Marche, Lord Glanhen."

"Thank you for telling me about Mount Grace," Amarantha said. She hoped that her polite and kind manner might stop whatever was happening here, whatever sense of vengeance this woman had against her. "So you left the castle and found work in Bronllys? Do you work at the tavern where I saw you?"

That seemed to harden the woman's expression again. "I did not find work," she said, annoyed. "My entire life was taken from me. My son, his wife… we had nowhere to go. But we always knew that we would regain Mount Grace and it was William Marshal who helped us gain the establishment in Bronllys. To everyone there, my name is Madam Iris and I am the proprietor of The Three Cocks. That is all I have ever gone by since my return, for if anyone knew that Lady le Marche was still in close proximity to the castle, it might get back to your father. We escaped him once. We might not escape him again."

Amarantha wasn't sure where to take the conversation from that point other than to ask the obvious. "And me?" she said. "What do you wish from me?"

The anger returned to Lady le Marche's expression. "You are going to help me regain my castle," she said. "My castle in exchange for your life. I am certain your father would want to save his daughter."

It was simple enough but it was also horrifying. Amarantha struggled against a surge of fear. "You are going to ransom me? By yourself?"

Lady le Marche looked as if she might slap her again but, instead, she stood aside and pointed off to the east.

"Do you see those woods on the rise?" she said, watching Amarantha nod. "On the other side of those woods is the River Wye. But more importantly, there is someone important in the woods."

Amarantha could see the dark line of trees in the near distance. "I do not understand," she said. "Who is in the woods?"

"An army," Lady le Marche hissed. "You asked if I was to ransom you alone? Of course not. My Gere paid for Irish mercenaries to come to Wales and help him wrest Mount Grace from your father and the Irish have finally arrived. My dear son did not live to see this day and The Marshal and his foolish knight have delayed too long in doing what they promised to do, so I am taking matters into my own hands. I should have done it a long time ago."

Not much of what the woman was saying made much sense, but that didn't matter at the moment. Amarantha had a bad feeling about what was to come next.

"And that means you will ransom me to my father?" she

asked.

Lady le Marche nodded. "Indeed, I will," she said. "My son brought eight hundred Irishmen to Wales and he paid them well, but there may not be a battle at all now that I have you. The fool that The Marshal sent, the man who calls himself Morgan, refused to use you as leverage, but I would not rest until I had you. You fell right into my lap when you visited The Three Cocks and you are the key, my dear. You are going to regain my castle for me."

It took Amarantha a moment to realize that the old woman had spoken Morgan's name. She knew they had known one another because she had seen them together. But now, the old woman was speaking of Morgan as if he were something more than just a customer in her tavern.

Perhaps he was.

"Morgan of Mercia?" she said, confused. "But he serves de Winter. He told me he serves at Thetford."

Lady le Marche shook her head. "He serves William Marshal," she said. Then she held up a finger as if to lecture Amarantha. "The Marshal sent him to pose as my dead son and lead the Irish to victory against your father at Mount Grace. But he refused to use you against your father, the dolt. There is more than one way to win a battle."

Amarantha felt as if she'd been kicked in the gut. So Morgan wasn't who he said he was? He'd already lied about being married, although he'd explained his reasons well enough. But now... now he had also lied about where he served? *Who* he served? Was he really a knight for William Marshal? Confused, not to mention grossly disappointed, Amarantha couldn't help but show it.

"I do not understand any of this," she said, her frustration mounting. "Morgan and you… you plan to destroy my father?"

Lady le Marche nodded. "That is why Morgan is here," she said. "He is to help me regain Mount Grace, any way he can. Even through you."

Another kick to the gut. So all of the man's kindness and the warm flicker in his eyes were all a lie? He'd effortlessly charmed her and she had let him, when all of it had evidently been to get close to her father.

Or perhaps Lady le Marche was lying.

The woman was clearly mad. Perhaps none of it was true. Perhaps all of it was true. Amarantha was horribly confused and struggling not to become despondent about the situation, but she couldn't help but notice that Lady le Marche was simply standing there, looking off towards the east where she said the Irish were encamped.

"How do you know they're there?" Amarantha asked, the early morning breeze lifting her hair. "The Irish mercenaries, I mean. How do you know they're there? Have you seen them?"

Lady le Marche glanced at her. "Because I was told they were here, outside of St. Arvans," she said. "The villagers have seen them and they confirmed their location when we came through last night. They tell me that a small army is camped right over there near the river's bend, so that is where you and I are going this morning."

The thought of being presented to Irish mercenaries frightened Amarantha deeply. "I do not suppose I can talk you out of this," she said, hating that she sounded fearful. "My lady, I've lived a pleasant life. My father has soldiers, but I've never even seen a battle. I teach peasant children to read. I've never harmed anyone. I do not want to be the instrument of my father's destruction."

Lady le Marche was resolute. "Your father is a warlord," she said. "How can you not have experienced a battle?"

Amarantha shrugged. "I do not know," she said. "I simply never have. I supposed I've been fortunate in that respect."

Lady le Marche's features screwed up. "Do you mean to tell me that when you were first called to Mount Grace, that you did not even recognize that there had been a siege?" she said in disbelief. "You did not see the obvious signs?"

Amarantha was coming to feel stupid. "I told you that the place looked worn," she said. "They were working on the walls, but no one said anything about a siege. Or… or mayhap they did and I did not listen. All I was told was that the king came into possession of the place. I was not told how."

Lady le Marche sighed sharply. "It is a good thing you are so lovely because you are surely as stupid as a sheep," she said. Then she reached down and pulled Amarantha to her feet. "Come along. We are going into the woods to find the Irish."

Unfortunately, Amarantha's hands were still tied behind her back, so she was at a distinct disadvantage to resist in any great capacity and she was utterly terrified of being presented to a bunch of ruthless mercenaries. The mere thought nearly put her into a panic.

"My lady, *please*," she said softly, tears filling her eyes. "Please do not take me to them. They will want to hurt me and I… please do not do this."

But Lady le Marche was unsympathetic. She grabbed Amarantha by the arm and began dragging her off the road. "They will not hurt you," she said. "An injured hostage is not worth much. But I cannot vouch for them taking a pound of your flesh. Are you a virgin, Girl?"

Amarantha burst into tears and hung her head. Lady le

Marche had her answer. Without another word, she began pulling the weeping girl towards the tree line to the east.

Hollis de la Haye's daughter was about to pay for the sins of her father.

CHAPTER FOURTEEN

The Three Cocks

"AND WE HAVE been searching for her ever since."

Bric and Alexander were listening to Morgan speak of Hollis de la Haye's daughter, who seemed to have vanished off the face of the earth. It was early morning at The Three Cocks tavern and the usual smell of baking bread was heavy in the air. It was a cloudy morning after a night of rain when an exhausted Morgan appeared to tell them about the missing lady.

"The same lady you saved from the robbers in the church?" Alexander said.

Morgan nodded. "The same."

"The lady who came to apologize to you for the fiasco at the feast at Mount Grace?"

"Aye."

Alexander pondered the information. "Then I take it you are helping search for her to further endear yourself to de la Haye?"

Morgan hesitated a moment before replying. "Aye," he said.

"Those are my orders, are they not? To gain de la Haye's trust?"

Alexander nodded slowly, but it wasn't in agreement. It was because he was digesting the situation as a whole. He was seeing things that Morgan was not and, truth be told, they hadn't seen Morgan all day yesterday. Now, things were starting to make some sense.

Alexander didn't like it.

"What about the agents in the mines?" he asked. "You were supposed to meet with them yesterday and since you never returned to the tavern, I assumed that you did."

Morgan shook his head. "I did not," he said. "The lady disappeared and I've been looking for her ever since."

Alexander cocked his head. "Morgan, forgive me, but that is not your mission," he said. "I understand why you are doing it, but it is taking you too far off task. You need to be meeting with the agents in the mine and with the Irish right now. Use this chaos to your advantage."

"What do you mean?"

"Start this revolution while de la Haye is looking for his daughter," Alexander said as if it were the most obvious thing in the world. "Now is a perfect time while de la Haye is in disarray and half of his men are out of the castle. Did you not think of that?"

Morgan gazed at him a moment. "Nay," he said. "I was only thinking on my directive. To earn de la Haye's trust."

"A trust you will earn only to betray, which will not matter when the revolution begins," Alexander said. Then he eyed the man for a moment. "Morgan, what are you not telling us? You should have seen this opportunity, yet you did not. You are only focused on finding de la Haye's daughter. *Why?*"

Morgan was being increasingly backed into a corner where

the only way out would be a confession he didn't want to make. He wasn't even sure how to make it or what to say, only that it wasn't something he wanted to speak of. He felt like a failure for even entertaining thoughts of Amarantha and his uncontrollable attraction to her. Hell, he hadn't even kissed the woman, but he knew that was only a matter of time. That sweet face and those delectable lips were infiltrating his thoughts and now… now, Alexander was on to him.

He could see it in the man's eyes.

Averting his gaze, he hunted wearily for the nearest chair.

"You are not going to like my answer," he said quietly.

Bric was looking at him critically as Alexander stood over him. "What is it?"

Morgan sighed heavily, shaking his head as if the entire situation and his reason were the most ridiculous things on earth.

"Because de la Haye's daughter…" he said, then stopped himself. It was a moment before he could continue. "She's the most spectacular woman I've ever seen. She's beautiful and intelligent. She teaches peasant children to read. She has a sense of compassion and understanding. She's not an ordinary woman, Sherry."

Alexander didn't seem surprised by the answer. He glanced at Bric, who simply lifted his eyebrows. They both knew what it was like to love a woman, as they were both married to women they adored. More than adored. The women they were married to were their entire lives, so they had a great deal of understanding for something like this.

But that didn't make it optimal in this situation.

"And you have feelings for her," Alexander said softly.

Morgan shrugged. Then he nodded. "Christ, I do not know

what I'm feeling," he said. "All I know is that right now, I am in turmoil. She has clearly been abducted and the rain last night has washed away any evidence we might have located. It's like she simply vanished."

Alexander wasn't unsympathetic. "Of all times for you to fall for a woman, on a mission is not the preferred setting."

Morgan forced a smile, but it was without humor or warmth. "Scold me," he said. "It is less than I deserve."

"I am not going to scold you," Alexander said. "You cannot help what you feel. But you should have been more guarded."

Morgan nodded wearily. "I know," he said. "I tried. Believe me, I did. But Amarantha is beyond any woman I've ever met. I think I knew the moment I first saw her that she was... different."

"And you let her in."

Morgan sighed faintly, as if it took all of his strength to do so. "And she does not even know it," he said. "That's at the bottom of this – she does not even know it. I've not spoken a word to her about anything other than common subjects – her father, the church, the lies I've concocted about my background. She has no idea who I really am or what I feel."

"And that is where your professionalism has taken a stand," Alexander said. "I'm proud of you for that, Morgan. You did not let your feelings destroy your common sense, no matter what you felt. That is the mark of a good agent."

Morgan didn't seem to feel too bolstered by the praise. They were just words to him, but at least Alexander wasn't berating him. He actually felt relieved that his little secret was out in the open.

"Maybe so, but you know I have to find her," he said, gazing up at Alexander. "I could not live with myself if I walked away,

Sherry. It's personal now."

Alexander knew that. He also knew that all of the scolding in the world wouldn't change Morgan's position, so that's why he hadn't done it. There was no point. What was important now was to get Morgan back on track while also helping him deal with the disappearance of the lady.

"I understand," he said. "If it will help you focus on what is important, then I will reason this out with you. First, we must discuss your meeting with the agents in the mines today. That must take place quickly because Bric is ready to ride with you to the Irish mercenaries. You *must* get to them, Morgan. With de la Haye searching for his daughter, now is the time to strike. You do understand that, don't you?"

Morgan nodded. "I do," he said. "And I agree. But the lady..."

Alexander put a hand on his shoulder. "Now we shall talk about her," he said. "Let us work through this quickly and succinctly. Mayhap I will see something you do not. When was the last time you saw her?"

"The day before yesterday," Morgan said. "She had come here to apologize to me for the infamous feast. I came back to my chamber to get my possessions and when I returned, she and her cousin were gone. I assumed they'd gone to the privy. Her cousin returned but she did not."

"And no one saw her leave?" Alexander said. "Did you ask Lady le Marche?"

Morgan was prepared to tell him that he hadn't, but it occurred to him he hadn't even seen Patience. Then in recalling the conversation he'd had with her that same day where she demanded he use Amarantha as leverage against her father, he sat up straight and looked at Alexander with wide eyes.

The warning bell was going off in his head, and loudly.

"The day that Amarantha disappeared, I saw Patience leave in a wagon," he said. "I did not think anything of it at the time, but now… Christ, I wonder if… oh, my God."

He bolted to his feet but Alexander stopped him. "Where are you going?"

"To find Patience le Marche."

"She is not here," Alexander said. "Bric and I went looking for her at dawn but no one has seen her in two days."

Morgan's eyes widened. "My God," he muttered. "It *has* to be her."

"What do you mean?"

Morgan clapped a hand to his forehead as realization hit him like an avalanche. "When Lady Amarantha was here in the tavern, Patience recognized her," he said. "She wanted me to abduct her and use her as a hostage against her father. She thought that surely the lady's father would surrender the castle in exchange for his daughter's life but I told her that it would not work. I told her we must stay the course and follow the plans that have already been laid, but she was unhappy about it. *Very* unhappy."

Alexander was starting to catch on. "And you think she took de la Haye's daughter, anyway?"

"It's the only answer," Morgan insisted. "She left in a wagon, which was full of hay. Lady Amarantha had to be buried under the hay."

Things were starting to make sense now, pieces of the puzzle coming together. "But where would she take her?" Bric asked. "If she took her out of Bronllys, where would she go? If she'd gone straight to de la Haye, you would have known that. She would have done it already."

Morgan nodded, thinking hard on the conversations he'd had with Patience since meeting the woman. He was trying to figure out if there were any clues in things the woman had said.

"Nay, she hasn't gone to Hollis yet," he said. "Which means she is either hiding Amarantha somewhere or she's gone or… wait a moment. She could not go to Hollis alone. He'd simply kill her and take his daughter back. Even Patience would know that. She'd have to have protection."

"What *kind* of protection?" Bric wanted to know.

Horror swept Morgan's expression as he realized the answer to that question. It was the most logical thing he could think of.

"Patience no longer has an army behind her," he finally said. "But her son bought one."

Now, Alexander and Bric had the answer, too. "She's gone to the Irish mercenaries," Bric said, slapping his thigh in realization.

Morgan nodded, sickened as he became convinced of it. "Wouldn't you?" he said. "She's got an entire army near Chepstow, an army her son has already bought and paid for. She's taken Amarantha to the Irish and they are going to use her as leverage for the surrender of Mount Grace. Christ, it all makes sense now. That bloody woman went behind my back and abducted Amarantha, anyway."

Alexander and Bric could see that Morgan was quickly becoming distressed about it, so Alexander took charge. Maybe Morgan wasn't in love with Lady Amarantha yet, but it was clear he was fond of her. *Very* fond.

That kind of emotion could be crippling.

They had to act fast.

"Then you must find the agents in the mine immediately,"

he said. "Get to the bottom of the support in the mines and do it quickly. Once you find out what you can, you and Bric will head to the Irish mercenaries immediately. I'm sure they will not hurt Lady Amarantha if they think they can use her for their gain, so I believe there is a little time, but not much. You must move quickly, Morgan. I realize this is difficult if you truly have feelings for the lady, but you are going to have to think with your head and not your heart. Do you understand me?"

Morgan did. Above all else, he was a knight and he followed orders. His feelings for Amarantha weren't clear yet, but they were strong enough to muddle his mind and create a sense of apprehension in his chest. He was ashamed about his reaction but, in a sense, he didn't care.

He wasn't ashamed of what he felt for her.

"I do," he said. "Father Nicodemus was going to locate them for me, but I've not seen him since then. I'm going to the church."

"We'll go with you."

Morgan unlocked the door. "Stay alert," he said. "The last thing we need is for de la Haye's men to see us all together and wonder who you two are, so we must be careful."

They were in agreement. All three of them were in casual clothing, at least as far as knights went – leather breeches, tunics, but with an array of both hidden and revealed deadly instruments on their bodies. Broadswords were left behind, tucked under beds. No one wanted to look threatening, or stand out to suspicious or curious townsfolk, so it was with this in mind that they went about their business.

Separately, so they wouldn't attract attention as a group, the three of them headed for St. Mary the Virgin.

$\mathscr{CS}$

"Escaping the mining camp once is difficult but slipping out twice is a damned miracle." A man with dark hair, dark eyes, and skin tanned from time spent in the sun was hissing the words. "We've come twice, Father. I do not know if we can come a third time. Where is The Marshal's contact?"

Father Nicodemus was facing off against two enormous men in the dark recesses of the church. They were the contacts from the mine, men that had arrived at Mount Grace several months prior, displaying their prowess with a pickax and obtaining a position as miners because they were so physically strong.

They were brothers, not born in England, but rather from a land far away. They used that to their advantage and pretended not to understand the language spoken by the miners or the men from Mount Grace very well, which afforded them a world of opportunity to listen to conversations that would otherwise not have taken place in front of them.

They had a wealth of information to give to the man who had been sent to replace Gere le Marche.

But that much-anticipated meeting hadn't worked out as planned. Somehow, the brothers had managed to make it out of the *Brenin Arian* mine without being seen. It was an extremely difficult feat because Hollis de la Haye kept a heavy guard at the mines to ensure no one escaped. Once a miner, always a miner they would say. But here they were, in the church for the second time in two days, and Father Nicodemus knew that time was of the essence.

But there was a problem.

"Your contact is out looking for Hollis de la Haye's daughter," Father Nicodemus told them. "She was abducted from town two days ago and he is helping in the search. If you can wait here at the church, I will go over to The Three Cocks and see if he has returned. I will try to locate him, but you must wait here. He has been eager to speak with you before he goes to the Irish mercenaries and brings them to Mount Grace."

The first man nodded. He was big and seasoned, with intense eyes, a rather long beard, and long, dark hair that was tied up in braids. He had the look of a wild man about him, or at the very least, an overworked miner.

But that was his intent.

"We can only stay a few hours at most," he said. "We must return at the changing of the guards so our return will go unnoticed, so you only have a few hours, Priest. However, if we must leave, then you will tell our contact that the mines are ready to revolt."

Father Nicodemus nodded. "I assumed as much," he said. "How many of le Marche's men are left?"

"About thirty," the man said. "Out of an army of a thousand, that isn't much, but it is enough. Also…"

He was cut off when the door to the church suddenly lurched open. As the two agents quickly slipped back into the shadows, Father Nicodemus immediately moved towards the men who were entering his sanctuary. They were backlit by the light coming in through the door, so Father Nicodemus didn't recognize Morgan until the door shut and they were within a few feet of each other.

His eyes widened.

"Morgan!" he gasped. "Where have you been? I went to find you yesterday and no one seemed to know where you were until I heard about Lady Amarantha's disappearance. What happened?"

Morgan's face was lined with fatigue. "I think Patience took her."

"What?" Father Nicodemus gasped. "Why would she do that?"

"Because she grew angry with me when I would not abduct Amarantha so she could be used as leverage against Hollis surrendering Mount Grace," he said. "She brought it up to me two days ago when Amarantha came to The Three Cocks. She wanted me to abduct the woman and use her against her father, and I would not do it."

Father Nicodemus shook his head with disgust. "God's Bones," he muttered. "I did not think she would actually do it."

"Then she has spoken of it before?"

The priest shrugged. "More in passing," he said. "Lady Amarantha comes into the village often and Patience knows who she is. She has mentioned it before, but I never thought she was serious."

When Morgan realized that, he struggled not to become angry. "Why did you not tell me this?"

Father Nicodemus lifted his hands in a helpless gesture. "Because I never thought she meant it," he said. "It wasn't something she spoke of on a regular basis and I had forgotten. Truly, I did not think it was important."

Morgan's irritation had the better of him. "It was quite important because she followed through," he said. "I spent all day looking for Amarantha, along with hundreds of Hollis' men, but it occurred to me this morning that Patience must have taken her. No one has seen her in two days and I saw her leaving The Three Cocks on the day Amarantha disappeared. Now you have confirmed that it is all true."

Father Nicodemus was genuinely distressed. "Great saints," he swore softly. "I am very sorry, Morgan. But what was Lady Amarantha doing in The Three Cocks? Her father would never allow her to visit such a place."

"She came looking for me," Morgan said. "But we will discuss that later. First, let me make introductions. These men with me are my friends and comrades, Sir Alexander de Sherrington and Sir Bric MacRohan. They serve The Marshal, too."

Father Nicodemus found himself looking at two enormous men, clearly men of power and skill simply by the way they held themselves. They looked like elite knights to the bone.

"My lords," the priest greeted them. "I am Father Nicodemus."

"Father," Alexander greeted. "We've come because we need to meet with your contacts from the mines. We…"

"Ask and you shall receive."

The two agents from the mine emerged from the shadows, smiling at men they knew very well. While Bric and Morgan grinned at the sight, Alexander appeared incredulous.

"Addax?" he gasped. "And Essien? *You* are the contacts in the mines?"

Addax al-Kort and his younger brother, Essien, reached out to hug men who were close friends and comrades. Essien, young and impetuous, kissed Bric loudly on the cheek and was rewarded by a slap to the face.

Everyone started laughing.

"I should have known The Marshal would send some of his best," Alexander said. "Usually, I know everyone he sends into a situation but he never told me that he had sent you. What a pleasant surprise."

"Surprise, indeed," Addax said. "There is much to tell, Sherry, and little time. It is a good thing you came when you did."

Alexander grew serious very quickly. "We've only just arrived," he said. "There are eight hundred Irish mercenaries waiting just north of Chepstow, but we must know how conditions are in the mines. Are they ready to revolt?"

Addax nodded. "Indeed, they are," he said. "I was just telling the priest that there are about thirty le Marche men, men from Oliver le Marche's army who are ready and willing to lead the miners against de la Haye's army. They have been made aware of Gere le Marche's desire to bring Irish mercenaries into the fight, but that has been something spoken of for years."

"Since John took the castle, I am sure," Alexander said. "And the mood is one of revolt?"

Addax nodded. "It has been since Gere le Marche began making contact with some of the le Marche men that John had forced into conscription in the mines," he said. "He told them that he was bringing help to regain his castle and they have patiently waited. This day has been a long time coming, Sherry. And the Irish are here?"

"They are, indeed," Morgan said, stepping in. "After this meeting, Bric and I are heading south to find them and bring them north to Mount Grace. I believe it would be wise to discuss tactics, or at the very least, a signal that will let the miners know that the Irish are ready to attack. That way, the miners can revolt at the same time. Coordination is key."

"How far is the mine from the castle?" Bric wanted to know. "I've not even seen the castle yet."

Addax and Essien looked at him. "Mount Grace sits on a rise," Addax said, using his hands to demonstrate. "There is a small vale to the north and the mine is on the next rise. Over the years, le Marche and his ancestors have built tunnels and walls to protect the mine and the miners' village, so it is well protected and, when John took possession of Mount Grace, the mine and the encampment became a prison. The miners are not fond of the de la Haye soldiers."

"Can the miners make their way into the castle when the time comes?" Bric asked.

This time, it was Essien who answered. "There are two tunnels that go from the miners' encampment into the sublevel of the north wall of the castle," he said. "That is how they bring the ore into the castle and prepare it for shipment. In fact, there is a large shipment being prepared right now in those sublevels."

"Who prepares the shipments?" Alexander wanted to know.

"The miners," Essien said. "There are fifty miners in those sublevels at any given time."

"And even more when we prepare to strike," Morgan muttered. "How soon is the shipment moving out?"

"In a few days," Addax said. "The wagons are nearly at capacity, so they cannot hold much more. I would say four days at the most."

Morgan looked at Alexander. "And it will take a day to get to the Irish, a day to muster them, and a day to move north," he said. "When they open the gates to move the shipment out…"

Everyone understood the implication, most of all Alexander. "They will make it easy for us to breach the gatehouse and get inside," he said. "We spoke of a signal for both armies to strike in unison. I would say this is it. When they open the gates to move the shipment out, we move."

"Then we must hurry," Morgan said. "We must get to the Irish encampment with the information, but I must also locate

Amarantha. I know she's there, Sherry. There is nowhere else she could be."

"Amarantha?" Addax repeated. "De la Haye's daughter?"

He'd heard the name working in the mines, so he knew who she was. Alexander nodded his head. "Aye," he said. "There has been a… complication."

"What complication?" Addax asked.

It was Morgan who answered. "Patience le Marche abducted Hollis' daughter with the intention of ransoming her," he said quietly. "I am certain Patience took her to the Irish, the only army she has, and she's going to use the woman for leverage. Amarantha's life for the return of Mount Grace."

Addax's eyebrows lifted in surprise. "I'd not heard this."

"That is because no one knows," Morgan said, laboring not to let his feelings show through too much. "Hollis, of course, knows his daughter is missing and he has been looking for her for two days, but he does not know what we figured out – that Patience took her. And I intend to get her back."

So much for not letting his feelings show through. He'd made the statement with more passion than a man should have unless he had an eye for the lady in question. Addax was wise enough to sense that there was more to the story and not ask about it, but Essien opened his mouth. The moment he did so, however, Alexander shook his head at him and Essien quickly understood the silent command.

It was a question for another time.

"Then it seems as if this will be a complex undertaking," Essien said as if he'd intended to say it all along. "Has anyone sent word to de Velt yet? It was my understanding that he wants to be part of this."

Alexander nodded. "I will send him word today," he said.

"He's still at his properties on the Marches, so I will tell him that he needs to muster his army immediately and head to Mount Grace. However, he cannot make it here in two or three days. Four days is the soonest I would expect to see him."

"Then we must try to oust de la Haye from his castle until help arrives," Morgan said, looking at the men around him. Some of the very best warriors and spies he'd ever seen. "Addax, how many miners are there?"

Addax cocked his head thoughtfully. "Several hundred," he said. "The mine itself is not that large, but the vein is thick with ore. The more miners, the more ore that is produced."

"And how big is de la Haye's army?"

"A thousand or more," Addax said. "Have you been inside of Mount Grace yet?"

Morgan nodded. "I have, but not enough to see how many men he has," he said. "With several hundred miners and eight hundred mercenaries, we should be able to do what we were sent to do."

"Unless the Irish are stupid and try to use de la Haye's daughter as a bargaining tool," Essien said. When everyone looked at him, perhaps with some annoyance on Morgan's behalf that he'd brought the woman up again, he put up his hands in supplication. "I am sorry, Morgan, but it must be said. We cannot pretend that de la Haye's daughter could not be a big factor in all of this. If the Irish want to use her as leverage, why would we not let them? Hollis surrenders Mount Grace, there is little to no bloodshed, and Hollis has his daughter returned to him. Would that not be the best of all solutions?"

He wasn't wrong. If they could get away with regaining Mount Grace without any fighting, that was indeed the best of all solutions.

Except for one little thing.

They would be bargaining with Lady Amarantha's life.

One by one, they turned their attention to Morgan.

Alexander and Bric knew more about his attraction to Amarantha than Addax and Essien did, but they all knew there was something unspoken to a certain extent. It was in everything about Morgan when the subject of Hollis' daughter came up. When Morgan saw that everyone was looking at him, he sighed faintly. They were expecting a response and perhaps even permission to let such a thing take place.

But he wasn't going to give it to them.

He decided to make his position abundantly clear.

"You should know that Hollis has asked me if I would court his daughter," he said. "You should also know that I have feelings for her. I do not know how or why or even what they really are, but I know that they are there and they grow stronger by the hour. Hollis is our enemy and I accept that. But his daughter is not my enemy. She has no bearing on her father's loyalties, nor does she care. I find the idea of using her as leverage extremely distasteful and, quite honestly, I'd rather fight my way into Mount Grace than let her be used in a game that men play. She does not deserve that. She's probably terrified at this moment and rightfully so, and I will tell you now that if any of those Irish animals touches her, they will become my enemy and I swear they will regret such an action for the rest of their miserable lives. I'll bring the de Wolfe armies down on them and they will not survive."

He was growing agitated, speaking with emotion that knights didn't usually infuse into critical conversations. It was highly indicative of those feelings he'd mentioned. But Essien wasn't going to go without a fight.

"Morgan, you know I do not discount your feelings, but you have to look at it from our perspective," he said, indicating his brother. "We have been here for months. You have not. We have seen this situation from the inside of that silver mine and to say conditions are deplorable is an understatement. To say that men are dying in those mines on a daily basis is true. To say that Hollis de la Haye is a brutal overlord is even more true. I do not know his daughter and that is where you have the advantage on me, but I can tell you that from my perspective, if one small woman can end the turmoil for those miners and le Marche men, then I say let her. Why would you not?"

He wasn't trying to be belligerent and Morgan knew it. He'd known Essien for a couple of years and he liked the man. There was something wild and untamed and joyful about him at times, something Morgan had appreciated, but as he spoke of the men in the mines and Hollis' management of them, he could see the weariness in his eyes. The man was plain tired of everything he'd been through.

He wanted it to end.

They all did.

But that didn't mean Morgan could agree with him.

"Because if Hollis refuses to exchange Mount Grace for his daughter, then her life is forfeit," he said simply. "Did you stop to think of that? I do not know Hollis well, but I know he supports the king in all things. Mount Grace does not belong to him. If de la Haye is the ambitious bastard everyone paints him out to be, then he could very well refuse to exchange Mount Grace for his daughter. Probably not an easy choice, but he cannot give up what he does not own and he does not own Mount Grace."

Alexander had been watching the exchange carefully. It had

the potential to blow up, so he stepped in. He felt that he needed to.

"Let us go on the assumption that Hollis will not accept his daughter in trade for Mount Grace," he said. "Lady Amarantha was not a component of this situation until two days ago, so let us assume she is still no longer a component. We have a plan to follow and I believe that we should. Morgan, you and Bric head south to find the Irish. Addax and Es, you two return to the mines. The signal to attack will be when the gates of Mount Grace open to move the silver ore out. Once those gates open, we move and we do not stop until Mount Grace is ours."

"But what if the Irish are not in position by then?" Addax asked. "Do we still ask the miners to revolt and hope they survive? I do not believe they can do it alone."

He had a point. Alexander looked at Morgan. "You will send word to Father Nicodemus when the Irish have arrived," he said, gesturing to the priest who had remained completely silent throughout the exchange. "He will get word to the miners that the Irish are ready. Then, when the gates open, we charge."

"I will tell them," Father Nicodemus said, watching all eyes turn to him. But his focus was solely on Morgan. "But you... *you* are fond of Lady Amarantha? *Truly* fond of her?"

Morgan could see the surprise in the man's eyes. "Aye," he said. "Truly fond of her."

A hint of a smile creased Father Nicodemus' lips. "Then I am pleased," he said. "She is a good woman, Morgan. Too good for that peacock Farran."

Morgan's eyes glimmered with mirth. "I am glad you approve."

"I do," the priest said, but he grew serious. "I pray you find her, Morgan. And I also pray you can forgive me for what I am about to tell you."

"What are you going to tell me?"

Father Nicodemus cleared his throat softly, looking to the men who were focused on him. "Simply this," he said. "You must remember that I have been hoping for the ouster of Hollis de la Haye since he took command of Mount Grace. And I am not the only one."

"Why should I forgive you for that," Morgan said. "I know you have been loyal to the House of le Marche."

Father Nicodemus held up his hand. "That is not what I meant," he said. Then he looked around the group, rather nervously. "I was not going to speak of this because if the truth was ever known, this man's life would be at risk. When I said I am not the only one loyal to le Marche, I meant that there is another. He serves at Mount Grace."

Morgan's eyebrows furrowed curiously. "Who?"

Father Nicodemus lowered his voice. "Kenan," he said. "I could not tell you all of this, Morgan. I lied to you when I said I did not know that Kenan had served at Mount Grace. I knew very well. He and Gere were in league with one another, with Kenan feeding Gere information directly from Hollis. What Hollis knew, Gere knew. That is how he was so able to plan for the Irish mercenaries and move them here. Kenan knows they are coming."

That brought a load of bricks tumbling down on everyone, but Morgan most of all. His eyes widened in shock.

"And you told me none of this?" he hissed. "Why in the hell not?"

Father Nicodemus struggled to hold his ground. "Because I did not trust you," he said. "You said you were from William Marshal and you said you were here to pose as Gere le Marche, but I did not know that for certain. I did not trust you completely. But I do now. Addax and Essien know you and, now, I can tell you the truth. You must forgive me for not doing so sooner. Kenan will do what he can from inside Mount Grace, but we cannot give him away."

Morgan looked directly at Addax and Essien. "Did you know this?" he asked. "About de Poyer?"

Addax shook his head, looking extremely doubtful at the priest. "De Poyer is part of the rebellion?" he said, incredulous. "In all of the times I have met with you, you never told me this. Why not?"

"Because Kenan asked me not to," Father Nicodemus said. "The man is a pain in my side and abrasive as sin, but we have one thing in common – trust. He trusts me and I trust him. I would not give him away and he would not give me away. His position is so precarious that I could not tell you for fear that somehow, someway, it would get out. You see, Kenan loved Oliver le Marche like a father but he moved to Kenilworth at the request of his own father. He wanted to return to Mount Grace to serve Oliver when he was knighted, but his father would not let him. His father wanted him in a more prestigious house."

"Like de la Haye," Addax said knowingly. "I understand now. He went to de la Haye and when the man assumed command of Mount Grace, Kenan came with him. By coincidence?"

Father Nicodemus nodded his head. "Purely by coincidence," he said. "But once he came with Hollis, he recognized Patience in town and through her, became reacquainted with Gere. He has always been in favor of overthrowing Hollis and returning the castle to Gere and Patience, but he is a lone man.

What could he do alone?"

Morgan was trying very hard not to feel frustrated or duped by a priest who failed to tell him everything but, in hindsight, he understood. Father Nicodemus was protecting a very big secret. Morgan had to earn his trust.

It seemed that he had.

He had to force himself to calm.

"He does not know about me, does he?" he asked.

The priest shook his head. "Nay," he said. "He knew that The Marshal was sending someone to help, but he did not know how or why. Patience never told him the details, only that help was coming. But mayhap he figured it out when he saw you."

Morgan nodded. "Mayhap," he said. "In that event, you should get word to Kenan that we have a plan in place for the siege of Mount Grace. At least he can be prepared. If he helps us regain the castle, I am certain that Sherry will give him an excellent recommendation to The Marshal. Mayhap he'll be able to remain at Mount Grace once The Marshal takes control."

"I am certain he would appreciate that," Father Nicodemus said. "Kenan has had a love affair with Mount Grace since childhood."

"So I was told," Morgan said. But he eyed Father Nicodemus for a moment. "Any additional lies or half-truths I should know about?"

The priest shook his head. "Nothing," he said. "But I am sure you understand why I had to be careful."

Morgan did but he was still perturbed. He shrugged his shoulders and looked away as Alexander stepped in.

"It seems that we are set," he said. "Addax and Es, I know your time here is short. Return to the mines and we will send you word as soon as the Irish arrive."

Addax and Essien nodded, shaking hands with Bric and Morgan and Alexander before rushing off to arrive before the changing of the guards with Father Nicodemus on their tails. That left Morgan, Alexander, and Bric standing alone.

Alexander turned to Morgan.

"I was not going to say this in front of Essien, but he has a point about Lady Amarantha," he said. "If she can end this quickly, I would not be opposed to that."

Morgan's jaw ticked. "And if she can't? Do we simply sacrifice her because we were looking for the easy way out?"

Alexander wasn't particularly happy with what could have been taken as an insult. "I am not looking for the easy way out, Morgan," he said. "I am looking for the simplest way with the least lives lost. You should be looking for that, too."

Morgan wouldn't back down. "When we reach the Irish encampment, I am going to find Amarantha and take her to safety," he said. "You may as well know that. I will not let them use her."

Alexander grunted softly with regret. "And leave Bric with the Irish? You would leave him exposed while you run off with the lady to get her to safety?" he said. "What about Bric's safety?"

"I can take care of myself," Bric said, siding with Morgan. "Sherry, what if the woman hostage was Christin? What would *you* do? Would you allow her to be a sacrifice to win a war for you?"

Christin was Alexander's wife. A braver, more beautiful woman had never lived in his opinion, but it brought everything into focus for him. Not that he hadn't been focused before – he'd simply been more focused on the outcome. It was simple not to be sympathetic to a faceless woman he'd never met before.

But Morgan had.

After a moment, he conceded.

"Very well," he said. "Do what you must do, but do not give yourself away and make it to the battle at Mount Grace. This is your mission, Morgan. Do not abandon it."

Morgan could have been insulted, but he knew Alexander was a fair man. There were other men involved in this operation and although Morgan was concerned about Amarantha, he couldn't forget those who were risking their lives.

Him included.

"I would never abandon something I had taken an oath to fulfill," he said. "Sherry, I realize that I have never had a mission that has depended solely upon me. I have always been in support of men like you and Bric, Maxton and Caius and the rest of the Executioner Knights. This is my moment to shine, as was once told to me, and I will carry out my orders. I *will* shine. But I do not believe we should use Amarantha to achieve this goal and if that makes me weak, then I suppose I am weak. I would not be in favor of using any woman in so dangerous a position."

Alexander could see something at that moment that he didn't see much of in the Executioner Knights and that was the fact that Morgan hadn't yet become hardened. He was still a deep-feeling, deep-thinking man, something the older members of the group had long since learned to compartmentalize.

Morgan hadn't learned to do that yet.

The truth was that Alexander was one of the best assassins the world had ever seen. He had achieved that terrifying reputation by killing anyone he was told to kill and using people – men or women – to achieve his goals without a second thought. He was hardened in that respect, but he'd not lost his ability to feel. He was reminded of that every time he thought of his wife. She had restored what he thought he'd managed to kill – his emotions – but Morgan was still young. He didn't have the background of serving in The Levant like many of them did. His experience had come from his duties and adventures in England.

The man still had a heart.

Alexander couldn't fault him that.

In fact, he envied it.

"Then get her away from the Irish," he said simply. "That is all I can tell you. But do not fail as Gere le Marche. You were charged with this and you will see it through."

"I will, Sherry. I will or I will die trying."

Alexander watched Morgan and Bric as they slipped from the church and out into the dusty street beyond. For a moment, he pondered Morgan's last words.

I will or I will die trying.

God, he hoped it didn't come to that.

CHAPTER FIFTEEN

H IS NAME WAS Ryan O'Magnan.

Amarantha knew that because she'd heard Patience shout the name, the name of the man her son had contact with. Dragging Amarantha behind her, she'd walked into the encampment that smelled heavily of smoke and human habitation shouting the man's name. There were several cooking fires and the men around those fires had stood up, looking at the wild-haired woman curiously. Even more men had come out of the trees, watching the procession of two women – and one of them bound – as they walked into the heart of the encampment next to the river's edge.

Ryan O'Magnan!

Somewhere back in the encampment, a man with the sides of his head shaved and the top of his red hair long and stringy appeared. He was big – a tall man with muscles on his bare arms and a bushy, red beard – and he eyed Patience quite curiously. There were several men with him, surrounding him, each one of them looking quite confused until Patience shouted that name again and the man with the shaved sides told her to shut her lips because he was Ryan O'Magnan and she was making enough noise to call forth the dead.

Patience practically threw Amarantha at Ryan O'Magnan's feet.

"My name is Patience le Marche," she said. "My son is the man who brought you here to regain Mount Grace. I've come to you on his behalf."

Ryan's brow furrowed with curiosity. "Why?" he said. "Where is your son, Lady le Marche?"

"Dead," Patience said flatly. "He is dead, but you have been paid and I have come to assume command. We are going to Mount Grace and we are taking this woman with us. Our battle has already been won."

Ryan's gaze moved from the slightly unhinged old woman to the young woman on the ground at his feet. She was dirty, and her arms were tied behind her back, but even he could see how utterly exquisite she was.

That made him quite interested.

"Who is this?" he asked.

Patience pointed to Amarantha, who was trying to push herself into a sitting position. "That is the daughter of the commander of Mount Grace," she said loudly and proudly. "He will surrender the castle in exchange for his daughter. No blood will need to be shed, but I want you to go with me to the castle as a show of force. We will demand the release of my castle or we will kill his daughter right in front of him."

Ryan's gaze was riveted to Amarantha as she finally managed to sit up. A random tear streamed down her right cheek and he crouched in front of her so he could get a better look at her. What he saw did not displease him.

"I didn't know English lasses were so comely," he said after a moment. "What's your name, Girl?"

Amarantha met his eyes, flinching at what she saw. He was big, burly, and barbaric. In her mind, that was what she had expected of an Irish mercenary and all she could see in his face was her pain and destruction.

"My name is Amarantha," she said hoarsely.

He nodded faintly, looking her over one final time before reaching out to pull her to him. She stiffened and gasped, terrified he was going to do something terrible and humiliating to her right in front of everyone, but he pushed her onto her side and pulled her around until her bound arms were facing him. Producing a dirk, he cut through the ropes.

Amarantha gasped in relief as her arms were freed.

"There," Ryan said. "That's better, isn't it?"

Both of Amarantha's arms were asleep and the skin was worn raw where the ropes had been too tight. She struggled to rub some feeling back into them.

"Aye," she said, eyeing the man. "Thank you for your kindness."

He grinned, flashing big teeth, and stood up. Reaching down, he pulled her to her feet. His gaze lingered on her a moment longer before returning to Patience.

"Now," he said. "You say you are Patience le Marche?"

Patience wasn't thrilled he'd untied Amarantha but she didn't fight him on it. "Aye," she said. "My son, Gere, paid you for your services through William Marshal's men in Ireland. Gere was supposed to meet you here, but he died of a fever several months ago. I have taken up his cause and will lead you to Mount Grace and to victory."

Ryan looked her over, humor tugging at his lips. "You do not look like a warrior," he said, listening to his men snicker.

"We've come a very long way, Woman, and we are in no mood for foolery."

"I assure you that there is no foolery."

"What's the situation at Mount Grace?"

Patience frowned. "It does not matter what the situation is," she said, pointing to Amarantha. "We have Hollis de la Haye's daughter. We can go to the castle and demand their surrender or Hollis' daughter will die."

"Are you prepared to kill her if he refuses?"

Patience was a little taken aback by the question. She had truly believed the Irish would praise her for bringing such an asset into their encampment but, instead, they seemed apathetic… suspicious almost. Certainly they weren't hailing her as a hero to the cause.

That angered her.

"You will do what you were hired to do," she said. "I will not lift a finger. You were paid to fight and kill and that is exactly what you will do if de la Haye refuses to surrender."

Ryan had a smile playing on his lips, but it wasn't one of humor. "Woman," he said slowly. "You give a great many orders to men who do not know you. I was expecting to meet Gere le Marche here and that is what I will do unless you can prove to me that you are who you say you are. As it is, you're just a madwoman spouting threats."

That was an unexpected turn as far as Patience was concerned. It never occurred to her that the Irish wouldn't believe her. But as she struggled for something convincing, Amarantha saw the situation for what it was – the Irish weren't about to follow Patience blindly. They wanted proof and Patience couldn't give it to them.

There was an opportunity here.

Amarantha was willing to take a chance that her salvation was in mucking up the waters.

"She *is* a madwoman," she suddenly said. "She is not who she says she is. She killed Gere le Marche and his mother because she wants Mount Grace for herself. She is greedy and dishonest!"

That turned the Irish back to Patience, whose eyes flew open wide at the betrayal. "That is not so!" she cried. "The little bitch is lying!"

Amarantha hoped to save herself in the chaos. "It *is* true," she said, breaking down in loud sobs and hoping that would make her more believable. "She abducted me. I am the wife of a knight and she abducted me and is forcing me to pose as the daughter of this man named Hollis. I do not even know him!"

She carried on, greatly confusing the Irish, who were looking at Patience as if she'd done something heinous to the woman.

Ryan was frowning at her.

"Who *are* you?" he demanded. "Tell me your real name, Woman, or you will not like my response."

Patience could see that the tides had turned against her. This was shocking, something she hadn't expected. She'd assumed they would take her word for it as to who she was and who Amarantha was, but now… now, Amarantha was turning the tables on her. The victim was now becoming the aggressor. Horrified at the turn of events, Patience put up her hands as if to protect herself from the angry Irish.

"My name *is* Patience le Marche," she insisted. "I am the wife of Oliver le Marche, Lord Glanhen and lord of Mount Grace. My son is Gere. The castle was taken from us by John and his royal troops."

"Where is your son?" Ryan barked.

"Dead!" Patience cried. "He is dead, I told you this! And this woman is the daughter of the man who stole my castle away from me!"

Amarantha let out a squeal of distress. "She is lying!" she said. "She grabbed me and hit me on the head and is forcing me to pretend to be the daughter of this man. Look at my head! Look at the blood!"

To prove her point, she peeled back the hair on the left side of her head, near her face, and there were indeed streaks of dried blood from where Patience had hit her. That seemed to confirm everything she was telling them and the pendulum of mistrust swung in Patience's direction.

"So you've been lying to us?" Ryan said to her. "We do not take kindly to liars. Give me your real name or I will throw you in the river."

Patience could see that they disbelieved everything she'd told them. Somehow, Amarantha had managed to get them on her side. The only thing Patience could do was run. She'd have to run back to Bronllys and tell Morgan what had happened. Her only hope was in the man she'd tried to circumvent and although she'd told the Irish her son was dead, if they believed her to be a liar, then they would believe she was lying about that, too.

It was the only hope she had.

Men were starting to move in her direction, threateningly. Fearing for her life, Patience began to run. She wasn't sure which direction she was running in, only that she had to run. She had to get away. She had to find the wagon and make it back to Bronllys.

Unfortunately, the forest was working against her.

Over the eons, the River Wye had created steep cliffs on the west side of its path. There were cliffs of limestone all the way down through Chepstow and to the mouth of the River Severn. Not knowing the area and having a poor sense of direction in her panic, Patience ran straight for those cliffs. Strangely enough, no one was chasing her at that point. They simply watched her run to the edge of the trees, stumble because she realized there was a drop off, and then tumble all the way down to the river. They could hear her screaming all the way down.

And then… silence.

For Patience, Lady Glanhen, her end came because of her own haste.

Patience was impatient no longer.

☙

AMARANTHA HAD NO idea what they were going to do with her.

After the incident with Patience, she thought that she would be free to go, but the leader, Ryan, had other ideas. He'd taken her straight to his camp and put her in his tent, ordering food and drink brought to her. He'd even had a bucket of hot water brought to her, lugged by a woman who was surprisingly young and busty. She smiled openly at Amarantha as she set the bucket down, even going so far as to hand her a rag and a small, well-used piece of soap.

Amarantha had never been so grateful in her entire life.

She was still in the pretty purple gown she'd dressed in when she'd gone to see Morgan at The Three Cocks, only the dress wasn't made for travel or even strenuous wear and the fabric was torn and stained, fraying at the seams. It was a complete loss, but it was all she had, so Amarantha used the water and soap to wash her hands and arms and face and even her lower legs, washing away two days of dirt and fear. She even tried to wash some of the dirt off the purple dress, but she ended up ruining it more than it already was.

Still, it was amazing how much better she felt after a wash.

Using her fingers and some of the water, she combed through her hair as much as she could, smoothing it and taking out the dirt and tangles, before braiding it into a thick single braid and tying it off with part of her torn hem. The same wench who'd brought the water also brought the food – it was simple stuff, roasted fish from the river as well as beans and carrots cooked together, like a stew.

She ate until she could hold no more.

The sun had gone down over the land and the sounds of night were heavy in the air. Amarantha found herself listening closely to every chirp, every crack or snap. There was an encampment all around her and she could hear men talking and laughing, but not in a language she understood. *Irish mercenaries*, she kept telling herself. Men who had saved her from Patience and her scheme, but saved her for *what*?

That was the question.

The reality was that she was a hostage.

Truth be told, there was more than her current situation on her mind. Ever since Patience had told her about Morgan and how he wasn't who he said he was, the information weighed more and more heavily on her. She'd tried not to give it any credit, but Patience had seemed so certain. Amarantha didn't know Morgan very well and she'd only met him a handful of times. But in those times, she'd felt something for him she'd never felt for anyone.

As if a whole new world had opened up.

She didn't know why she felt that way, but she did. Even

when she was under the impression that he was married to another, somehow, she couldn't move away from him. She had thought that it would be better to have him as a friend rather than not at all, but that notion was quickly dashed. If he'd asked her to be his mistress, she would have done it because the attraction between them had been far too strong. Frankly, she'd been weak. She would have gladly given up life as Farran's wife to become Morgan's mistress.

That was the sad fact.

And now… now, Patience had succeeded in planting suspicions. Morgan was a knight who served William Marshal, not de Winter as he'd said. He'd come to Mount Grace to pretend to be Gere le Marche, who was evidently Patience's son. That was the family from whom Mount Grace had been taken. Amarantha felt stupid that she didn't even know the circumstances of how her father had come to be garrison commander of the place. King John had stolen it from a family and that family wanted it back.

It was all so very confusing.

But it was also very eye-opening.

Her father knew the situation exactly, of that she was certain. He knew how he came to be garrison commander of Mount Grace and she was positive that Patience hadn't been lying about that. It was true that no one had ever told Amarantha about her father's activities, or just how dirty the man could play, but she'd heard rumors. She would have had to have been deaf and stupid not to. She'd heard the whispers of servants and soldiers when they didn't think she'd been listening. She'd always ignored it because Hollis was her father, after all. He went to great lengths to ensure she thought well of him.

But deep down, Amarantha knew the truth was much different. And it was never more evident than now.

Nay… Patience hadn't been lying about that.

Amarantha had always lived in a genteel world, protected from the raw brutalities of life, but the past few days had seen that change dramatically.

Everything was closing in on her.

"Lady?"

Startled by the voice outside the tent, Amarantha looked up in time to see Ryan flipping back the flap and stepping in. He had an oil lamp with him, a crude thing made from earthenware, but when their eyes met above the flame, he smiled.

"Ah," he said. "You're awake. I wondered if you would be."

He came into the tent, which was low-ceilinged and not like the tents her father utilized. These tents were made of oiled canvas, without color or adornment, round and with two center poles and little else other than they were held down by stakes. And the tent wasn't very large, either, which made her recoil away from Ryan as he entered the dwelling. But he didn't come any closer. Instead, he crouched down next to a big, wooden chest.

"Did you get enough to eat?" he asked her.

Amarantha nodded as he opened the top of the chest and began rummaging around. Trying to find what he was looking for, he began pulling things out.

"The soap and water? Did it help?"

Again, Amarantha nodded. Ryan continued to hunt around in the chest, realizing she hadn't answered with words and finally eyeing her in the dim light.

"I heard you speak earlier, so I know you can," he said. "Why so silent now? You had plenty to say earlier."

Amarantha sat on the ground with her knees up to her

chest, her arms hugging her legs. "I still do," she said. "I do not wish to be a troublesome guest, but may I ask a question?"

"You may."

"May I go home, please?"

Ryan didn't reply right away. He continued to pull things out of the chest, clearly looking for something. When he had what he was looking for, he folded it up clumsily and extended it to Amarantha.

"Here," he said. "That garment you're wearing will not hold up another day."

Amarantha didn't take the clothing right away. "It was not meant for the abuse that it has seen."

"I know."

"You did not answer my question."

"Get out of that dress and I will."

Amarantha wasn't thrilled with that reply, but she also wasn't surprised. "If I am to go home tomorrow, I do not need to wear anything else."

"I never said you were going home tomorrow."

Growing annoyed, and fighting down her fear, Amarantha took the clothing he had extended to her and set it down on the ground next to her.

"You are the man known as Ryan O'Magnan," she said. "My name is Amarantha. Now that we are properly introduced, I would like to have a conversation with you about my presence here in the encampment. I would very much like to go home. I was abducted by a madwoman and brought here. I do not want to be here. I have a… a husband and family that are missing me. May I please go home?"

Ryan went from a crouch to sitting on his buttocks, watching her in the weak light of the oil lamp.

"You are the most beautiful woman I have ever seen," he said, almost wistfully. "Your husband is a fortunate man."

"He is a knight."

"What is his name?"

"Morgan of Mercia."

Ryan cocked his head. "Mercia," he repeated. "That is an ancient kingdom."

Amarantha nodded. "Very old," she said. "His family is very old and very rich. If you return me unharmed, I am certain he will pay you handsomely."

"Do you have children?"

Amarantha almost told him that she didn't but thought better of it. If he thought she was a mother, he might be more sympathetic.

"Aye," she lied. "Twins with pale hair and a newborn. I must not be separated from my baby."

"All boys?"

"All boys."

Ryan nodded faintly, still looking at her intently. It seemed as if the man had something on his mind and he seemed to want to talk. His manner was quite placid. Truthfully, he wasn't behaving like any mercenary she had ever heard of. The man in front of her wasn't behaving like a mindless barbarian. He was rather thoughtful and introspective.

"You've been a good wife to your husband by bearing him sons," he said. "What are their names?"

Amarantha tried not to appear as if she didn't know the answer to that question. "Henry and Richard," she said the first names that came to mind, former kings of England. "The baby's name is Geoffrey."

Having no idea that they were the only names she could

think of fast enough, all of them Plantagenet men, Ryan smiled faintly. He was thinking of blond-haired twins and a fragile newborn. He'd gotten a good look at Amarantha when she'd been dragged into camp and he'd taken note of her large breasts, tiny waist, and flaring hips. He could only imagine the delight her husband must have taken putting his seed into that beautiful body and with those generous hips, she was able to birth three sons. Probably quite easily from the way she was built.

The woman was made to breed.

"Your husband is a fortunate man," he said again. It had been a long time since he'd been around a decent woman and even longer since he'd been around one of such beauty. "I am certain he wants you back. I know I would."

There was something in his tone that Amarantha didn't like. In fact, he was looking at her steadily, his eyes moving down her neck, her shoulders, lingering on her body that was all folded up as she sat on the ground.

"He must be frantic right now," she said. "May I go home on the morrow, please?"

A smile flickered across Ryan's lips. "How badly do you want to leave?"

"Very badly."

"Enough to do what I ask?"

She looked at him curiously. "What will you ask?"

"Stand up."

Amarantha was growing increasingly apprehensive. Something in the way he was looking at her made her uncomfortable. Slowly, she unwound her arms from her legs and stood up from the cold ground. The silk garment wasn't holding up well at all, unraveling at the seams as she tried to keep it together. Ryan pointed to the dress.

"Remove it," he said quietly.

Amarantha looked at him in shock. "Please," she begged. "Please do not hurt me."

He shook his head. "I am not going to hurt you," he said. "But if you want to go home on the morrow, you will do as I say. Will you obey?"

She was beginning to tremble. "And if I do not?"

"I will strip your clothing off of you and keep you as a prisoner."

It was no choice at all. Biting her lip to keep from weeping, there was something defiant in her actions. If he wanted her to strip, then she would, damn him. Feeling more contempt than she knew was possible, she began to untie the garment, loosening it at the seams. Because it was in such terrible shape, it came right off, falling in a pile at her feet and leaving her in her shift. She'd lost her hose and shoes long ago, so the shift was all she had between her and the Irish mercenary.

Chin up, she looked at him defiantly.

He picked up the clothes on the ground and pushed them against her chest.

"Now," he said. "Put them on."

Amarantha slapped a hand over the clothing on her chest so it wouldn't fall to the ground. She was so stunned that he hadn't asked her to strip completely or, God help her, something worse that she looked at the man, dumbfounded.

"That is all?" she said. "Just… put the clothing on?"

He was over near the tent flap. "Did you want to do something more?"

Amarantha shook her head almost violently, quickly unfolding the clothing to see what would go on first.

"Nay," she said quickly, moving swiftly to put on the clothing. "I will wear this. May I still go home tomorrow?"

"We will discuss it tomorrow."

She froze as she prepared to pull a long tunic over her head, made of very fine wool. "But you said I could if I did what you asked of me."

"I am not finished asking."

Sighing heavily, Amarantha continued to dress in the fine woolen shift, a large woolen apron that was more like a dress with a front and a back and the sides cut away, and a thin woolen cloak that matched the apron. It was actually quite well made and comfortable, far more comfortable than the silk garment she'd been wearing.

All the while, Ryan had been watching her.

"I thought it would fit you," he said quietly. "You wear it well."

In spite of the awkward situation, Amarantha ran her hands over the apron, smoothing it. "It is well-made," she said. "Thank you for the use of it."

"Thank my wife," he said. "It belonged to her and she made it with her own hands."

Amarantha looked up at him. "Did she come with you?"

"She's dead. I carry her clothing wherever I go to remind me of her."

Suddenly, the Irish mercenary took on a human side and the clothing became something more than just a garment. Amarantha wasn't sure what to say to him but, somehow, sympathy seemed appropriate because she could see the grief in his eyes. Maybe that's what she'd been seeing all along when he looked at her.

"I am sorry," she said quietly. "I hope your memories of her are strong and good."

He nodded. "Verily," he said. "She was a bastard, you know. Her father was an English lord."

Amarantha wasn't so sure she wanted to comment on that because his tone inferred that it was an unwelcome subject.

"What was her name?" she asked, hoping that was harmless enough.

"Ciara."

"That's a pretty name."

He smiled faintly. "It suited her," he said. "She named our daughters Nora and Alaina, but she died giving birth to our son. His name was Eoin and I buried him with his mother. Do you know why I came to Wales to fight another man's war?"

"Nay."

"Because I want to kill Englishmen like the one who fathered my wife and then ignored her all her life. Does that shock you?"

Amarantha shook her head. "Nay," she said. "Is that what you tell your daughters?"

He looked at her as if surprised by the question. "I do not speak of it to my children," he said. "Even now, my mother tends them while I lead my men against an enemy I am paid to hate, but no one has to pay me to hate the English. That comes naturally."

Amarantha watched him closely. "Yet you do business with the English," she said. "What I mean is that you took money from one Englishman to kill another. Isn't that right?"

He nodded. "I am paid to fight other men's wars."

"And it does not matter who it is?"

"I do not care if the money comes from the devil himself. If he wants me to fight his war, I'll do it for the right price."

"Have you always fought other men's wars?"

Ryan nodded faintly, his expression taking on a distant cast. "My father did it," he said. "I do it. I have done it quite a lot since my wife died."

Amarantha pondered that for a moment because, somehow, it seemed like the man was finding an outlet for his grief in the wars he waged. "After my mother died, I did not see my father for two years," she said. "He simply… left. He said he was off to fight for the king, but I heard him tell my grandmother that he had to leave because he could not look at me. I looked too much like my mother. Every time he looked at my face, he saw her. We are still not terribly close."

That gave Ryan pause. "I suppose there is some truth in that," he said after a moment. "I can understand a man feeling that way about his daughter."

"Is that the way you feel about your daughters?"

He cocked his head thoughtfully. Then he snorted with some irony. "I do not know," he said. "I have never thought on it that way, although leaving them behind… it is easier to pretend that Ciara and my wee lasses are at home, waiting for my return. Mayhap I live in a fantasy world when I am fighting other men's wars. It makes me forget the pain I must return to."

It was a tragic admission, but one that Amarantha understood because of her father. It wasn't that Hollis wanted her to always think well of him – it was perhaps because he didn't want to have any more of a relationship with his daughter than he already had. He had his world and she had hers, and it was true that she looked a good deal like her mother as Everelda often commented.

Perhaps that was the reason Hollis kept her at arm's length most of all.

"I'm sorry you've known such pain," she said. "I do not know what it is like to lose my husband, but I have lost those dear to me. Mayhap, with time, you will be able to look at your daughters and find joy. Do not do to them what my father did to me – his apathy towards me all of my life has been difficult. One feels very lonely when a parent does not show a child affection."

Ryan was listening to her, but it was difficult for him. As if he were listening to something he didn't want to hear but knew he should. The conversation with the captive had taken an interesting turn for him, certainly not something he'd expected nor anticipated.

There was a humanity to Lady Amarantha that was rare.

"Tell me something, Amarantha," he said. "Do you love your husband?"

"Did you love your wife?"

"Very much."

"Then we are the lucky ones, you and I. Marrying for love."

Ryan nodded but he looked as if he wanted to say more on the subject. He hadn't spoken of Ciara since her death, so to speak on it with a perfect stranger was… odd. But in the same breath, it was also cathartic. He appreciated it but couldn't tell her so. He didn't know how.

He ended up averting his gaze.

"You may sleep in my bed tonight," he said, pointing to the pallet on the ground. "I will see you when morning comes and we will discuss Mount Grace and what you know of it."

"I do not know much. My husband serves at Thetford, in Norfolk."

Ryan simply lifted his eyebrows as if to accept her word for it, but something told Amarantha that he didn't. Perhaps there was some part of Patience's ramblings that had his attention. Perhaps he thought Amarantha knew more than what she was telling him. In any case, Amarantha was prepared for an interrogation on the morrow.

God help her… she hoped she survived it.

CHAPTER SIXTEEN

"WHAT DO YOU want to do?" Bric asked, mouth full. "They don't seem to be preparing to leave. They look quite settled in."

Morgan could see that. They'd entered the town of St. Arvans before dawn and, after a brief discussion with a sleepy tavern owner, they were told that there had been a small army camped about a mile out of town, along the edge of the River Wye. They'd been there for quite some time, so everyone knew about them.

Now, Morgan and Bric did, too.

They hadn't been difficult to find. They'd set up camp in a collection of trees and they'd cut down enough trees that they'd made a clearing out of it. Literally, they'd made their own village. Morgan and Bric had been watching for the better part of a couple of hours before moving back to St. Arvans, into a tavern that was tiny, stale, and dark. Their horses were in the stable behind the tavern, being fed and watered, as they settled down with a big bowl of porridge and honey, yesterday's bread, and watered ale.

And that's where they found themselves at the moment. That's where Bric's question had come from. As they shoveled in the food, they pondered the situation out there along the river's edge.

"I have been thinking about it," Morgan said, chewing. "I think we must take a two-front attack."

"What do you mean?"

"Simple," Morgan said. "You will show up and present yourself. Tell them you're a soldier looking for work and you heard about them. Give them some story, any story, that will make them feel a kinship to you. You're Irish, after all. That should mean something to them."

Bric was following. "So I tell them I'm looking for work," he said. "I'm a bachelor knight or a lone assassin."

"Exactly. You're in it for the money and ask them if they can use your sword."

"I'm sure they will."

"Me, too," Morgan said, swallowing the bite in his mouth. "The second part of the attack is this – while you're keeping the attention of the leaders, I'll slip into camp and look for Amarantha. Where would you keep a woman you wanted to protect?"

Bric took a big drink of watered ale before replying. "In the middle of the encampment so she could not escape easily," he said. "I'd have her under guard."

"Patience is probably with her."

"What are you going to do about her?"

Morgan shook his head with regret. "The woman has gone off on her own," he said. "I have to assume she is no longer allied with The Marshal or me or our cause. She is trying to force this by taking Amarantha as a hostage and using her against her father."

Bric took a big bite of bread and butter. "If I were Patience, I would even reveal The Marshal's plans," she said. "She's a bitter, desperate, old woman and she's trying to coerce the Irish into doing her bidding. Her son paid them and she wants to use them. Mayhap she feels as if she doesn't even need The Marshal or his men anymore. She doesn't need you. That brings about the question – did she tell them Gere was dead? If so, then you cannot pose as Gere. They will know it is a lie."

Morgan nodded. "That is where you come in," he said. "Find out what you can about that – why they are there, who they are fighting for. See if you can find out what Patience has told them. I cannot make an appearance until I know. If they have been told Gere is dead and I walk in pretending to be Gere, that will be a problem."

That was an understatement and Bric couldn't disagree. "Agreed," he said. "I'll head into camp and find out what I can while you hunt for the lady. But be cautious – if you are discovered…"

"If I am discovered, you do not know me," Morgan said firmly. "You know nothing about me. If I am discovered and put under restraint, or worse, it is up to you to see the mission through. Do not worry about me, Bric – your job will be to make sure this mission is successful. And Bric?"

"Aye?"

"Get Amarantha to safety," Morgan said softly. "No matter what happens to me, please make sure she is safe."

It all sounded rather grim. Bric nodded briefly, praying this whole situation wasn't going to fall apart because of a skittish old woman. Truth be told, however, from the moment Morgan had set foot in Bronllys, nothing had gone according to plan.

Bric could only hope this was the exception.

Morgan, too.

Of everything he'd ever done in his life, this was the most important. He wasn't sure how or why it ended up that way, but Amarantha was involved. A woman he hardly knew, but a woman he'd felt a connection to from the moment he'd met her. He simply couldn't let anything happen to her. Something told him, deep down, that she was going to mean more to him than anything in the world. That he'd found his everything.

He wanted to make sure they had a chance to see if that was true.

They finished their meal in silence and when it was finished, they headed off towards the trees near the river separately. Bric came in from the road and Morgan headed east, planning on coming down through the northern part of the tree line and skirting the cliffs along the river. He was going to take the most camouflaged path he could find to get to the camp and keep watch from there.

As Bric led his horse across the meadow and into the encampment from the west, Morgan came in from the north, through the trees. He was surprised to see that there were no guards protecting the encampment, but the Irish had been there so long that there didn't seem to be a need. The villagers knew they were there and, for the most part, they stayed to themselves, so there wasn't any sense of threat. There were too many of them for the gangs of outlaws that roamed the woods and they were far enough away from any fortress that no one living in a fortress even knew they were there. Therefore, there were no perimeter guards.

As Bric made his way into camp on the opposite side, Morgan lay in wait, watching.

Waiting for an opportunity.

When a sleepy, groggy Irishman with rather fine clothing and a big, woolen scarf over his head moved towards the latrine pit that had been dug near the river, Morgan had his opportunity. He followed the man to the pit and when he squatted to purge himself, Morgan clubbed him over the head with a heavy branch. He split the man's skull easily and dragged him off into the trees, stealing all of his clothing before throwing him into the river and watching the body float for a few moments before sinking in the current.

Once the body was out of sight, he put the dead man's clothing on, including the scarf over his head, and lingered on the edge of the camp, more camouflaged than ever now that he was in the garb of the mercenaries.

For Morgan, the mission began in earnest.

CB

IT WAS MORNING.

The dawn was clear for the most part, with high clouds that hinted at a threat of rain later in the day. The trees were alive with birds and as Amarantha lay there, listening to the chatter, the tent opening was pushed aside and the busty wench entered.

The woman had food with her on a small wooden plank, like an offering, and extended it to Amarantha as she sat up from the messy pallet. More of the beans and carrots and fish were the fare of the day but Amarantha was so ravenous that she ate it without complaint, every last morsel of it, and afterwards, more hot water was brought in for washing. The wench stayed with her, helping her wash her neck and even washed her feet, which were dirty from having lost her shoes. The wench supplied her with crude leather slippers that were well worn and a bit too small, but Amarantha wasn't picky.

She took them and was grateful for it.

The wench was a little more solicitous this morning, in offering to comb her hair and braid it, and Amarantha let her. She asked the woman her name, but there was a language barrier. Eventually, the wench revealed her name to be Roisin, pronounced *Ro-sheen*, but there wasn't much more she could tell Amarantha, who didn't speak Gaelic. They spent a lot of time making gestures and smiling at one another.

Just as Roisin finished with Amarantha's hair, the tent opening widened and Ryan stepped through. Roisin immediately scampered out, pushing past him and nearly tripping in her haste. But Ryan didn't seem to notice.

His focus was fixed on Amarantha.

"Did you sleep well?" he asked.

"Aye," she said, eyeing him anxiously. "May I return home this morning?"

Ryan smiled weakly. "Those are the first words out of your mouth, are they?" he said. "Well, I suppose I do not blame you, especially if you have an infant waiting for you."

"Aye," she said, remembering her lies from the day before. "A child needs his mother."

"True," Ryan said. His gaze lingered on her, as it so often did when he came around her. As if he couldn't stop staring at her. "If I agree to let you go, I cannot let you go alone. I would not feel right doing so. A beautiful woman like you would be a target for an unscrupulous man, or worse."

Amarantha was both excited to hear he was considering it, but not so excited that he evidently intended to send her with an escort. In fact, he never even asked where she lived and she struggled to come up with something very quickly. It never occurred to her that he'd send someone to escort her.

Think, Girl, think!

"I do not think it is necessary for you to send me with an escort," she said. "I can go into town and send word to my husband to come for me. I will stay safely in the tavern in town."

Ryan frowned. "That place?" he said. "There is but one tavern in St. Arvans and it is full of the dregs. People only in the actual sense, but they're downtrodden and dirty, like animals. I cannot let you go there and wait."

She shrugged, trying to downplay the danger. "I will lock myself in a chamber," she said. "No one will bother me."

"Do you have any money?"

She shook her head. "I do not," she said. "But I can ask my husband to bring money."

Ryan scratched his head and sat down on the only chair in the tent, a sturdy three-legged stool. He seemed pensive, as he always did, as if there were something more on his mind. Amarantha watched him anxiously, waiting for him to give the word that she could go. Or perhaps she couldn't. In either case, she wanted to know because the ambiguity of her immediate future was starting to wear on her.

"Since yesterday and the appearance of you and that madwoman, I've made a decision," he said. "It is very possible she was not mad at all. She seemed quite convinced of her information."

"I know."

"She seemed quite convinced that she was who she said she was and that you were who she said you were."

"Aye, that is true."

He stopped scratching his head and looked at her. "I will

not become angry if you tell me the truth," he said. "If you tell me the truth, then I can better make decisions for myself and for my men. You see, I want to return to Ireland and to those little girls I left behind. They are all I have. But I cannot do that if I do not know the truth of the matter. I am putting myself in danger if I do not know everything I should know and my children will have lost both parents if I do not return home. Do you understand that?"

Amarantha nodded solemnly. "I do."

"Then I will ask you a question and you will tell me the absolute truth," he said. "If you do not and I find out later that you have lied to me, I will throw you to my men and let them take you to sport. Is this clear?"

Amarantha was utterly horrified. "You threaten me?"

"I promise you," he said quietly. "I am not a man who likes intrigue, Lady, so I will ask you a question and you will tell me the truth. Will you do this?"

Amarantha was backed into a corner. She had no doubt that he would do what he said he would do and she very much didn't want that to happen. But she was terrified to tell him the truth. She'd been lying the entire time to him. But she could see, in his eyes, that it would go very badly for her if she wasn't truthful now when he was asking her to be.

Her entire body began to tremble with fear.

"What is your question?" she asked weakly.

His eyes were intense. "Was there any truth to what that madwoman said?"

Amarantha sighed faintly, closing her eyes as she realized that it was a question with many answers. Many, many answers.

But she could only give him one.

She lowered her head.

"Aye."

"What part of it?"

"All of it."

"Then you are the daughter of the commander of Mount Grace?"

"I am."

"Are you married?"

"I am not."

"Then there are no children."

She shook her head and replied, "Nay."

He sat forward, leaning his elbows on his knees, his focus never leaving her lowered head.

"But there is someone you love."

Tears filled Amarantha's eyes. It wasn't that she loved Morgan. She didn't know him well enough yet. But what she did know was that she was enamored with him. She was enamored with him and, at this moment, she was terrified that she would never see him again. She was terrified that she was going to end up like Roisin, a camp follower, but not by choice.

She broke down into soft weeping.

"Aye."

Ryan nodded, digesting the information. "Thank you for telling me the truth," he said. "What do you know about Gere le Marche and his quest to regain Mount Grace?"

Amarantha wiped at her eyes. "Not as much as you, I am sure," she said, sniffling. "You see, I live at Mount Grace, but my father keeps me well away from his business. I did not even know that the king took it from the le Marche family until recently. My father only told me that the king came into possession of the castle and appointed him garrison commander, but nothing more than that. I did not know anything about le Marche trying to regain his castle until a very short time ago."

She continued to sniffle and wipe her eyes and Ryan watched her, feeling some sympathy. He'd been around enough grifters and conmen to know a lie when he heard one, which was why he'd had suspicions about her story from the beginning. She didn't lie very comfortably. But at the moment, he didn't have any suspicions. She was clearly frightened and getting the truth from her had been shockingly easy.

That told him the woman had no idea how to lie and maintain the façade.

"What do you do at Mount Grace while your father is forcing men to work in the mine?" he asked.

She glanced at him. "You know about the mine?"

"I do not think it is a great secret," Ryan said with a tinge of irony. "Gere le Marche paid me with silver ore from the mine, so aye, I knew of it. Is it still operating?"

Amarantha nodded. "Aye," she said. "But I do not know anything about it. I am sorry. As I said, my father keeps me out of his business."

"Which brings me back to the question of what you do all day at the castle."

She shrugged, still sniffling a little. "I am chatelaine," she said. "I tend to the keep and the kitchens and the hall. Once a week, I go to the church in Bronllys and teach peasant children how to read."

"You know how to read?"

"I do. Do you?"

He grinned. "I do," he said. But his smile soon faded. "Do you think your father would surrender Mount Grace in exchange for you?"

Amarantha could only shrug. "That is difficult to say," she

said. "Will you kill me if he does not?"

"Nay."

"Then what will become of me?"

"Do you want to come back to Ireland with me and be the mother of two little lasses?"

He said it with a smirk but she wasn't sure if he was jesting. Something told her that he was possibly serious, which concerned her.

"Are you giving me a choice?" she asked.

"Not really," he said. "If your father will not take you for the castle, then I will take you for my wife."

Her eyes widened. "Wife?" she stammered. "But… but there is someone I love. Please… please let me return to him."

"We cannot always have what we want in life."

That reply only fueled her distress. "All my life, my father has controlled me," she said. "He has tried to convince me to marry a local warlord, a man who simply looks at a wife as a possession, but I do not want to be a possession. I want to marry a man I love. I want to bear his children. I want him to listen to me when I speak, to have respect for my thoughts. You told me you loved your wife and if that is true, can you imagine forcing her to marry someone other than you? Can you imagine how she would have felt? Please… you have proven to me that you have intelligence and compassion. Please show mercy."

Ryan began cracking his knuckles, perhaps not entirely pleased that she wasn't eager to run off to Ireland with him, but he knew that was his pride talking. Amarantha did make a compelling argument.

But his pride might not be able to take her rejection.

"So I am not good enough to marry?" he said. "You do not think that you could ever love me?"

Amarantha shook her head. "'Tis not that," she said. "It's simply that my heart can only go to one man and I have chosen him. If you do not have my heart, you have nothing of me. Surely you do not want a wife like that."

Ryan didn't, but his pride was still wounded.

"I will make you no promises," he said after a moment. "It seems to me that this battle may already be over when I offer you to your father, so we will move out today. I am tired of waiting for Gere le Marche to show his face and if he is truly dead, then there is no longer any reason to wait."

He stood up and Amarantha stood right alongside him.

"Wait," she said. "With Gere le Marche dead, and now his mother, there is no one to turn the castle over to. You would be securing it for a family who no longer exists. Don't you see? You would be fighting for no reason at all."

He looked at her, realizing she had a hell of a point. He didn't know why that hadn't occurred to him until now. "There are no more members of the le Marche family?"

Amarantha shrugged. "I do not know," she said honestly. "But I was told that only Gere and Patience escaped when John confiscated the castle. I do not know if there are any other members of the family."

Ryan was back to scratching his head again. "Then if that is true, I could merely take the castle for myself," he said. "I am in my line of work to make money. What makes more money than a silver mine?"

Amarantha eyed him. "You would take Mount Grace?"

"Mayhap then you will want to marry me if I live in your home."

Amarantha didn't have anything to say to that, at least anything he would want to hear. She simply hung her head, trying to come up with something that wouldn't offend him.

"I do not think the Welsh would be happy to have an Irish mercenary in their midst," she said.

She avoided commenting on marriage altogether, but Ryan was a patient man. His pride wasn't, but his mind was. He didn't push her.

At least, not yet.

"The Welsh be damned," he said. "They are not my concern at the moment. In any case, many thanks for your truth and for your information. I have some preparations to make."

He started to step away but she skipped after him. "When may I return home?"

He stopped and she crashed into the back of him. Reaching out, he pinched her chin gently between his thumb and index finger and gave her a little shake.

"Stop asking," he said, a glimmer of humor in his eyes. "You will know as soon as I decide."

Amarantha pulled from his grip, eyeing him unhappily, but she wisely kept her mouth shut. At least, about that. She had a feeling he wasn't jesting when he told her to stop asking, so she wisely backed down.

But not entirely.

"May I at least… well, if you are going to make me wait, at least let me do it comfortably?" she asked. "May I use the privy?"

He chuckled. "I've got a pot for you."

"I do *not* want to use a pot."

"Then you can use the trench near the river."

That didn't sound much better, but Amarantha nodded reluctantly. Still chuckling, he took her by the hand and pulled her out into the morning sunshine, speaking Gaelic to a nearby man and pointing to Amarantha. Before she realized it, she had a male escort to the privy and she wasn't entirely happy about it.

"I do not know about Irish women, but English women feel the need for privacy for things such as this," she said rather staunchly, pointing to the guard. "I do not need a witness."

That only seemed to amuse Ryan even more. "He will not watch you piss," he said, saying something to the man in Gaelic and watching him laugh. "Nay, he will not watch you piss. He is only there for protection."

"Protection from what?"

"From the wild animals in the trees," Ryan said. Then he pointed towards the river. "Go, now. Do what you must and hurry back. I may have more questions for you."

Begrudgingly, Amarantha trekked after the Irishman who seemed to speak little of her language. When they reached the trench near the river, she turned her nose up at it and pointed to the trees. He shook his head and there was something of a battle until she simply lifted her skirts and headed towards the trees.

There was heavy foliage inside the tree line and she slipped in behind it, waving the man off when he tried to follow her. She simply gestured to him that she would be very quick and come right out again, but she needed the privacy. Several feet away, he understood and turned his back.

With a sigh of relief, Amarantha squatted down and lifted her skirts a little, relieving herself in the dirt. When she was finished, she stepped out of the foliage but she was still in the trees. She hadn't taken two steps when someone grabbed her from behind.

And the fight was on.

CHAPTER SEVENTEEN

R YAN COULD SEE a man coming.

With his prisoner off relieving herself, his attention was focused on an enormous man with hair so blond that it was white leading a worn-out steed. He watched curiously as the man drew close and one of his men told him to halt. The man leading the horse stopped immediately.

"*Ciallaíonn mé tú aon dochar*," he said loudly. *I mean you no harm.* "*Shíl mé go bhféadfá fear maith a úsáid. Tá a fhios agam conas troid.*"

It was native Gaelic, Irish to the bone.

I thought you could use a good man. I know how to fight.

Ryan stepped forward.

"Who are you?" he asked in Gaelic.

Bric didn't move forward, instead focusing on Ryan who was looking at him with both suspicion and curiosity.

"My name is MacRohan," he said. "I'm a hired man by trade. If a lord needs a sword, then I am his man. I heard about an Irish army down in Chepstow, so I have followed your trail. There are those in St. Arvans who say you are a mercenary

236

army and you are looking for good men. Do you have a place for me?"

Ryan moved a little closer, looking Bric over. "Where are you from?"

"Newry."

Ryan cocked his head. "My mother was born there. MacRohan, you say?"

Bric nodded. "What's your mother's name?"

"O'Neill."

"O'Neill from Camlough?"

Ryan stared at him. Then, he grinned. "You know it?"

"My uncle was from Camlough."

That seemed to be enough to gain Bric entry into the camp. Ryan motioned him forward. "Come," he said. "My name is O'Magnan. This ragged bunch is my lot, but they're a good lot. They fight hard. Have you been wandering long, MacRohan?"

Bric nodded. "Long enough," he said. "I can find a position if the English don't hate the Irish too much. But lately, it has been difficult. There seems to be a lot of Irish rage around here. That's why I thought I could throw in with you, whatever you may be doing. Do you have a job for me?"

Ryan nodded. "North," he said. "A place called Mount Grace."

"In Wales?"

"Aye," Ryan said.

"What's the task?"

Ryan glanced at him. "Evidently, the English king stole it from some bastard who wants it back," he said. "He paid me well, but I was just informed that he's dead. Now, I've got a man who has paid me to fight for him, but he's not here to accept his victory or his prize."

Bric pretended to be moderately interested when, in fact, Ryan just told him exactly what he needed to know. It confirmed everything Morgan had suspected – that Patience had taken Amarantha to the Irish mercenaries. It also confirmed that Patience had told Ryan of her son's death. If Ryan knew that Gere was dead, then that changed everything for Morgan.

They would have to rethink their approach.

"What do you intend to do?" he asked. "And, more importantly, can you use me?"

Ryan's easy grin returned. "I don't know," he said. "Can I?"

That was Bric's cue to prove his worth, at least as much as he could. Returning to his horse, he unsheathed his magnificent broadsword, swinging the weapon in a series of very controlled moves that were quite impressive. Still swinging, he moved to the nearest tent and sliced through the rope supports in shockingly precise order. As the man inside yelled because the tent came down on him, Bric stopped swinging.

"Well?" he said. "*Can* I?"

Ryan and the men standing around him burst into laughter. Ryan motioned for Bric to come near and held out his hand so he could get a look at the sword. As soon as Bric handed it over, Ryan's smile vanished and the tip of Bric's very sharp sword ended up pointed at Bric's throat.

The laughter stopped.

"Enough games," Ryan growled. "Who are you? Who has sent you?"

Bric didn't flinch. In fact, he'd been half-expecting such a thing because Ryan's acceptance of him had been far too easy. He simply stood there, gazing steadily at the man who held a sword to his throat.

"No one has sent me," he said. "My name is MacRohan.

Bric MacRohan. I'm a hired sword and nothing more."

Ryan's eyes narrowed and he inspected the hilt of Bric's very expensive weapon. "This is not the sword of a hired man," he said. "This is the sword of a knight."

"Who says I am not a knight?" Bric said. "Do you truly think earls and kings will hire me if I am not equipped with the best weaponry money can buy? Of course it is expensive. *I* am expensive. But jobs have been few and far between lately, which is why I tracked you down. If you do not need me, then I'll be on my way, but no man calls me a liar. I am what I am."

Technically, he *was* a liar, but that was immaterial at the moment. He stared down Ryan just as Ryan was staring him down. After several long and tense moments, Ryan finally lowered the sword and handed it back to Bric.

"Very well," he said. "But you are clearly elite. Why are you a hired sword and not sworn to some lord somewhere?"

Bric took his weapon carefully. "Because the lord I was sworn to was not an honorable man," he said. "I do not serve men of dishonor. That is all I will say about that."

Ryan accepted it. Whether or not he really believed Bric was a hired sword was debatable, but he was willing to go on a little faith.

Besides… the man had great skill which could be useful.

"You're throwing in with a lot of mercenaries," Ryan said. "Do you find us without honor?"

"If you keep your word, I do not."

"I keep my word. Always."

"Good," Bric said. "So do I. Now, when are we moving to this Welsh castle?"

Ryan's suspicious gaze hovered over Bric for a moment longer before turning away. "More than likely on the morrow," he said. "With the man who paid me dead, I could do one of two things – fulfill his task or simply go back home. Mount Grace has a silver mine and it is a very wealthy castle, so if I can take the castle, the property and the mine belong to me. I've never had a castle before."

Bric learned a great deal with those few sentences. "You plan to stay?"

"Why not?"

Bric lifted his eyebrows. "Because the Welsh might have something to say about a gang of Irish taking one of their castles."

Ryan waved him off. "They're a bunch of wild animals, the Welsh," he said. "They fight among themselves too much and that weakens them. I can hold the castle, have no fear."

Interesting, Bric thought. *He's going to take it for himself, but The Marshal will have something to say about that.*

"I wish you luck," he said. "I'll help you claim it, but I won't stay to help you keep it."

Ryan looked at him, laughing, and Bric cracked a smile. "Where's your sense of adventure, Lad?"

Bric snorted. "Intact," he said. "But that is not an adventure. It's madness."

Ryan laughed as he continued to lead Bric into the heart of the encampment.

CHAPTER EIGHTEEN

"**S**HUSH," SOMEONE WAS hissing in her ear. "Amarantha, stop fighting. It's me. It's Morgan!"

Startled, Amarantha stopped wrestling with the arms that had grabbed her long enough to turn and see Morgan's face just a few inches from her own. With a soft cry of shock and delirious relief, she threw her arms around his neck and squeezed.

"Morgan!" she gasped. "You found me!"

She was happily strangling him and as much as he relished the feel of her arms around him and her body pressed against his, this wasn't the time to enjoy such a thing. It was ironic that their first real physical contact had to be under these circumstances, but he was grateful.

Grateful he had been right about Patience and he'd been fortunate enough to locate her.

"Shhh," he whispered, putting his hand over her mouth gently. "Your guard is out there, listening. I need you to call him into the trees."

She blinked in surprise. "What?" she breathed. "Why?"

"Just do it. Hurry."

He unwrapped her arms from around his neck, kissed her hands, and then darted off into the bushes. Bewildered but willing to do as she was told, Amarantha stood up, brushed off her dress, and called to the guard. He was several feet away, still facing away from her, and because of the language barrier, she had to call him a few times before he turned around.

Heart pounding, Amarantha motioned him over and he gladly followed her right into the trees. He was smiling at her, perhaps lewdly, when Morgan suddenly jumped out of the trees and threw the man into a headlock. As Amarantha watched in terror, he slowly suffocated the man to death.

Morgan slipped the man down the cliffs and into the river.

Morgan watched the body drift down the river, blending in with the murky waters before finally submerging before turning around to find Amarantha. She was right behind him, watching the body along with him, and he grabbed her by the hand and began to run.

Amarantha went happily and willingly.

They ran along the river's edge, towards the northeast, until they came to a clearing where Morgan had tethered his horse. He swiftly mounted, pulling Amarantha on behind him, before spurring the animal onward.

Onward to freedom.

℃

IT WAS IMPORTANT to go as fast as the horse could possibly move.

Time was of the essence. Morgan knew that and he suspected that Amarantha did, too. At some point, if not already, the Irish would realize she hadn't returned and they would go searching for her. Who "they" were was of little matter – Patience and the Irish in general – but they would realize she was missing and go on the hunt. They wouldn't find her, nor would they find her guard, and Morgan estimated it would take about an hour for them to figure out she was gone and so was her guard.

Would they think her guard abducted her?

There were probably a thousand things they would suspect, but in the absence of the guard, the most logical suspicion would be that the guard absconded with her. They would most definitely go in pursuit if they were serious about using her as a hostage. Morgan didn't want to take her back to St. Arvans because he thought that might be the first place they would go to look for her. He believed that their only real chance of slowing down their pursuers was to try to wipe out his trail in the trees.

But it wasn't easy.

Moving through the trees initially and not along the road cost time, but if they were hunting for Amarantha, it was important to not give them a trail to follow and even more important not to be out on the open road. He wasn't completely familiar with this area, so he took what he felt was the most logical direction – northeast – following the curve of the river. He wasn't keen on seeking shelter anywhere nearby because taverns or inns could be raided. Doors could be breached.

He was going to have to find someplace safe for them both.

Perhaps their flight north was made a little worse by the fact that it was a bright, beautiful day. The sky was a clear blue and puffy, white clouds scattered across the sky in the gentle breeze. The waters of the River Wye were their usual muddy color, full of silt, as they made their way along the cliff's edge. The sun was shining brightly on anything that moved. Once or twice, Amarantha tried to speak but he shushed her softly.

He didn't want anyone hearing a woman speaking.

Anyone who might be hunting for her.

The Wye Valley was an outstanding area of beauty, with thick forests lining the river and hills reaching for the sky. It would have been peaceful and lovely had they not been so wrought with apprehension. At one point, the forest thinned out and there was a small road that led north. Morgan made the decision to come out of the trees. He felt that he'd muddied up his trail enough. Up on to the road, he spurred his animal into a run.

Unfortunately, the horse wasn't the most dependable mount and the fast running only went so far. Eventually, the animal slowed down and couldn't go any faster, and Morgan was seriously wondering what they were going to do about it when he caught sight of something in the distance.

A church's steeple.

An idea struck him.

He'd been worrying about finding a safe place for them and perhaps this was it. Not even the Irish would violate the sanctity of a church. At least, Morgan hoped not, but their horse was quickly losing strength and they had to find someplace to hide for the time being.

He headed straight for that steeple.

A rather large church spread out before them, much larger than anything Morgan would have expected in this sleepy but serene valley. Part of it was timber, but part of it was stone, as if they were adding on more buildings with the stone from the original timber church. There was a wall around the place, but the door leading into the sanctuary was exposed for the most part. There was a path off the road that led to the sanctuary and Morgan reined his horse onto that path and continued along the side of the walled cloister, beneath the shade of some giant elm trees.

There, he pulled the horse to a halt and climbed off.

"Now," he said, his hand on Amarantha's leg as he focused intently on her. "We can speak. I am sorry I cut you short, but if we were being pursued, I did not want you to give us away. Or even if there were only people around, voices carry. I wanted our passing to go without notice."

Amarantha smiled wearily at him. "I realize that now," she said. "I was not trying to jeopardize us."

He smiled in return. "I know," he said. Then he paused, simply drinking in the sight of her. "Are you well, sweetheart?"

Amarantha's breath caught in her throat and tears sprang to her eyes. He peered at her with concern.

"What is wrong?" he asked. "What did I say?"

She shook her head. "You called me sweetheart."

"And this offends you?"

"Nay. But… am I?"

His smile returned. "You are mine."

"Am I truly?"

"If you want to be. Do you?"

She sniffled, struggling to regain her composure. "I have a question for you first," she said.

"What is that?"

"Do you serve William Marshal?"

That wasn't the question Morgan had been expecting. He'd already lied to her so much, about who he was and the fact that he was married, though he'd come clean with that one. Still, he just couldn't stomach one more lie to her.

Not one more excuse.

Gazing at the woman, he realized that he was going to accept Hollis' offer of courting her. He'd made that decision as he and Bric had ridden south to find the mercenaries. Morgan wanted to marry Amarantha and he wanted to spend the rest of his life getting to know this brave, compassionate woman with the body of a goddess and the face of an angel. The time she'd spent away from him, in danger, had been some of the worst moments of his life. He knew it was mad to think so – he knew it was mad to think that a woman he'd only known a few short days could get under his skin so much, but the truth was that she had.

She was embedded in him.

Now, she was asking him a direct question and he suspected why.

He sighed heavily.

"Did Patience tell you that?" he asked.

Amarantha nodded. "She told me you had come on the orders of William Marshal to pose as her dead son."

"What else did she tell you?"

"That this was just another mission for you." She paused, gazing at him with some pain in her expression. "Does that mean none of this was real?"

He was shaking his head even before she finished. "It was real, Amarantha," he insisted softly. "The way I feel when I look at you. That is real. My interest in you. That is very real. You asked me if I serve William Marshal. The answer is that I do. I was ordered to come to Mount Grace, assume the identity of Gere le Marche, and lead the Irish mercenaries to victory over your father. My orders are to take Mount Grace in any way that I can."

There it was. The truth, as she had asked for it. Only she hadn't expected it to be so shocking. Well, perhaps not shocking, but certainly, she felt disappointment and fear.

She thought she saw the situation clearly.

"You are going to use me as leverage so my father will surrender Mount Grace, aren't you?" she asked quietly. "That is why you were friendly with me."

Morgan began shaking his head again. "Never," he said. "Why do you think I just took you away from the mercenaries? I did not want them to use you. I will not use you, I swear it. I may be a lot of things, but a dishonorable man is not among them. If I swear to you that you will be safe with me, then I mean it. I will protect you to the death, Amarantha. Always."

She believed him. It was such a passionate plea that any doubt she might have had, any fear, had been dissolved. Although the man had told her multiple lies since they'd first met, this didn't feel like one of them. She could see his sincerity in everything about him. Her gaze finally moved to the church with its dark stone and timbers.

"Then why have you brought me here?" she said. "Are we going to hide in a church?"

"I am going to marry you."

Her head snapped to him in shock. "You're *what*?"

"Marry you," he said evenly. "That last time I spoke to your father, he asked me if I would consider courting you and I have decided to accept. In fact, I have moved beyond the courting and have gone straight to marriage. We are marrying today."

Amarantha stared at him as if the man had grown another head and those fears and doubts so recently dashed returned with a vengeance. "And then what?" she said, growing agitated. "Do you think by marrying me, my father will simply surrender

Mount Grace because you are my husband? What if he does not surrender? What will you do then?"

Morgan could see that she was taking the situation in the opposite direction – one of angst and fear rather than one of hope and joy. She was still suspicious. He hadn't expected this turn and was coming to think that perhaps any sense of warmth and attraction between them might have been one-sided.

Perhaps she simply didn't feel the same way he did.

"My lady," he said, lowering his voice in the hopes that would calm her down. "My name is Morgan de Wolfe. My uncle is the Earl of Wolverhampton. I serve William Marshal and I have come to Mount Grace to effect a change in who possesses the castle and its riches. That was my mission. My only mission. What I did not expect was to meet someone like you. I knew the first time I looked at you that you were someone of great interest to me and by our third encounter, I was smitten. What I feel for you has nothing to do with your father or William Marshal. It has everything to do with you. If you do not feel the same way about me, then I shall return you to Mount Grace, or anywhere else you wish to go, and I will not trouble you again. Tell me now what you wish to do so there are no misunderstandings."

By the time he was finished, her manners weren't so agitated. In fact, she'd cooled down rather quickly. He heard her sigh faintly, sharply, as if forcing herself to regain her composure.

"De Wolfe," she finally said. "I've heard the name."

"I would think so."

"Where were you born?"

"Cheslyn Castle, my father's outpost."

"Where is it?"

"Northeast of Wolverhampton by several miles."

"Do you truly intend to take Mount Grace from my father?"

"I do. It is not his."

"It belongs to the king."

"Who stole it from the House of le Marche."

She cocked her head, trying to reason out the situation in her own mind. "Then who will command it, if not my father?"

"More than likely Ajax de Velt."

That brought a reaction. "The Dark Lord?" she said. "I've heard my father speak of him. He is a great enemy of the king."

"He is."

She paused, mulling over the next step in their startling conversation. "What happens to my father when you oust him?" she asked. "If he is not killed in the battle, what will become of him?"

"I am sure he will return to Craswell Castle, won't he?"

"You know of Craswell?"

"I know a lot of things."

"You will not arrest him in the name of William Marshal?"

"That is not what I have come to do."

Amarantha pondered that for a moment. "He will always support the king, you know."

"And I will always support William Marshal." Morgan cut her off when she tried to speak again. "You've not yet told me what you wish to do, my lady. Shall I take you home? Or will you marry me?"

He was actually giving her a choice in the matter. In spite of everything, the choice was still hers. He could have very easily forced her into marriage, but he didn't. Amarantha couldn't honestly say she had ever been given a choice in any major decision in her life, so it was quite surprising.

But it also told her what kind of man Morgan de Wolfe was.

De Wolfe. Of course she'd heard that name, like everyone else in England. They were a major house, dedicated to the crown usually, but they hated John and were closely allied with Christopher de Lohr and William Marshal. Even Amarantha knew that. Somehow, that made him more prestigious than Morgan of Mercia could have ever been. It was true that he'd lied to her about his identity at first, but she understood why.

What mattered was that he was being truthful now.

She gazed at the man, inspecting his dark hair and hazel eyes that were golden in some light. He was still the most beautiful man she had ever met, a man who was evidently more elite than she had imagined. She'd been attracted to him from the start, too. She remembered when she'd thought he was married, how drawn she was to him. How she'd envied his wife. The truth was that she didn't know him well at all, but what she did know, she liked. Her attraction to him was positively magnetic and something she couldn't deny. She would regret it if she did.

Just perhaps, this was one chance in life she needed to take.

"It seems rather foolish to be speaking of this," she finally said. "We hardly know one another."

Morgan nodded. "That is true," he said. "But sometimes, one meeting is all it takes to know you are meant for a woman and she is meant for you. I've known men who have married a woman they knew for years, yet that didn't make them any happier. It simply meant they knew what kind of woman they were marrying. What do I know of you? I know you teach children to read. I know you are kind and compassionate. And I know that you are decisive in your opinions. What I do not know of you, I can learn. What I cannot learn, I can feel."

A smile spread across her lips. "That is very poetic."

"It is true," he said. "Now you know how I feel. How do *you* feel?"

Amarantha looked at the man for a moment longer before sliding off the horse. Her dress caught on the saddle and he helped her straighten it out, for which she thanked him. Then they stared at each other for several long seconds, a thousand questions and a thousand answers filling the air between them.

What I cannot learn, I can feel.

She could, too.

"I want to learn with you," she said softly. "And feel what I cannot learn. Every day will be an adventure, I think. But I am willing to share that adventure with you, Morgan. But I have one request."

"Name it."

"That you will never lie to me again, no matter what. Will you do this?"

He nodded faintly. "I am not a liar by nature," he said. "I am a man who values trust and honesty above all. But serving William Marshal means I must sometimes deviate from that because it is my duty or I will risk my life unnecessarily if I am truthful."

"I will never be a duty."

"Nay, you will not."

"Morgan?"

"Aye?"

"Are you ever going to kiss me or are we simply going to talk?" she asked. "Mayhap you should kiss me and then we will decide for certain if we should marry."

He laughed softly at the surprising request. "A marriage decided on one kiss?"

"I am sure marriage has been decided on less important

things."

She had a point. With a grin, he pulled her into his arms, feeling her warmth and softness against him and he swore, at that moment, that he had never before held a woman for no woman he had ever embraced had felt like this. It was as if this were the first time he'd ever touched a woman because Amarantha's scent and feel and heat erased every memory of any woman he'd ever had.

Gone.

There was no hesitation as he slanted his lips over hers.

Heat. Soft. Delicious. She was all of those things as he suckled her gently, suckling the breath right out of her and still suckling more. His tongue licked at her lips, begging for an invitation to enter her mouth, and when she timidly opened her lips, he took full advantage of it. He could have so easily continued because the more he tasted, the more he wanted, but he simply couldn't take the time now. Mercenaries were probably after them at this very moment, so he reluctantly pulled away only to see that she was half-dazed in his arms.

His smile returned.

"Well?" he said huskily. "Do we marry?"

She swallowed hard, trying to regain her senses. "We do."

That was what he wanted to hear. Taking her by the hand, he held on to her as he grabbed the horse's reins and walked up to the sanctuary door. He didn't see a stable, at least not an obvious one, and he didn't want to leave the horse exposed, so he took the animal through an open gate and tethered it next to a font that had water spilling into it. It was probably holy water, at the very least spring water, and the horse began to slurp water as he led Amarantha back around to the front of the sanctuary.

Quietly, they entered.

There were children and a few men at the far end of what was a very long, very big sanctuary. Truly, Morgan was quite surprised to find such a big church in the middle of a quiet valley. Still clutching Amarantha, he made his way to the front of the sanctuary where a couple of the boys caught sight of them and ran for one of the men. Morgan could see by the heavy woolen robes that it must have been a priest. The boy pointed to them and the priest set down the cup he was wiping out and headed in their direction.

"I think Father Nicodemus will be very disappointed we did not let him perform the mass," Amarantha muttered.

Morgan's eyes twinkled with mirth but he was prevented from answering as the priest came upon them, looking at them curiously. He was an older man with a very round face and red cheeks, reeking as if he hadn't taken a bath in years. They could smell him from where they stood.

"May I know your business, children?" he asked.

"We wish to be married, Father," Morgan said, resisting the urge to pinch his nose at the stench. "I am prepared to pay well for it."

The priest blinked as if confused by the request. "Marriage?" he said. "When?"

"Now."

"At this moment?"

"Aye."

The priest shook his head. "I am afraid it is not as easy as that, my son," he said. "You are not a member of this parish, are you?"

Morgan didn't reply. He dug in a satchel slung over his shoulder, the one he'd removed from the horse when he'd left it tied near the well, and removed his purse. He held up two gold crowns in front of the priest.

"Nay, I am not from this parish," he said. "Nor is she. She is of age and has given her consent, and I am of age, also. I will pay you two gold crowns to perform the mass and give us a chamber in which to consummate the marriage. Do it now, and send someone to feed my horse, and I'll give you another gold crown. A fourth gold crown is yours for denying you ever saw us, to anyone who asks. Is this in any way unclear?"

The priest was looking at the gold crowns. That kind of money would feed the priests and members of the parish for months. This was a big parish and there were many who attended mass, but it was expensive to run a church this big.

It wasn't as if they were rich.

"Marriages are recorded and the book is available for all to see," he said hesitantly. "I could deny seeing you, but your name would be in the book."

"If you did not see us, then how would anyone know to look in the book where events are recorded?"

He had a point. He also flashed the two gold coins again as incentive. Staring at the coins, the priest deliberated the proposal for about a half a moment longer before stepping forward and snatching the money out of Morgan's grip.

"Give me a moment," he said.

He ran off with a few acolytes and Morgan's money, but returned shortly with another priest and the records book, bound with leather and with yellowed vellum pages.

After that, things happened quickly.

Dressed in peasant clothing and without his family or friends present, Morgan de Wolfe and Amarantha de la Haye were joined in matrimony during a swift mass. The truth was that, legally, they didn't need the mass. Sometimes, it was as simple as them stating that they took each other as a spouse and most marriages were conducted at the entrance to the church. That was the traditional way. But Morgan wanted the mass and he wanted it recorded so that it could never be contested, by anyone. He was thorough that way. As soon as the blessing was given for the marriage, the second priest who had accompanied the first filled out a line in the book of births, deaths, and marriages as Morgan supervised.

And with that, he had himself a wife.

Morgan gave the priest the additional coins he had promised him. One of the boys took them out of the sanctuary and towards a series of outbuildings towards the river. There was a large dormitory that they passed by and then several smaller chambers next to the dormitory that were timber and not stone. It was that mix of building materials that they'd noticed from the start and the child opened one of the doors, indicating for them to enter. Amarantha went inside, timidly, but Morgan asked the boy to bring them some food and drink in about an hour. The boy ran off without even acknowledging the request.

Shaking his head at the skittish child, Morgan followed Amarantha into the chamber.

It was dark inside, so dark that he hit his knee on the end of the bed. As he grunted and rubbed at the offended kneecap, Amarantha found a flint and stone and lit the taper. As a warm, golden glow filled the room, Amarantha got a good look at the chamber and groaned.

"God's Bones," she muttered. "We would have done better had we stayed out in the forest."

Morgan chuckled, looking around at the chamber. It was small, with an equally small bed shoved against the wall. There was a mattress and a woolen blanket but little else.

"God's Bones is right," he said. "Evidently, they think this is a suitable place to consummate a marriage."

"I wonder if they get such requests."

He chuckled. "I doubt it," he said. "But since they know what we're going to do, I will look around to make sure there are no holes from which to watch us. The last thing we need is a celibate audience."

Amarantha giggled in spite of herself. "You don't think they'd really do that, do you?"

He shrugged. "God only knows," he said. "I've known some priests who are more corrupt than any men I've ever known, so who's to say?"

Amarantha sat down on the bed, gingerly. "Let us hope these priests are not interested in things that do not concern them."

Morgan put his satchel down on the only table in the room, a tiny thing with a little stool. He kicked the stool with his boot only for the thing to collapse.

"It looks like the furniture in this chamber was made for dwarves," he said. "But I suppose it does not matter. It will be suitable for our needs."

He turned to see Amarantha sitting on the bed, looking rather forlorn, and it occurred to him that he'd been rather callous about consummating the marriage. He'd spoken of it as if it were simply an act, a necessity to seal the marriage, and nothing more. He didn't want to start off this marriage by sounding like a cad.

He could only imagine how she must be feeling.

"I know this has happened quickly," he said gently. "I realize you must be frightened, but I swear to you that there is nothing to be frightened of. I promise that I will be as gentle as possible, but I know you understand that this marriage must be consummated. For it to be binding, so no one can ever break the bond, we must…"

He gestured to the bed, inferring what must take place and hoping she got the message. She did, as evidenced by her pink cheeks.

She understood everything.

"I know," she said. "But you were correct when you said this has happened very quickly. I can hardly believe that we are actually married."

He tried to sense regret in her tone, but there didn't seem to be any. Just disbelief. He went to her, putting a tender hand on her head.

"I swear you will not regret it, Amarantha," he said softly. "I will do everything I can to be a kind and attentive and understanding husband. I suppose I've never given any thought to what kind of husband I would want to be, but now… now, I have. I want to be the best husband I can be because it would crush me to see you unhappy."

She looked up at him, smiling. "I promise to be the best wife I can be, also," she said. "I've always wanted to marry a man I was fond of. Nay, not just fond… a man I love. I think it would be terrible not to love the person you were married to."

"I agree."

Her cheeks started to pinken again. "Do you suppose we could learn to love one another? Is that too much to hope for? Or is it a silly, romantic notion that only women have?"

He smiled. "I do not think it is a notion that only women have," he said. "I have several friends who love their wives desperately. I have always envied that. Shall I tell you a secret?"

"Of course."

"I am very glad I have the chance to have my own love story."

It was a sweet thing to say. Amarantha smiled broadly, bashfully, thinking that he was being very romantic. Perhaps he didn't even realize it.

But she did.

"Well," she said, looking around at that small bed. "What do we do next? I apologize if I sound naïve, but I've never consummated a marriage before."

"Nor have I."

"But you *do* know what to do, don't you?"

He nodded. "I believe I can navigate these tricky waters," he said. "The first thing we should do is pull the blankets down to the floor. That bed is not nearly big enough for us both."

He was making it seem unimportant, like a task they both had to accomplish and had to work together in order to do so. By making it seem not so hugely critical, he was able to calm Amarantha a little. She worked alongside him, pulling the woolen blankets off the bed and spreading them on the hard-packed ground and fashioning a big bed of sorts. It wasn't comfortable, but it would get the job done.

But soon enough, they were finished fussing with the blankets and there was nothing else for them to do but get on with it. He was looking at the bed, wishing he didn't have to take her here, when he felt her gaze upon him. Glancing up, he met her eyes.

Amarantha was looking at him expectantly but also with some trepidation. He could see it in her eyes.

He sighed faintly.

"You become more beautiful every time I look at you," he

said softly. "You make my heart beat so. I do not even know when that started, my heart fluttering like a silly squire's, but it happens every time I look at you. I know it always will."

She smiled at his very sweet words. "Do you feel as if you cannot breathe?"

"I can hardly breathe."

"I feel the same way."

Reaching out a hand to her, she put her left hand in his and he pulled her down onto the blankets. As she sat down, he knelt, still holding her hand.

"This is not how I imagined I would take a wife and I am certain this is not how you imagined you would take a husband," he said. "As of this moment, you belong to me. You will belong to me forever, come what may. I wish I had all the time in the world to properly introduce you to something that is going to bind us in more ways that you can imagine, but there is not time. This must be done quickly. That does not mean it is unimportant. On the contrary – that means it is very important. *You* are very important."

Amarantha didn't seem particularly nervous. At least, not outwardly. "I know," she said. "I wish I was as poetic as you are but, alas, I am not. However, this moment reminds me of something I read in one of my father's books."

"Oh?"

She nodded. "A very old poem," she said. "Older than almost anything else in his collection. I do not remember all of it, but I do remember the most important lines."

"What are those?"

She smiled, squeezing his hand.

"Bridegroom, dear to my heart," she murmured. "You have captivated me as I stand trembling before you."

He lifted her hand and kissed it. "That is beautiful," he said. "But is it true?"

She nodded sincerely. "Very true."

Gently, he cupped her cheek and tipped her face up to meet his. "Good," he murmured. "Because I tremble as I kneel before you, Amarantha. I suspect I always will."

With that, his mouth claimed hers hungrily. His arms went around her instinctively, pulling her into the curve of his torso. Waves of satisfaction and warmth rolled over him as he clutched her against him, his mouth feasting on hers.

Morgan knew he was lost the moment she began to respond to him with her soft mouth. He lost himself in her honeyed lips, his enormous hands moving to her hair, savoring every sound, every taste, every movement she made. He couldn't even think, surrendering to his desire faster than he'd ever surrendered to anything in his life.

He could not have resisted her.

Emotion overwhelmed him.

He was more forceful in his kisses than ever before. With supreme gentleness, he lay her on her back and began untying the garments she was wearing. They'd done a decent job of concealing her curves, but he knew what was underneath it all. Now, those curves, that delicious body, belonged to him and he was ready to experience it. Everything came off under his eager hands, including his own clothing. But somehow, his lips never left her mouth.

In little time, they were both naked.

Amarantha should have been self-conscious at the very least, but she couldn't seem to manage it. There was something so fine and natural about what they were doing. When Morgan finally paused to catch his breath, he moved down beside her, looming over her, his big hand on her hip as he looked her over from her neck to her toes.

Arousal didn't begin to cover what he was feeling.

Her skin was like silk, perfect in every way. Her breasts were large and firm, with big nipples, and those beautiful hips flared in such a way that he could hardly wait to plant his body between them. But he could see that she was panting heavily, from his kisses and perhaps a little fear, so he resumed his kisses, gently, before rolling his big body on top of her.

Morgan's enormous body enveloped her in power and heat. His mouth left her lips, devouring her neck as he moved down her body. He tasted every inch of flesh on her shoulders and arms, moving to her chest and depositing tender kisses on the swell of her breasts. A big hand finally moved to fondle a tender breast as his lips found her nipples, moving from one to the other hungrily.

Beneath him, Amarantha squirmed with delight.

She was running on instinct. Everything he was doing to her was new and naughty and thrilling and utterly consuming. His weight on her was significant and she instinctively parted her thighs, allowing his lower body to slip between them. He was such a big man that he nearly swallowed her up with flesh and warmth, yet his touch was incredibly gentle and passionate. One hand slipped beneath her to grasp her tender buttocks and she lifted her pelvis, somehow helping him gain hold. It seemed completely natural for him to grasp her there.

She wanted more.

More was what Morgan was about to give her.

Amarantha was in a haze of passion as he moved down her belly, kissing every piece of flesh he could come into contact with. She was thinking of how much she was enjoying this moment, that it truly didn't seem as frightening or painful as other women had led her to believe. She was thinking that she wasn't embarrassed that she was naked beneath him because he was so big, she felt completely concealed.

Protected.

Adored.

But those thoughts flew from her mind when he grasped her buttocks with both hands and brought her private core to his mouth.

The groan that pealed from her lips was filled with ecstasy.

Amarantha's eyes rolled up into her head as his mouth began to work her virginal center. He worked her with his tongue, ignoring the fact that she was a maiden. He was being as gentle as he could be but, even so, his lust had the better of him. This woman and her beautiful body threatened to destroy his control and all he wanted to do was taste her. Every part of her.

He had to have more.

As his tongue licked her into a frenzy, he could feel his lust for her building. But it was more than lust – it was quickly becoming a need. He needed the feel and taste of her as much as he needed to breathe. When he manipulated her taut little bud of pleasure and felt her body convulse, he suddenly lifted himself up, put his engorged manhood at her threshold, and thrust himself into her.

Amarantha gasped at the sting of possession, but it was a quick sensation. It was there and then it was gone. Morgan thrust again and again, seating himself completely as she lay beneath him, legs flung open wide. It seemed so intuitive to spread her legs for him, inviting him deep into her body when she'd never invited anyone there before. But with Morgan, it was instinct.

Everything with him was instinct.

Timidly, she put her hands on his buttocks, feeling the smooth, taut skin as he coiled them and gently began to thrust. With one hand on her buttocks and the other on her breast, Morgan impaled her on his phallus again and again, listening to her gasps of delight, feeling her body respond to his as he had never experienced in his life. It was as if she were made for him, every part of her, and he fit within her like a piece of a puzzle.

He'd found the person who completed him.

Their tender kisses resumed and he kissed her cheeks, her neck, before claiming her lips once more. He could feel her body rattle with his powerful thrusts, her soft gasping in his ear that encouraged him. She was so utterly divine that his end came faster than he wanted it to, but he simply couldn't help it.

Even after he climaxed, he continued to thrust into her and was rewarded when her body released around him. Her tender walls pulled at him, demanding his seed, and he gave her all that he could. At least, for the moment. There would be much more to come in the days ahead. Not wanting the moment to end, however, he continued to move within her, to kiss her, to caress her buttocks and breasts. Those gorgeous, full breasts that drew his lust. When he finally slowed his movements, he knew quite irrevocably that something important had happened to him. As if the heavens had opened up and shown him what he had been looking for all his life.

It was the beginning of something he couldn't begin to comprehend.

Amarantha rested in his arms, breathing heavily with exertion, and Morgan held her tightly, his gentle kisses raining on her hair and face, her shoulder, until he felt himself growing hard again and he resumed another round of tender thrusts. Amarantha moaned softly as he moved within her once again, her arms wrapped around his neck as she completely turned herself over to him.

Though he knew they should cut this short and quickly leave, Morgan couldn't seem to. He took her again on that old woolen blanket, holding her softness against him as he made love to her, his actions infused with everything he was quickly coming to feel for her. When they each finally found their release, it was together, and Amarantha began to weep softly, completely overwhelmed with what had transpired. When she had awoken that morning, nothing could have prepared her for what the day would bring.

Exhausted and overcome, she fell into a deep sleep with his body still embedded in her and he did not have the heart to move her. He lay there and held her tight, his body against hers, and thinking that this moment, in this place, was the most precious experience he'd ever had.

With the most precious wife he'd never expected.

CHAPTER NINETEEN

"T AD IS NOT a man to take what does not belong to him," one man was saying to Ryan. "It would not be like him to run off with your prisoner. Something must have happened to them both."

Almost three hours after he last saw Amarantha head off with an escort in tow, Ryan and his men were still looking for both her and the escort. Ryan thought he knew all of his men, most who had been with him for many years, but the disappearance of Tad MacKenna and his lovely prisoner had him seething.

He was furious.

There was no trace.

All of the men had been out looking. They'd combed the woods, the river's edge, the fields and trees to the west, and St. Arvans. In fact, they'd descended on the village like locusts looking for the pair, which stirred up the locals who'd had a strict policy of not bothering the mercenaries if they didn't bother them. But the search for Amarantha and Tad destroyed that invisible barrier and the villagers were up in arms over the mercenaries who had all but wrecked their village.

To Ryan, that meant they had to go.

They were going, anyway.

"Christ and his bloody saints," he grumbled. Then he held out his hands for emphasis. "Did the man really run away with her? 'Tis like they bloody well disappeared into the air!"

Ryan, a usually calm and congenial individual, was as angry as anyone had seen him. That is, anyone but Bric.

He'd been watching the entire situation unfold carefully.

About a half-hour into the search for Amarantha and Tad, Bric knew for certain that Morgan had found her and spirited her away. Because he'd served on the Marches on occasion between de Lohr and de Velt, whenever his liege, Daveigh de Winter, had been asked to send support, Bric had spent some time in the area.

He knew the region marginally well and he knew that there was nothing to the east for many, many miles. He knew there was an abbey to the northeast, several miles away, and there was an array of villages around. If he were Morgan, he would have taken her to the abbey for safety, but he wasn't sure the mercenaries knew there was an abbey to the northeast. It was true they'd been there for a few months, but in the short time he'd spent with them, Bric was under the impression that they hadn't strayed far from where they were camped.

That would work to Morgan's advantage… hopefully.

While the search was going on, he'd hung back and let the others do the work, but there had been a strategy to it. If he was a hired sword, and clearly Irish, then it would stand to reason that he wouldn't know the area very well. He kept waiting for Ryan to ask him to help search, but the man never did. He bellowed to his men to search the area and search the village, completely forgetting about Bric, until one by one his men returned empty-handed.

And Bric just stood by and watched it all.

Finally, one of the last groups of men returned from searching, having gone south towards Chepstow. The thought was that Tad might have taken her to Chepstow to secure a cog and take her back to Ireland, but they didn't get as far as Chepstow before returning. That frustrated Ryan to no end and he raged at his men while they stood around nervously.

That was when the entire focus of the group changed.

"The villagers from St. Arvans are arming themselves, Ryan," one man told him. "We upended the village from one end to the other looking for Tad and the lady and they've not taken kindly to it. Do we stand and fight?"

Ryan knew about the upset villagers. He'd heard reports from his men returning from the search, but now he was being reminded of it yet again.

He grunted unhappily.

"We've lived in harmony with them for the past few months, and now this," he said with regret. "They cannot understand that we're looking for a missing woman?"

"I do not think they care, Ryan," the man said softly.

Ryan shook his head. "I'm sure they don't," he said. "But I will not fight them. I have been paid to fight at Mount Grace and I will not waste men or weapons beating back some villagers, so let us break down the camp. We ride within the hour for Mount Grace. Sooner if the villagers appear. Get to it."

He clapped his hands and men started to move, rushing all over the place in their haste to break down their semi-permanent encampment. Bric, having nothing to break down, was still standing aside, watching everything, when Ryan caught sight of him. Chewing his lip with thought and frustration he made his way over to Bric.

"Do you know this area, MacRohan?" he asked.

Bric shrugged. "Not very well," he said. "I've traveled mostly in Norfolk and in the south. Wales is full of Welsh and I avoid them if I can."

Ryan smiled thinly. "Agreed," he said. "But we are moving to Mount Grace before the day is out. You've heard my men – the villagers of St. Arvans are out for blood after we raided their town today. Not that I blame them, but I've no desire to fight off villagers. My fighting is better suited for castles and sieges, not peasants with pitchforks."

Bric scratched his head, looking around the encampment. "With your men packing up, do you want me to continue the search for the lady and the man that ran off with her?"

Ryan shrugged, the anger he'd so recently been feeling turning to defeat. "If you'd like," he said. "I'm not sure where you could look where they have not, but it is worth a try. Where will you go?"

Bric was still looking around. "Your men have gone north and south and west," he said, pointing. "No one has gone due east."

"The river is to the east."

"One can cross the river."

That idea intrigued Ryan. "Then go," he said. "We will be on the road within the hour, so you can find us heading north to Mount Grace."

"What road will you be taking?"

Ryan gestured towards the northwest. "I do not want to go through St. Arvans," he said. "I know there is another road in that direction that heads north. 'Tis a bit out of the way, but it will take us past Raglan and from there, to Mount Grace."

"I will find you there," Bric said. "And what does this woman look like so I know her on sight?"

Ryan's gaze took on a distant hue. "Brown hair and dark eyes," he said. "The face of an angel and a body…"

He made the exaggerated shape of a woman, with big breasts, little waist, big hips. Truth be told, Bric had never met Amarantha, but this wasn't the first time he'd heard tale of her figure, so he suspected he would know her when he saw her without benefit of an introduction.

"I understand," he said. "Her name?"

"Amarantha," Ryan said. "And the man with her – Tad – is a good fighter, so watch him. Just get her back if you can, but if he tries to kill you, do what you must to defend yourself and the lady."

Bric simply nodded and turned away, heading off to find his horse, which had been placed in a corral with many others. When he finally collected the animal and headed off, he immediately went southeast because he knew that Ryan was more than likely watching him.

There was a bridge to the southeast and Ryan would assume that was where he was going, and he did. It took him about an hour to reach it, a few moments to cross it, and then he was riding with all speed north on the other side of the river, up to the crossing near Tintern.

It was Tintern Abbey he would be visiting.

Something told him he would find what he was looking for.

CHAPTER TWENTY

Mount Grace

THE ORE WASN'T ready for shipment in four days.

It was ready in two.

The Irish weren't anywhere to be seen when the wagons were readied and covered with oiled canvas, and Kenan assigned about two hundred men to guard the five big ore carts. It was mid-morning on a bright but cold day as the order was given to open the gates and purge the ore carts from the outer bailey.

Somehow, Essien had made it out of the mines and into Bronllys to tell Alexander what was transpiring. Father Nicodemus had been alerted, also, but the decision had been made by Addax to begin the battle with or without the Irish and Alexander couldn't get word to him in time to wait. Bric and Morgan hadn't been heard from and a messenger boy that Alexander had sent south towards St. Arvans to see if he could spy the incoming Irish army hadn't returned, so they were flying blind. But Addax had the miners prepared and ready, and when the gates opened, the opportunity to flood the outer bailey of Mount Grace was too good to pass up.

The rebellion, for the remains of the le Marche army, had begun.

The day they'd waited five years for was upon them, Irish army or no.

With a muttered curse, Alexander had donned his armor, mounted his steed, and charged up to Mount Grace with Essien behind him just as the miners began to flood from the tunnels and out into the bailey. The gatehouse was swarmed right away by men bearing weapons that they'd been fashioning in secret for the past five years, sharp blades that cut and sliced and killed many Mount Grace soldiers who were caught off guard.

As Alexander and Essien charged in through the gates, they noticed that the first thing the miners had done was disable the gates so they couldn't be closed. The gates were massive panels of oak and someone had set fire to them and the ropes that held them. While that was happening, more miners had flooded into the inner bailey and, even now, nasty fighting was going on at the smaller inner gatehouse.

This gatehouse had a portcullis, which a gang of miners were tying ropes around and using ponies from the mine to pull off its track. Someone had made it into the smaller gatehouse above and had destroyed one of the wheels that raised and lowered the portcullis. With that destruction and the ponies pulling it off the track, the inner bailey was exposed.

It was bedlam.

The Mount Grace soldiers had grown lazy over the past five years. No battles and only a skirmish or two had left them unprepared for a rebellion that had come up from beneath them, through the tunnels and into the castle. There was a wooden troop house built against the outer wall, one that housed about five hundred men at any given time. Led by Essien, miners tied up the doors and barred the windows and set the structure on fire. The sounds of dying men filled the air as the entire troop house went up in flames.

Alexander had never met Hollis or Kenan and had to be told by Addax when the men joined the battle. Hollis seemed to be directing everything from the keep while Kenan charged out astride his big, brown warhorse. He rushed out into the outer bailey, sword wielded, and seemed overwhelmingly surprised to see a fully armed knight in the midst of the fighting along with two burly miners who swung a sword better than most.

Worst of all, the Mount Grace soldiers were stunned into inaction. When the miners first flooded the outer bailey, they stood curiously and watched them overrun the ward. When they moved into the inner bailey and went for the gatehouse, that's when the soldiers seemed to jar out of whatever trance they'd been in. That's when they started to fight back, but once they did, the miners turned on them and began to kill with those crude blades they'd made over the years.

Very quickly, the battle turned into a bloodbath.

Alexander, Addax, and Essien were in the middle of it, cutting down Mount Grace soldiers and leading the miners. It was Alexander and Addax who charged into the inner bailey, with Essien holding the outer bailey, and ran straight into Kenan, who was mostly trying to defend himself from the miners more than he was actually taking the offensive. Addax knew him on sight and, given what Father Nicodemus had told them, he pointed him out to Alexander. The two of them charged the man, boxing him back against the wall of the inner bailey.

Kenan was armed with an enormous broadsword but, so

far, he hadn't tried to fight them. But it was clear he was prepared to defend himself. Addax lowered his sword to show that he wasn't a threat.

Yet.

"De Poyer," Addax said. "We are from the stable of William Marshal. We have come to take Mount Grace in the name of the Earl of Pembroke. We have reason to believe you will support this action."

Kenan's focus moved between Addax and Alexander, slowly, contemplating the words. "Who told you this?"

"Father Nicodemus."

Kenan sat back in his saddle as if struck by the news. "Then you have not come to kill me?"

"Not unless you try to kill us."

Kenan kept his sword up, but his body language changed. "You are truly from The Marshal?" he asked as if still in disbelief. "And these miners? Are they part of The Marshal's army?"

Addax glanced around at the small army of gleeful but determined miners. "They are not part of The Marshal's army," he said. "But they are led by men who used to be part of Oliver le Marche's army. They know how to take this castle back."

"Where are the Irish mercenaries?"

Alexander and Addax looked at one another, realizing that everything the priest had told them about de Poyer was true. At least, so far.

"We're not sure," Alexander said. "Their arrival is expected at any moment. The miners were supposed to wait for their arrival and once they were here, the attack was to be coordinated when the gatehouse opened to transport the ore. Since the ore shipped before the Irish could arrive, it seems the miners have gone on without them."

Kenan nodded, watching a gang of miners obliterate some soldiers who were trying to protect the armory. "The miners will kill me if I do not defend myself and the keep," he said. "Hollis is in the keep, watching everything."

"He will not come out and fight?" Alexander asked.

Kenan snorted rudely. "That man?" he said. "He's a coward. Unless he has the upper hand and can beat down someone smaller and weaker, he will not fight. He will hide and let others do the fighting for him."

Alexander peered at him curiously. "Then if the Irish were to try to use his daughter to force him to surrender Mount Grace, he would not?"

Kenan shook his head with disgust. "Nay," he said. "If there is a chance he will end up a prisoner or in the shameful position of surrendering, he will not do it. Do the Irish have her, then?"

"We do not know," Alexander said. "Morgan and another knight have gone to the Irish to try and locate her, so if she is with them, they will find her."

Kenan was silent for a moment. "Morgan of Mercia," he said. "He's a Marshal man, isn't he?"

Alexander nodded. "He was to replace Gere le Marche and lead the Irish over the de la Haye forces."

The light of understanding came to Kenan's eyes. "I thought so," he said. "The man didn't look like a simple knight to me, following orders from his commander. He looked like he eats babies for breakfast and slays men in his sleep."

Alexander started to laugh. "I would not go that far, but being a de Wolfe, you would not be much wrong. He is elite."

"De Wolfe?" Kenan said with surprise. "He's Wolverhamp-ton?"

"His uncle."

Everything was coming clear, for both sides, and Kenan finally lowered the sword he'd been holding aloft since he was cornered.

The gesture was obvious.

"You have no chance of getting into that keep unless I do it for you," he said. "But I have one request."

"What is it?"

Kenan's dark eyes grew intense. "That when I capture the keep, you tell William Marshal that I am the one who did it," he said. "I want to stay at Mount Grace after Pembroke takes control. Will you do this?"

Alexander nodded without hesitation, remembering they'd mentioned this very thing during the conversation in the church. "Aye," he said. "You will have a place of honor when the new commander takes his post."

That seemed to give Kenan a good deal of relief. "Good," he said. "Then gather about twenty men and come with me. Your men will form a barrier to prevent anyone from leaving the keep, Hollis included. I will flush him out."

"He will put up a fight?"

"Leave him to me."

He sounded determined. Alexander and Addax exchanged glances as Kenan headed off towards the keep with Alexander trailing after him as Addax went to collect as many miners as he could find on such short notice. He gathered twenty-two in short order before heading off towards the keep and forming a barrier in front of the entry door.

It was the last frontier.

☙

IT WAS EARLY morning at Tintern Abbey.

Although Morgan had only intended to stay at the abbey as long as it took to marry Amarantha and consummate the marriage, they'd both fallen into a heavy sleep after consummating not once, but three times. Not even the boy bringing them food an hour later and rapping on the door could wake them, so they slept all the rest of the day and all night as well.

It had been Morgan who had awoken first, about an hour before dawn, groggy and having completely lost track of time. Amarantha was still sleeping and he'd carefully disengaged his body from hers, covering her with her clothing before quickly donning his own and leaving the chamber to find out what time it was. Or even what day it was. He'd been completely disoriented until a kitchen servant told him that it was an hour before lauds, or the morning mass.

That's when Morgan realized he'd stayed longer than intended.

Taking what food he could carry from the kitchens – bread, cheese, and wine that had been watered down with boiled apple juice – he took it all back to Amarantha, who had risen and dressed by the time he returned.

Just the sight of her did his heart good. In the weak light of the taper she'd lit, she was just finishing with the braid in her hair when he entered. Their eyes met and she smiled, he smiled, and all was right in the world. Morgan kissed her forehead, her cheek, and finally her lips before he ever spoke a word.

"It is nearly dawn, sweetheart," he said softly. "I found what food I could. Let us eat and be on our way."

Amarantha took the bread and cheese and wine from him, setting it down on the floor next to her as he went about securing his satchel.

She yawned.

"Did you intend for us to sleep all day and all night?" she asked, jesting with him.

He chuckled. "Nay," he said. "But once I was in your arms, I forgot all sense of time."

She smiled at him before taking a big bite of the mostly stale bread. "As did I," she said. "I have never felt safer or more content in my life."

He glanced at her as he tied up the satchel. "Any regrets?"

She shook her head firmly. "None," she said. "For the first time in my life, I feel… joy. Satisfaction. I am not certain how else to describe it, but it's a wonderful euphoria."

He grinned. "Strange," he said. "I was just thinking the same thing."

She smiled broadly as he approached her and she broke the stale bread in half, handing part of it to him. He took an enormous bite.

"It is too bad we cannot stay here and enjoy this protection and privacy," she said. "Even though we slept on an old blanket on the floor, I will have nothing but wonderful memories of this moment."

"I am glad," he said, swallowing what was in his mouth and taking another bite. "But I promise you that I will provide much better for you than a cold floor and an old blanket."

She broke the cheese up and handed him the larger portion. "Where will we go now?"

He began eating the cheese. "Back to Mount Grace," he said. "But first, I will take you to Father Nicodemus and he will hide you until this is all over."

She looked at him with some concern. "Hide me?" she said. "From whom?"

He swallowed the bite in his mouth. "Everyone," he said quietly. "But mostly from the Irish since they are going to be at Mount Grace also. Since I am returning to fight a battle, I do not want you part of that. I want you well protected, so the best thing for you would be to remain at the church until everything is over."

Amarantha understood that, though her heart was still heavy for many reasons. "Do you think the Irish will be looking for us? For me?"

"Possibly," he said. "It is best not to tempt fate and hide you away."

She took a nibble of the cheese in her hand. "They were not cruel to me, you know."

"Who? The Irish?"

She nodded. "The leader's name is Ryan," she said. "He was not unpleasant. I suppose I always imagined mercenaries to be bloodthirsty fiends, but he wasn't like that at all. He was rather kind. He gave me these clothes to wear when my dress was ruined. He spoke of his dead wife, his children. He seemed like a normal man."

Morgan lifted an eyebrow. "A normal man who takes money to kill men he does not know," he said. "Though I am glad he was kind to you, I still do not want him to have the opportunity to get his hands on you again."

"And hiding at the church is the best hope against that."

"Exactly."

Amarantha fell silent again, taking another bite of her cheese before speaking. "When you go to Mount Grace, remember that Everelda is there," she said. "You… you will not let anyone hurt her, will you?"

He could see how concerned she was. "Of course not," he

assured her. "I will make it a point of finding her and taking her to safety, I swear it. I will not let anyone hurt her."

That brought measurable relief. "Thank you," she said. "I am sorry if it was offensive to even ask that question, but I wanted to make sure you remembered her. She will be very frightened. I know that you look at my father as the enemy, but…"

He cut her off gently. "Your father is not my enemy," he said. "Your father is a man who serves the man who is my enemy. If you are concerned for your father's welfare, know that I will not kill him unless he tries to kill me. I am allowed to defend myself in such a case."

She nodded quickly. "Of course you are," she said. "I did not mean to suggest otherwise. My father and I have never been close, but he is the only father I have. Mayhap you will let him return to Craswell and simply stay there."

"I will consider it," Morgan said. "But much is out of my hands, you know. The Marshal is my liege and if he makes a decision about your father's fate, I must obey."

"I know."

"But I will do what I can to make sure your father is treated fairly."

She smiled weakly. "That is all I can ask," she said. "But I was wondering something else."

"What?"

"When all of this is over, where shall we live?"

"Where do you want to live?"

She shrugged. "I have lived at Mount Grace for the past few years," she said. "Before that, I was at Warwick Castle."

"Where were you born?"

"Craswell."

He lifted his eyebrows. "If your father does not survive the battle, then Craswell will go to you as his only child?"

She nodded. "I am the Craswell heiress."

He grinned. "Ah," he said. "I've married an heiress."

He said it rather comically and she giggled softly. "Such as it is," she said. "Although I will say that Craswell doesn't do too badly. There are six villages on our lands and my father is never without money."

"A *rich* heiress."

Her laughter grew. "I probably should not have told you," she said, watching him snort. "But it will become yours, as my husband, when my father dies. I think you will make a fine Lord Craswell."

Morgan reached out a hand to stroke her hair affectionately. "You are the only thing I care about," he said. "Not some lordship. But back to the question of where we will live – my post, believe it or not, is Richmond Castle in Yorkshire."

She looked surprised. "All the way up there?"

"All the way up there."

"Is that where we will live?"

He nodded. "I am the garrison commander," he said. "That is only a recent appointment, however. My liege, Caius d'Avignon, married last year and assumed his wife's properties, leaving me in command of Richmond, which belongs to The Marshal. When I am finished with my mission here, I will return to Richmond and you will go with me. I think you will like it there. It is a vast place with a lovely village. I know the people will love you."

The idea of a lovely Yorkshire post fed Amarantha's imagination. She imagined wild, green fields, a stalwart castle, and happy people.

"It sounds lovely," she said. "I look forward to it."

He smiled. "As do I," he said. "But first, we must get through the situation at Mount Grace. There is much to come before we can go to Richmond."

Amarantha took a last swig of the weak wine concoction before standing up. "I am ready," she said, brushing herself off. "As long as I am with you, I can face anything."

His smile faded and he cupped her chin gently and kissed her. "As can I," he said softly. "I am sorry for the hastiness of our marriage and the dirty floor upon which we spent our wedding night, but I am not sorry I married you. I would do it again, a thousand times over, the very same way as long as it was with you."

She put her hand to his cheek, watching him kiss her palm. "Shall we get on with it, then?"

"We shall."

Taking her hand, he grasped his satchel and headed out of the tiny chamber. The sun was just starting to lighten the eastern sky, a glow of pink and yellow upon the blue expanse of night. They moved swiftly and quietly across the compound, back to where Morgan had tethered his horse. But when they reached the spot, the animal was missing.

Curious, they began to wander around until they found a small kitchen yard attached to a small stable. Morgan poked his head inside to see his horse in one of the stalls, munching on some dried grass that had been spread around him. He was still saddled, but the bridle had been removed and hung on a nearby peg. Releasing Amarantha's hand, Morgan collected the bridle and had just put it on the horse's head when a deep voice filled the stale, dark air.

"I was wondering when you would make an appearance,"

came a decidedly Irish voice. "And I see you found the lady."

Amarantha gasped and turned towards the source as Morgan came out of the stall. A figure covered in a dark horse blanket was sitting in the dark, against the opposite wall, and as the blanket came off, Morgan breathed a sigh of relief.

"Damnation, Bric," he said. "You nearly scared the piss right out of me."

Bric stood up, brushing off the chaff. "Good," he said. "I meant to."

"How in the hell did you find us?"

"Simple," Bric said. "When the priests denied ever seeing you, I came straight to the stables to see if your horse was here and it was. So, I waited for you, but I have been waiting all night. Do you want to tell me what is going on?"

Morgan could see that Bric was looking right at Amarantha, who was looking at the enormous Irishman in fear. He suspected why.

"My lady," he said, reaching out to take her hand and pull her against him. "This is not an Irish mercenary, I assure you. Well, not much, anyway. This is Bric MacRohan, who serves The Marshal. A finer man you will never find but if you tell him I said so, I will deny it."

That brought Amarantha some relief as Bric dipped his head in her direction. "Lady Amarantha," he greeted. "The tales of your beauty were not exaggerated. In fact, they did not do you justice."

"It's Lady de Wolfe now," Morgan said quietly. "I married her yesterday."

Those softly uttered words told Bric everything he needed to know. "Ah," he said in realization. "That's why you spent the night here."

"Aye."

Bric's gaze lingered on Amarantha. "I must say that I am not surprised," he said. "When I deduced that you must have taken her to Tintern, I suspected there was more than one reason behind it. You have my congratulations, Morgan. I hope you will be very happy."

Morgan smiled weakly. "I already am," he said. "At least, given the circumstances, but those will change. We are heading back to Mount Grace."

Bric tore his gaze from Amarantha to focus on Morgan. "That is why I came to find you," he said. "The Irish are heading there, also, so you must avoid them on the road. They have not gone through St. Arvans because they tore the village asunder looking for the lady and the villagers are up in arms over it, so they sought to avoid a confrontation by taking the road further east."

Morgan nodded in understanding. "That was to be expected," he said. "So they hunted for her, did they? What do they think happened?"

"They thought her escort abducted her," Bric said. "They hunted for her but, surprisingly, they did not take the road to Tintern Abbey. When I realized that must have been where you'd gone because it made the most sense to me, I told them I would continue the hunt for the lady and meet them at Mount Grace."

"So they accepted you?"

"Mostly," he said. "I told the leader, O'Magnan, that I was a hired sword looking for work and he gave me permission to participate in the siege at Mount Grace. But everything you suspected was true, Morgan. Patience did bring the lady to the Irish so they could use her as leverage."

Morgan looked at Amarantha, who nodded to confirm what they already knew. "I did not tell you that she is dead," she said to them both, but mostly Morgan. "When she first brought me to the mercenaries, they did not believe she was Lady le Marche. I used that confusion to my advantage until they turned on her. She tried to run away from them but ended up falling into the river. She drowned."

Morgan hadn't know that about Patience. He hadn't even asked. He'd been so concerned with spiriting Amarantha away from the mercenaries that he hadn't really cared, but now he knew.

Good riddance, as far as he was concerned.

"It was unfortunate she chose to follow that path," he said simply. "But you are safe and that is all that matters. Now, we must return to Mount Grace and do it quickly. I may be a new husband, but I have a mission to fulfill that was entrusted to me long before I knew you. I gave my word to see it through and that is what I must do."

Amarantha forced a smile. "If I have learned one thing about you, it is that you are a man of honor," she said. "Wherever you go and whatever you do, I shall be by your side."

He smiled at her, a smile infused with both regret for what they were facing and delight for what the future would bring them. Giving her a squeeze, he turned to Bric.

"We had better depart quickly if the mercenaries are already heading north," he said, releasing Amarantha. "When did they leave?"

Bric went over to a darkened stall to pull his horse out into the light. "They were preparing to leave yesterday when I came looking for you," he said. "I suspect they did leave at the appointed time but stopped for the night. The moon was a sliver last night and it would have been difficult to travel that way. But I suspect they are already on the move again as we speak, so we should hurry."

Morgan was fastening his satchel to his saddle. "We will have the advantage, I think," he said. "We are already far enough north that we can make it to Mount Grace before they do if we move swiftly. I would prefer they not see Amarantha at all, so I will leave her off with Father Nicodemus before we proceed to the castle."

Bric couldn't disagree. In a hurry, they finished with the horses and headed out into the cold, dewy dawn.

CHAPTER TWENTY-ONE

E KNEW THAT Hollis was in here, somewhere.

Kenan was traversing the halls of a keep he'd traversed many, many times and for many, many reasons, but never a reason so important as the one he had now.

He had come to end five years of tyranny.

The keep was virtually empty and his movements were slow and deliberate. He searched every chamber he came across carefully, closing each door behind him, before moving to the next one. Since Mount Grace's keep was so large, he had a dozen rooms to search before he even made it to the living quarters above. All the while, he kept calling Hollis' name but, so far, there had been no reply.

It was a keep full of ghosts.

Given what was happening outside, it was strange that the place was so still. The servants seemed to have vanished. As Kenan moved up the stone stairway to the upper floors, he could hear sniffling and weeping. Following the sounds, he ended up in Amarantha's bed chamber with Everelda in a frightened ball on the bed. When she caught sight of Kenan, her tears came in earnest.

"Am I going to die?" she cried. "Please don't let them kill me, Kenan. I don't want to die."

Kenan came into the chamber, dressed to the teeth in armor and weapons. As he did so, Everelda's raven and Amarantha's pet cat came out from underneath the bed and jumped onto the mattress beside Everelda.

"No one is going to kill you, my lady," he said. "Stay in this chamber and you will be safe."

Everelda pulled the animals to her. "Do you promise?"

"I promise," he said. "Do not come out until I tell you to and you will be safe."

Everelda furiously wiped at her cheeks. "Is Amarantha here?" she asked. "Did they find her?"

Kenan shook his head. "They did not find her," he said. "Please do not worry over her right now. She will be found and I am sure she will be unharmed. But for now – remember what I told you. Do not leave this chamber under any circumstances. Do you understand?"

Everelda nodded, wiping at the tears that wouldn't stop flowing. Kenan turned back for the door.

"Do you know where Lord Hollis is?" he asked.

Everelda shook her head. "Nay," she said. "But I saw him going up the stairs to his chamber some time ago."

"He's not come down?"

"I do not know."

That was what Kenan wanted to know. As he reached the door, he paused and looked at her.

"Lock this door when I am gone," he said.

Everelda jumped up and ran to the door as he passed through it. When he heard her throw the bolt, he continued on up the stairs to the top floor where Hollis' chamber was located.

"Lord Hollis?" he called. "It is Kenan. Are you up here?"

He was immediately met by a muffled voice. About the time he reached the top of the stairs, the big, double doors that signified the master's chambers wrenched open and Hollis appeared with a sword in his hand. He was dressed how he usually dressed – a fine tunic and fine leather breeches – but he wore no armor. He owned some, and it was very fine, but he hadn't worn it in years. It probably didn't even fit anymore.

His sword glittered in the weak light.

"Thank God," Hollis said as he spied Kenan. "What is the situation? Who has attacked us? Tell me!"

Kenan came to a halt about ten feet away. "The miners, led by men formerly of the le Marche army and a few knights from William Marshal, have taken the castle," he said steadily. "They are asking that you leave in peace, my lord. I have come to escort you out. They promise you safe passage if you will leave willingly."

Hollis went from frightened and frantic to confused and disgusted. "Leave willingly?" he repeated, aghast. "Who has made these demands?"

"William Marshal," Kenan said evenly. "Gather what you can carry and let me escort you out."

Hollis' jaw dropped. "What do you mean you will escort me out?" he said with outrage. "I am not leaving. This is *my* castle."

Kenan's dark eyes glittered. "This is not your castle," he said, showing emotion for the first time. "This castle belongs to the House of le Marche and was brutally taken by deception by King John. William Marshal is restoring it to its rightful owner and you must leave. Will you gather your things?"

Hollis stared at the man for a few long and muddled moments. He was clearly trying to determine Kenan's loyalties although it seemed ridiculous to think the man was siding against him.

His brow furrowed.

"Kenan?" he said, more quietly. "What is the meaning of this? Why are you asking me to leave when you should be defending me to the death?"

Kenan faced him. "I am asking you to leave because you do not belong here," he said. "This castle belonged to Oliver le Marche, who was murdered when King John betrayed his trust and stole his castle. Oliver le Marche was a kind and generous man, and when I was a child, I fostered here. You did not know that, did you? Mount Grace was my home for a few years and Oliver was my mentor. I realize you did not kill him personally, but when the king stole his castle and installed you as the garrison commander, I could not stomach the sight of you in Oliver's place. For the past five years, it has taken every ounce of strength not to vomit when I saw you at the head of Oliver's table or sleeping in Oliver's bed. He was a good man who did not deserve what the king did to him and, now, justice is being served. Now – I will ask you one last time. Will you gather your things and leave peacefully?"

Hollis could hardly believe what he was hearing. To think that Kenan wasn't faithful to him, and evidently hadn't been all these years, put his world into a spin. Fear and rage bloomed hand in hand within his chest as he faced off against a knight who was far more skilled than he was.

Rage won out.

"Nay," he growled. "I will not leave and you cannot make me. If you try, I will kill you."

Kenan raised his sword. "Not if I kill you first."

Stricken with uncontrollable fury, Hollis charged Kenan. On any normal day or any normal circumstance, he would never have done such a thing but, at this moment, nothing was normal. Everything was muddled and uncertain. He ran towards Kenan with his sword leveled, certain above all else that Kenan wouldn't fight back. Defend himself, yes, but not fight back.

He was wrong.

Kenan had enough time to drop to one knee as Hollis drew close and lifted his sword, slicing into Hollis' chest and belly. Hollis screamed and brought his sword down on the top of Kenan's left shoulder, cutting through mail and leather and wool and flesh, cutting the man as he fell away, mortally wounded.

For Kenan, however, it wasn't a mortal wound, but a wound that began to bleed profusely. Hand over the wound to unsuccessfully staunch the blood flow, he stood up and loomed over Hollis as the man bled out all over the floor of the stair landing. For a moment, Kenan simply stared at him, watching the blood pool and feeling a sense of satisfaction he hadn't expected.

An ending to the Mount Grace nightmare.

"That was for Oliver," he murmured.

Hollis' sightless eyes were staring back at him.

ᙯ

"SEE THE SMOKE?" Bric muttered.

Morgan did. He could see the smoke in the distance, black and heavy, rising up above the tree line. They'd seen it for miles but now that they drew closer to the castle, they suspected that it was, indeed, coming from Mount Grace.

Morgan growled, low in his throat.

"Something has started," he said. "The Irish haven't even arrived… have they?"

Bric had no idea. "Unless they had wings and flew to Mount Grace yesterday, I would say that they have not," he said. "Damnation. They must have opened the gates early and the miners took advantage of it."

"It *was* the signal," Morgan said with regret.

"It was. And they evidently answered it."

That caused both men to dig their heels into the sides of their horses, encouraging the animals to move faster. Morgan's horse was carrying more weight with Amarantha as well as Morgan, so Bric was able to move faster. He tore down the road with Morgan trying to keep up, down the dirt road that was in relatively good condition. Morgan and Amarantha grew further and further back as Bric passed the church and came to the end of the town where the castle could be clearly seen.

It was in flames.

Bric didn't have his armor. That was at The Three Cocks, behind two locked doors and a locked closet, and he didn't have time to go and get it. He had his broadsword and that was about all he had, so he unsheathed his sword and headed up the road to the castle, charging in through the smoking, destroyed gates and into the outer bailey.

It was chaos.

"Bric!"

Someone was shouting his name and he turned to see Alexander, trying to catch his attention. Bric spun his horse around in Alexander's direction.

"What happened?" he roared. "Where are the Irish?"

Alexander had some gore on him, but not nearly what was

usual with him. In battle, he was always on the front line, always fighting fiercely, and was usually bathed in the blood of his enemies from head to toe. That was a typical look for him. But at this moment, he looked relatively tame as he tried to control his excitable horse.

"The ore shipment was early," he said, confirming what Bric and Morgan had suspected. "The miners were ready, the gates opened, and Addax made the decision to move without the mercenaries."

Bric looked around at the outer bailey in shambles. "Was it the right decision?"

Alexander was looking around, too. "It was," he said. "And I shall defend it to The Marshal. God only knows when we would have another opportunity like this one – gates open, miners at the ready, and the Mount Grace army off guard. It was the right thing to do. Where are the mercenaries?"

Bric threw a thumb in a southerly direction. "Coming," he said. "They departed yesterday, so they should be here sometime today, I would imagine."

"Good," Alexander said. "They can help us clean up this mess."

Hearing that statement brought Bric back to the conversation he'd had with Ryan the day before and a warning bell went off in his head.

"Wait," he said, holding up a finger to beg for patience as he remembered what he'd been told. "There is something you must know. We found the Irish mercenaries south of St. Arvans and we also found Lady Amarantha. She was unharmed, but more on her later. The mercenary leader, a man named O'Magnan, knows that Gere le Marche is dead. Patience is also dead, so I was told, so the leader is well aware that there is no living le Marche to claim the castle. He told me that he would like to claim the castle, and her riches, for himself, so that is why they are heading here. Not to help le Marche or The Marshal, but to claim it."

Alexander frowned. "God's Bones," he grunted. "Now we have to worry about them?"

"Indeed," Bric said. "How far out is de Velt?"

Alexander lifted his shoulders in a frustrated gesture. "Who is to say?" he said. "I sent the man word yesterday. He has only just received it and he still has to muster his army, so he will not be here in time to stave off the mercenaries."

Bric's jaw ticked faintly. "If they get in here, they will kill the miners and take the castle," he said. "I've looked that group over, Sherry. They are killers."

Instinctively, they both looked to the gatehouses. There were two. The gates at the main gatehouse had been burned and were still smoldering, but there was still the big, iron frame that had twisted but hadn't collapsed. The inner gatehouse had the portcullis that had been pulled off the tracks. The miners had been thorough in disabling the protection for the castle but in doing so, they may have sealed their own fates.

"Well?" Bric said. "What do you want to do?"

Alexander sighed sharply, turning his attention to the main gates and the iron frames with the wood burned out of them.

"We cannot let them in," he said. "If they get into the outer bailey, they can make their way to the inner bailey and the keep after that, so we must stop them at the threshold. Find Addax and Essien. Tell them the situation. Gather what miners you can find and get them to the main gates. We must prevent an Irish invasion."

Bric didn't hesitate.

He began to move.

⁊

"THE CASTLE IS under attack," Amarantha said fearfully. "Do you think they'll attack the town, too?"

Morgan had just pulled his frothing steed to a halt outside of St. Mary the Virgin. Grasping his wife by the hand, he rushed towards the entry.

"Nay," he said evenly. "I told you that the miners are revolting, so they have no reason to attack the village. When the Irish arrive, they'll be focused on the castle."

Reaching the doors, he gave a good shove and was shocked to find that they were locked. Father Nicodemus never locked the doors. Morgan began pounding on the door and Amarantha, realizing that it wasn't a good thing for them to be caught out in the open, began calling Father Nicodemus' name. She even ran around the side of the church, back where the walled cloisters were, and called his name several times. Morgan, who had been pounding on the front door, went around to find her and pulled her back with him.

He didn't want her out of his sight.

But their noise had caused a response. As soon as they returned to the main doors, one of the panels lurched open and Father Nicodemus appeared. His eyes were wide on Amarantha.

"My lady!" he gasped. "Praise God that you have returned safely. Come in, come in!"

He was motioning furiously. Morgan and Amarantha slipped into the dark sanctuary as Father Nicodemus slammed the door and threw the big bolt, locking them in. Then he turned to Amarantha but, for lack of words, simply went to her and hugged her.

She squeezed him tightly.

"Thank God," he said, verging on tears. "Are you well, my lady? I pray you were not hurt."

Amarantha smiled at the emotional priest. "I'm completely well," she said, releasing him and spinning in a circle so he could see her from all angles. "See? I am not hurt in the least."

Father Nicodemus was clearly relieved. "What happened?" he said. "Was it Patience?"

She nodded, her smile fading. "She took me to the Irish mercenaries and told them to use me as leverage against my father."

Father Nicodemus looked at Morgan. "Then you were correct all along," he said. "You knew it was Patience."

Morgan nodded faintly. "I was hoping I was wrong, but I am glad I was right," he said. "I would not have found the lady otherwise."

"True," Father Nicodemus said. "It is unfortunate that Lady le Marche could not wait for the plan to be executed."

Amarantha shrugged. "I suppose she was simply tired of waiting," she said. "She is dead, by the way. The mercenaries turned on her and she ran right into the river."

Father Nicodemus closed his eyes and muttered a quick prayer. "God rest the soul of a tragic lady," he said quietly. "But she is with her husband and sons now. She was not happy without them. I suppose if there is some mercy in this world, that is an example. For her, death was a good thing."

"Speaking of husbands," Morgan said, interrupting the reunion. "I am now the husband of Lady Amarantha. We were married at Tintern Abbey yesterday, so I have come to place my wife in your hands. I must go to the castle, but I want Amarantha to stay here where it is safe."

Father Nicodemus was beaming with joy. "God is indeed brilliant in his wisdom," he said. "You came to Mount Grace for a reason, my son, and it wasn't simply to help liberate the fortress. It was to find your destiny. Amarantha *is* that destiny."

Morgan grinned. "She is," he said, looking at her. "And I shall strive, every day, to be worthy of her."

"You already are."

Morgan was feeling humbled and the least bit embarrassed, but he couldn't linger over congratulations and kind words. He went to Amarantha and took her in his arms, kissing her sweetly right in front of the priest.

"I must go," he murmured before kissing her again. "I swear I will return as soon as I can."

Amarantha held him tightly, gazing up into those hazel eyes. "I will wait for you."

He kissed her once more before releasing her and heading towards the door. "No one is to leave this church, Father," he said to the priest. "Especially not Amarantha and you are not to admit anyone. The same Irish mercenaries who held her captive are heading for Mount Grace at this very moment, so she must be kept out of sight and safe. Is that clear?"

Father Nicodemus nodded, following him to the door. "She will be safe here, I promise," he said. "But Morgan… take care of yourself. I do not want to have to comfort your widow."

Morgan lifted the bolt, but before he stepped outside, he fixed the priest in the eyes.

"You won't."

Father Nicodemus believed him.

CHAPTER TWENTY-TWO

WHEN BRIC SAW Morgan approach, a cry went up.

Bric, Alexander, Addax, and Essien were at the front gates, trying to mend them enough so that they could stand some measure of onslaught from the mercenaries when Bric caught sight of Morgan coming up the road. He whistled loudly enough to rupture eardrums as men began looking around to see what had the knights so excited.

Astride the old warhorse who had seen better days, Morgan made it up to the gate before he was greeted by his comrades. He could see that everyone was working furiously on the gate, trying to untwist it and straighten it as much as possible. He was able to get inside the bailey as a hundred men worked on those gates, leaving his horse off where the others were gathered over in one corner of the ward that hadn't been damaged in the fighting.

"The miners did this damage?" he asked, looking at the impressive array of destruction. "We were wrong when we thought they could not handle the Mount Grace armies themselves. It seems as if they did quite well on their own."

"Addax led them," Bric said as Alexander, Addax, and Essien joined them. "But also, the remnants of Oliver le Marche's army showed excellent leadership."

"Those men have been schooling the other miners for years," Addax said. "I saw it as I worked with them. They trained when they were supposed to be on duty and learned what they could about tactics and fighting. I knew they had worked hard for it but I wasn't sure they could achieve victory without the support of the mercenaries, but I was wrong. They did this."

He held out his hand, indicating the ruined outer bailey. There were bodies of Mount Grace soldiers everywhere, being dragged into a pile by some of the miners.

"This is the best possible outcome," Morgan said. He looked at his friend. "You did well, Addax. And so did your miners."

Addax nodded in thanks, watching a group of miners struggle with the remains of the front gate. "But now we must deal with the mercenaries," he said, a hint of trepidation in his tone. "Bric told Sherry that they want Mount Grace for their own."

Morgan nodded. "So I have heard," he said. "Have they been sighted yet?"

"I have men at the edge of town and further on down the road that leads south," Alexander said. "They will notify us when they see them approach."

"They cannot be too far away," Bric muttered, scratching his head. "If they departed their encampment south of St. Arvans yesterday when they said they were going to, that would put them at any one of the small villages between St. Arvans and Raglan. If they spent a few hours encamped close to Raglan, which is an assumption, and started early this morning, they should be upon us within the next hour or so. That's just a guess, but I think it's fairly accurate."

"What we need are archers," Morgan said. "That gate will not hold long and we can put a hundred men there to hold the line but, eventually, the line will weaken. If we had archers aiming at the mercenaries, it would make them think twice before trying to breach the gatehouse."

Alexander nodded. "I have thought of that," he said. "There is an armory with bows and bolts, but they are in disrepair. I have men in the armory right now trying to repair what they can and get up to the walls. Truth be told, it looks as if de la Haye simply sat on his laurels and did very little for the readiness of his castle, which is quite surprising considering all he had to protect."

"Readiness was Kenan's job," Morgan said. "He is the one who should have kept everything in fighting order."

"Given that the man was secretly loyal to Oliver le Marche, it makes sense that he wouldn't keep anything in a state of readiness," Alexander said. "He wanted de la Haye to fall."

"Where is he?"

Alexander turned to the keep. "I sent him to the keep some time ago," he said. "He was supposed to find Hollis and force the man to surrender."

"He has not come out yet?"

"Nay."

"And you have not checked on him?"

Alexander shook his head. "He may be in the course of delicate negotiations with Hollis and I do not want to disturb that," he said. "He will show himself when he is ready. It seems to me that Kenan de Poyer has a stake in this almost as much as Gere or Patience did."

That was more than likely true. Morgan lifted his hand to shield his eyes from the glare of the sun as he studied the keep one last time. Nothing seemed to be happening so he turned away.

"I hope that Hollis listens to reason," he said. "I promised Amarantha that I would not kill the man. I intend to keep that promise."

Alexander looked at him. "That may be difficult to keep if he is combative, Morgan," he said. "I realize the man is her father, but…"

"He is my *wife's* father."

Alexander's eyes widened. "He's *what*?" he gasped. "You married the lady?"

"I did."

"When?"

"Yesterday, after I rescued her from the mercenaries," Morgan said evenly. "I took her to Tintern Abbey and married her."

Alexander was genuinely trying not to appear too shocked, but he looked right at Bric. "Did you know this?"

Bric cleared his throat softly and averted his gaze. "I did."

"And you did not tell me?"

"It is not my secret to tell, Sherry."

Alexander clapped a hand to his forehead in disbelief and turned away as Addax and Essien grinned at Morgan, silent gestures of congratulations. But those grins vanished when Alexander turned back around.

"Now we must deal with the fact that Hollis de la Haye is your *wife's* father," he said. Then he jabbed a finger at Morgan. "You told me that you had feelings for her but you were not sure what they were. You went from not knowing what you were feeling to marriage fairly quickly."

Morgan shrugged. "It was the right thing to do," he said. "You have a wife you love, Sherry. Surely you understand that a man must do as he must when it comes to a woman. I cannot explain it more than that."

Alexander's disbelief held out for a few seconds longer before he sighed heavily and shook his head.

"I understand more than most," he said. "And I, too, fell in love with my wife during a mission. I *do* understand. But The Marshal is going to think we're all mad because no sooner does he send us on a mission than we fall in love with women. It's a sickness."

Morgan began to laugh, as did Bric and Addax and Essien. Soon, they were all laughing when Essien suddenly caught sight of something at the keep. He stopped laughing and pointed.

"Look," he said. "The top of the keep."

Everyone turned to see that someone was taking down the royal standards that were flapping in the brisk breeze. As they watched, all four of them came down. Morgan looked at Alexander curiously. Alexander shrugged his shoulders because he had no real answers to give.

But then, another standard went up.

A single standard, smaller, of gray and yellow chevron stripes, was now waving in the breeze.

"Whose standard is that?" Morgan asked, puzzled.

"Le Marche," Addax said quietly. When everyone turned to look at him, he smiled weakly. "I've seen that standard. Some of the old le Marche soldiers in the mines still have their tunics."

It was most appropriate, even if it would be removed in favor of Pembroke standards at some point. But for now... now, the le Marche standards were flying again in honor of Oliver and Gere and all of the other le Marches who had once lived at Mount Grace. It was a rather poignant moment.

Alexander's dark eyes glittered as he watched.

"I suspect that means Hollis is no longer with us," he said quietly. "I am sure he would not have allowed Kenan to fly the le Marche standard if he was still alive."

"He would not," Morgan said, realizing he would have to tell his wife that her father had died in battle. "I am sure that Kenan has been waiting a long time for this moment. Mayhap we can keep it up for…"

He was cut off by yelling from the front gate. As the knights headed in that direction, a man broke through the line of men that were repairing the front gate, running frantically towards Alexander.

"My lord!" he shouted. "A small army approaches from the south!"

It was the news they'd been waiting for. "How far out are they?" Alexander asked.

"Less than an hour, my lord."

Alexander dismissed the man with a sharp nod of his head, turning to the group around him. Morgan, Bric, Addax and Essien were some of the best warriors he'd ever seen, men worth their weight in gold in a fight. Bric alone was worth three good knights in a battle and Morgan was worth more. He was a de Wolfe.

They were always worth more.

He looked straight at Morgan.

"Castle defenses will remain under my command," he said. "I want you at the gate with me. Bric, you will go to the keep and tell Kenan to remain inside and hold it. Then you will return to me, for I have a plan when the Irish arrive and I will need your help. Addax, rally your miners to the gate but leave enough to guard what Mount Grace prisoners remain. Essien, you are with the archers. Get them to the wall immediately and make sure they have at least ten bolts each. *Move.*"

Everyone separated. Morgan and Alexander were already heading to the gate, shouting to the men to hurry with what they were doing, and the repair of the twisted main gate continued in earnest. Word had spread throughout the miners that the mercenaries they'd been expecting had turned against them. That's all anyone knew.

Now, it was going to be the miners against the professional soldiers.

The ownership of Mount Grace Castle would soon be decided.

☙

"'TIS A GRAND castle," Ryan said as his army headed up the road to the smoldering castle on the rise. "I would like to spend my later years here, looking out over my empire and watching my grandchildren play at my feet. Aye, it suits me."

The men around him were grinning. All Ryan had been able to talk about on the entire ride north was Mount Grace Castle and how he was going to expand the mining operation by bringing over Irish workers. They would mine the silver twice as fast and make him twice as rich. For a man whose father and father's father had been professional soldiers, he was speaking of an entirely different life, which was pointed out to him. But, as he pointed out, neither his father nor his father's father had ever had such an opportunity.

The opportunity to own a rich Welsh castle.

They'd seen the smoke coming from the castle as they had approached from the south. That dark, heavy smoke could be seen for miles. As they drew closer, a certain stench began to hit them and they knew what it was. They'd smelled burning flesh before. By the time they reached the bottom of the road that led up to the gatehouse, they could see that the gates had been burned out and nothing but the iron frames remained. They could also see hundreds of men gathered at the open gates, waiting.

Waiting for the arrival of an ally.

They were in for a surprise.

Ryan had his men put their weapons away, at least for the moment. His plan was simple – to gain access to Mount Grace and then subdue anyone who resisted his attempt to take it. But he had to get into the fortress first. That was key.

But it looked like a committee was already waiting for them.

And they were armed.

Ryan put up a hand to his men, slowing their approach as he tried to figure out what was happening. He didn't see any fighting, only men with weapons forming a line in front of and behind the wreck of the main gate. They were all facing the incoming army and Ryan was seriously wondering why he was being met with an armed group until he spied a man he'd sent out to look for Lady Amarantha yesterday.

Bric MacRohan was at the gate.

The situation just got more puzzling.

With a heavy sigh, he called a halt to his army about half-way up the road and told his men to wait. They settled back as Ryan continued forward, followed by a couple of his senior men. At a leisurely pace that indicated he wasn't concerned of the resistance he was already meeting, he came to within a dozen feet of the men lining the gate entry.

His focus was on MacRohan.

"So you made it here before me," he said. "It looks as if the battle has already happened."

"It has," Bric said. Since he was the one who had made contact with Ryan and had established a rapport with him, Alexander decided that Bric should be the one to tell the mercenaries that they weren't welcome. "The miners were able to subdue the Mount Grace army without your assistance."

Ryan nodded, looking at the heavily armed miners behind Bric. "I see," he said. "Well, invite us inside and let us rest for the night. We'll feast and celebrate the victory."

Bric shook his head. "There will be no invitation to enter," he said. "You see, when I came to you yesterday, it was with a purpose. You suspected someone had sent me and even though I denied it, you should have gone with your instincts. Someone indeed sent me."

Ryan's brow furrowed. "Who would take the trouble?"

"William Marshal."

That caused Ryan's eyebrows to fly up in surprise. "The Marshal?" he repeated. "Pembroke?"

Bric nodded. "I serve the man on occasion and this was one of them," he said. "I came to locate a prisoner you had in your possession, a Lady Amarantha, but I also came to discover your plans. And you generously told me what they were."

Now, Ryan's suspicions on an armed line of men in front of the gatehouse was coming to make some sense. He grinned as realization dawned, looking at all of the armed men.

"Now I understand," he said. "They know I want Mount Grace for myself."

"They do."

"And they think to stop me?"

"They will."

Ryan laughed. "This is a group of untrained men, MacRohan, if that is even your name," he said sarcastically. "They cannot hold out against my skilled army. Fighting other men's wars is all we do. We will prevail in the end."

Bric turned to Alexander, who was standing a few feet away, and pointed to him. "O'Magnan, I will introduce you to Sir Alexander de Sherrington," he said. "He married a daughter of Christopher de Lohr. If you do not know that name, then you are more ignorant than I imagined. He is the Earl of Hereford and Worcester and he has an army of thousands. He can summon more men than you have ever seen in your lifetime. Sherry has something to say to you."

Alexander stepped forward, a very big man with black hair, black eyes, and an ominous presence. "O'Magnan," he said without a hint of respect. "I serve William Marshal directly. I know the situation at Mount Grace and I know why you are here. I know that Gere le Marche paid you handsomely to regain his castle for him, so this is a job you have already been paid for. To want more is to display incredible greed. Should you choose to move forward with your plans for Mount Grace, know the consequences of those actions."

Ryan eyed the big knight, grinning as if he hadn't a care in the world. "If you think to scare me with tales of angry Welsh, save your breath," he said. "I will be quite comfortable here at Mount Grace, so do not have a care for my situation. It does not concern you."

It was Alexander's turn to grin. "It is not the Welsh you have to worry over," he said. "It is not even William Marshal that you must worry over. Nay, O'Magnan. It's something much, much worse."

Ryan shook his head impatiently. "I'm not a child to be

frightened, so do not try," he said. "I will ask you one question, just once, and my actions will be dictated by your response."

"Go ahead."

"Will you vacate Mount Grace peacefully?"

"Nay."

Ryan lifted his shoulders. "Then this will not go well for you."

"Nor you," Alexander said. Then he lifted a finger as if to point skyward. "I would look at the walls if I were you."

Ryan did. At that moment, dozens of archers appeared, each one of them fully armed. The arrows were pointed right at Ryan, who lost some of his smile at the sight.

But not all of it.

"So you have archers," he said. "I do, as well."

"I'm sure you do," Alexander said. "But allow me to tell you how this will go if you succeed in your plans. Let us assume, for argument's sake, that your ragtag band of motherless malcontents is able to wrest Mount Grace away from us. We may look weak, but I assure you, we are not. But let us say that you take Mount Grace. It will not last, for we are expecting one of the fiercest armies in all of England, Scotland, and Wales to reinforce our ranks within the next couple of days. You may survive the battle with the miners and even with me, but you will not survive a battle with Ajax de Velt."

"Ajax de –?"

"The Dark Lord of Pelinom Castle."

Ryan was trying very hard to maintain his smile and his confident attitude, but the mere mention of Ajax de Velt wiped the smile cleanly from his face. He no longer had any reason to smile because he knew that name. English, Irish, Welsh, it didn't matter. All fighting men did. Ajax de Velt was more legend than man, a knight who took the art of warfare to a horribly brutal level that not even the most barbaric of men would cross. He'd come to Ireland a couple of times to assist William Marshal on his lands, and near Drogheda and up towards Belfast. Men whispered his name with the greatest of fear.

And that realization was enough to strike terror into his heart.

An fear a bhuaileann saighdiúirí, they would call de Velt.

The man who guts soldiers.

"You are trying to deceive me," he said after a moment. "Ajax de Velt is up near Scotland, so I've been told."

Alexander smiled thinly. "Once again, you show how ignorant you are," he said. "Jax de Velt has six castles on the Welsh Marches, the closest one being a two-day ride from here. He has already been notified that Mount Grace is in trouble and is mustering his army as we speak. Shall I tell you what will happen when he arrives and finds you within the walls of Mount Grace?"

Ryan had lost all of his humor. "You're lying," he growled. "Jax de Velt is nowhere near this place."

"Are you willing to take that chance?" Alexander asked. "His army is already on its way here. If you leave now, you may avoid him, but if you remain, he will more than likely trap you and take your men to sport. He'll ram poles up their arses so that they come out through their chests and post them along the road for all to see. He has no great love for the Irish so his tactics with you may be particularly brutal."

Ryan was quickly becoming agitated as well as scared and the fact that he was scared at all over a mere threat infuriated him. He was too proud to let an English knight bully him into submission, so without another word, he reined his horse around and headed back down the road where his men were waiting.

Bric and Morgan came to stand with Alexander.

"Well?" Morgan said. "What will he do?"

Alexander watched Ryan as he gestured wildly to his men. "I think he'll attack," he said. "You'd better let the men know. And get word to Essien to unleash the archers when the mercenaries draw close enough."

Bric headed off, but Morgan remained with Alexander, watching the mercenary and his army halfway down the road.

"Where do you want me, Sherry?" Morgan asked.

Alexander kept his gaze fixed on the mercenaries. "With me," he said. "Right here at the gate. This was your mission, after all. To wrest Mount Grace from the king. Now, you're going to have to keep it from that greedy Irish bastard. If he wants it, he's going to have to come through us to get it."

Morgan echoed his sentiments exactly, but he had what he thought might be a better idea. "They will never see such mortal fury if they try," he murmured. "But why wait for them to come to us? They are regrouping now. Why not charge them before they organize completely?"

Alexander looked at him, stricken by the suggestion. "Excellent idea," he said. "You're not just another pretty face."

Morgan grinned as he followed Alexander back to the gate where Alexander instructed the hundreds of miners to charge the mercenaries. He left about fifty men at the gate, plus the archers, and in very little time, the weary but victorious miners were charging down the road, straight at the mercenaries, who hadn't expected the offensive.

Morgan and Alexander were leading the charge.

Ryan was caught off guard by the rush of miners into his ranks. They were armed with crude but very sharp weapons and the blood immediately began to flow. Morgan went after Ryan in the definition of mortal fury, the man who had captured Amarantha.

This time, it was personal.

Ryan was mounted and, caught unexpectedly, was yanked off his horse by Morgan when the man grabbed his leg and pulled. He didn't have time to grasp his sword as he went over and Morgan came down on him with a weapon in his hand.

Ryan kicked him in the belly.

Morgan stumbled back as Ryan rolled to his knees, but Morgan was back on him again, not giving him a chance to get to his feet. The enormous broadsword with the wolf's head on the hilt, something all de Wolfe knights had, sliced into Ryan's torso. It cut him from his right side about midway into his gut. If Morgan had kept going, it would have sliced the man into two. Mortally wounded, Ryan collapsed to the dirt of the road.

Just like that, the mercenary king went down.

There was so much fighting going on around them that Morgan used his big boot to kick Ryan down the slope. Both sides of the road leading to Mount Grace dropped off sharply, and Morgan shoved Ryan halfway down the hill. He pursued him, preparing to deliver the final blow.

But he wanted Ryan to know why.

By the time he reached the man, he could see that Ryan was not long for this world. The man was lying on his back, breathing erratically and gazing up at the sky.

Morgan loomed over him.

"I suppose you knew your end would come in battle," he said steadily. "You fight other men's wars. It was inevitable. But

I wanted you to know why I did not spare your life."

Ryan looked at him, panting heavily and in a good deal of pain. "Go away, *Sassenach*," he muttered. "Let me die in peace."

Morgan didn't move. "You held my wife prisoner," he said. "Any man who would touch her will suffer at my hands. If she had been your wife, I am sure your position would have been the same. For Amarantha, you have earned this death, but because she said you were kind to her, I will make it merciful."

Ryan's brow flickered with realization. "Amarantha?" he said. "You… you have seen her?"

"I am the one who took her from your camp."

"And Tad? Her guard?"

"Dead. As you will soon be." Morgan bent over him. "But I wanted you to know why you've met your end."

Ryan realized that he had lost in this gamble. He'd lost everything and the understanding was more than he could bear. He'd never lost anything in his life. But he had now, in a dirty little Welsh town to a raggedy bunch of miners. For a man of his skill and prestige, at least in his own mind, it was an ignoble ending.

Defeated by a mob.

Closing his eyes, a lone tear trickled from his right eye, down his temple.

"Will you do something for me, *Sassenach?*" he asked hoarsely.

"What is that?"

"I have children," he said haltingly. "Two daughters. I want them to know that their dada died honorably. Will you at least put a dirk in my hand so that when my men come to find me, I will have died with a weapon?"

Morgan understood. In his last moments, Ryan was asking

for his dignity. He couldn't bring himself to feel sorry for the man, but he understood. As the battle up on the road waged, he removed one of his own daggers at his belt and put it in Ryan's right hand.

"There," he said, eyeing the man who was fading quickly. "Do you want me to hasten your death? I am not without mercy."

Ryan didn't say anything for a moment. Suddenly, his right arm came up with surprising speed and plunged the dagger Morgan had given him straight into his own chest, into his heart.

He was dead in an instant.

And that was the end of Ryan O'Magnan.

A bit stunned, Morgan stood over the man for a moment, understanding why he'd taken his own life. Ryan was a man who made his own life and determined his own destiny. In that realization, Morgan found it within himself to have a shred of respect for the man.

At least he lived and died by his own rules.

Removing the dagger from the man's chest, Morgan trudged back up towards the road, noting that some of the mercenaries had seen their leader laying down the slope. As Morgan approached the road, he shouted to Bric, who was in a fight with two of the mercenaries.

"Bric!" he called. "O'Magnan is dead. Tell them!"

Bric sliced one man through the neck and stabbed the other in the chest, both of his opponents falling away as he caught sight of Morgan with the bloodied dagger in his hand. He knew exactly what the man meant.

With O'Magnan dead, the battle was over.

"Clann mhac Éireann!" he boomed in a way only Bric

MacRohan could boom. "Tá do cheannaire marbh. Cuir síos do airm nó ní bheidh aon trócaire!"

Sons of Ireland! Your leader is dead. Put down your weapons or there will be no mercy!

The cry of Ryan's death was taken up by the Irish. Men began to point to the body down the slope to see for themselves. But the fighting didn't stop immediately; the miners were still in a fight for their lives, Addax and Alexander were still fighting in a pocket of men, and even Bric had to fend off another assault as he stood there. Essien had come down off the walls in complete disobedience of Alexander's orders and was fighting furiously with some of the Irish. But gradually, Bric's words sank in. The evidence was clear.

The fighting began to grind to a halt.

Your leader is dead!

Men began to rush down the slope towards Ryan's body. Seeing this, Alexander began to recall the miners. Addax and Essien took up the call and the miners began to retreat back towards the gatehouse, away from the Irish who were crushed by Ryan's death. As Morgan, Alexander, Bric, Addax, and Essien began to back up towards the gatehouse, covering the retreat of the miners, they could see several men collecting Ryan's body and carrying it back up the slope.

The five knights stood in a line just in front of the gates with the miners clustered behind them, watching as the mercenaries began to carry off their dead. They began to retreat down the road, away from the castle, and when it was clear that the battle for Mount Grace was over, someone began to cheer. Others took up the cry and, soon, the entire gang of exhausted miners was cheering loudly as the Irish mercenaries faded off down the hill, withdrawing as quickly as they could from the target they could not take.

A castle they could not conquer.

It was done.

Weary to the bone but elated, Morgan looked at Bric and Alexander, who began to laugh because of the cheering going on around them. Miners began patting the knights on the back, thanking them, physically demonstrating their jubilation. Essien came up behind Morgan and Bric, putting his arms around their necks and giving them an enthusiastic hug until Alexander cocked a dark eyebrow and pointed to the walls, indicating he was displeased with the man disobeying his order. But Essien merely grinned and kissed Bric's cheek joyfully.

He received a slap again.

A roar of laughter went up among the knights, who had lived to see another day. For the agents of William Marshal, it was a day well spent and a deed well done.

For Morgan de Wolfe, it was a mission that changed his destiny for the better.

In the end, he was richer for it.

EPILOGUE

Lioncross Abbey

"**A**ND THAT IS what happened, my lord," Morgan said. "We fought them off and they scattered in the wrong direction, straight into de Velt's oncoming army. You know what happened after that – the road between Bronllys and the border is lined with the corpses of the mercenaries. And now, you know everything that happened in the fight for Mount Grace and her silver mine. Do you have any specific questions?"

It was just after midday at Lioncross Abbey Castle, the magnificent home of Christopher de Lohr. Morgan, Alexander, Bric, Addax, and Essien were standing in Christopher's lavish solar, giving him a full report of what happened at Mount Grace a little over a month earlier. It had been quite a tale.

Christopher shook his head wearily.

"All of that," he said. "Christ, what a mess that was. What became of the miners?"

Alexander stepped in. "As you will recall, about thirty of them were the remnants of Oliver le Marche's army," he said. "Many of the miners have joined the new Mount Grace army, while the rest have decided to return to the mines."

"With much better working conditions and even a cut of the profits," Addax put in. "De Velt decided they had earned it."

Christopher nodded. "He is a generous man," he said. "I know that The Marshal turned the management of Mount Grace over to Jax, but Jax gave command of the garrison to Kenan de Poyer. I think that was a wise decision."

"Most definitely," Morgan agreed. "That was his only request in helping us regain Mount Grace – that he be allowed to remain. He has the utmost veneration for the castle. It means something to him, so it is only right that he should be the new garrison commander. He knows the men, the castle, the land. He will do well."

Christopher agreed, though he was still trying to digest the absolutely wild tale he'd been told about the battle for Mount Grace. It had been a short but eventful mission, one that had seen the objective accomplished even if had taken them some lengths to get there.

"And what about that fool who wanted to court Lady de Wolfe?" he asked. "Farren de Bonne? What happened to him?"

Morgan fought off a smile. "De Velt knew the man," he said. "Not well, but he knew *of* him. He is the lord of Talgarth Castle, a moderately important border castle. De Velt sent for Farran and the man showed up at Mount Grace but refused to go inside. Jax made him an offer to ally with Mount Grace and William Marshal or suffer the consequences and, of course, Farran agreed. But I do not think Jax trusts him very much."

"Not at all," Alexander grunted. "De Bonne is a selfish, fickle fool but the fear of de Velt's punishment will keep him loyal."

"It has kept me loyal for years," Christopher quipped to a

chorus of soft laughter. "Who else is left? Of course. Lady Everelda. I'm told that she is living with you and your wife, Morgan."

Morgan sighed heavily as the laughter turned in his direction. "That is true," he said sadly. "Not only do I have a new wife, but I have her cousin who clings to my wife like a barnacle. Having my wife to myself these days is a damned miracle. I draw the line at allowing Everelda to sleep in our bed."

Christopher fought off a grin. "She is returning with you to Richmond Castle?"

Morgan nodded. "She is," he said. "Truthfully, Everelda has nowhere to go, so there was never any question that she would come with us. But you can wager on the fact that I am going to find her a husband as soon as I can. Then mayhap I can have my wife back."

Christopher chuckled. "I wish you luck with that," he said. Then, he looked to the group around him. "Well? Is there anything else to report about Mount Grace?"

Heads were wagging back and forth, but Morgan spoke up. "The priest I told you about," he said. "Father Nicodemus? He is coming with me to Richmond as well. Richmond has its own chapel, you know. I've always wanted my own private priest."

"Ah, yes," Christopher said, rising from the chair he'd been sitting in for the better part of the morning. "I met the man when he arrived here with you. Now, I have my own report to send to The Marshal. Morgan and Sherry, he'll want yours, as well."

"Understood, my lord," Morgan said.

Men began to filter out of the solar and go about their business and that included Morgan. Alexander remained behind with Christopher, but Morgan wanted to see his wife before he began the long process of scribing a missive to The Marshal.

He couldn't go a few moments without thinking of her. She filled everything about him, like air in his lungs or blood in his veins. Perhaps his mission to Mount Grace had been a mad adventure, but he'd come out of it with the best possible prize.

The most beautiful woman in the world, by his side, for always.

Wandering the grounds in search of his wife, he found Amarantha, Everelda, and Father Nicodemus outside in a shady corner of the bailey as Amarantha read from one of her father's books to some of the younger de Lohr children and grandchildren. There were several. Christin, Alexander's wife, was sitting with one of her children on her lap along with Amarantha's cat, Palu, listening to Amarantha read a story about a monkey in a magic forest.

What was even more entertaining was Violet the Raven. She walked amongst the children, chattering and bickering, which delighted the children to no end. As a soft breeze blew the branches of the elm tree overhead, Morgan listened to the bird chatter in concert with his wife's sweet voice as she spoke of the monkey, who had a rat for a friend, and the rat would steal from the rich and give to the needy.

Amarantha was very good in her storytelling, dramatically conveying the part where the monkey and the thief-rat came to a magic well. That excited the younger children, who demanded to know what was in the well.

Morgan moved to where Amarantha could see him as he stood behind the children. He watched her as she told the tall tale, her features animated, her joy obvious. When the children began laughing loudly because the monkey threw the rat into the magic well, she laughed right along with them. Freely and without reservation.

Truth be told, he'd never seen her so happy.

Nor had he ever been so happy.

Morgan wasn't sure how he'd fallen so completely and hopelessly in love in just a month. He always thought he was a deliberate man, but the introduction of Amarantha de la Haye had changed his very fabric. Everything about him was different these days. The mission at Mount Grace seemed like a small price to pay for him to have found the love of his life.

And he did love her, more than he could possibly express.

When Amarantha looked up and saw him watching her, she smiled broadly and called him over. Reluctantly, Morgan went to her and between the two of them, they acted out a scene in the book where the monkey and the rat found a beautiful princess who granted them three wishes.

Morgan was the monkey, of course.

When Alexander showed up, looking for his wife and children, he was forced into portraying the rat, much to the delight of his little boys. He made a very good rat. Between Amarantha – the beautiful princess, the monkey – Morgan, and Alexander – the rat, they kept the children thoroughly entertained. It was a sublime day, eons away from what had transpired at Mount Grace those weeks ago. It was joy beyond measure and when Amarantha gave birth to a son the following year, that joy only deepened.

For the Executioner Knight and the daughter of the man he was sent to destroy, nothing could have prepared them for the deliriously wonderful life they would have together. Born of necessity and fed by desire, their love story became the stuff of legends.

What I do not know of you, I can learn. What I cannot learn, I can feel.

For Morgan and Amarantha, they had learned, and felt, everything.

Together.

CB THE END BO

Children of Morgan and Amarantha
Maxen
Ellis
Isolde
Brynn
Evan
Liam
Trevor
Gere

KATHRYN LE VEQUE NOVELS

Medieval Romance:

De Wolfe Pack Series:
Warwolfe
The Wolfe
Nighthawk
ShadowWolfe
DarkWolfe
A Joyous de Wolfe Christmas
BlackWolfe
Serpent
A Wolfe Among Dragons
Scorpion
StormWolfe
Dark Destroyer
The Lion of the North
Walls of Babylon
The Best Is Yet To Be

De Wolfe Pack Generations:
WolfeHeart
WolfeStrike
WolfeSword
WolfeBlade
WolfeLord
WolfeShield

The Executioner Knights:
By the Unholy Hand
The Mountain Dark
Starless
A Time of End
Winter of Solace

Lord of the Sky
Splendid Hour
The Whispering Night
Netherworld
Lord of the Shadows
Of Mortal Fury

The de Russe Legacy:
The Falls of Erith
Lord of War: Black Angel
The Iron Knight
Beast
The Dark One: Dark Knight
The White Lord of Wellesbourne
Dark Moon
Dark Steel
A de Russe Christmas Miracle
Dark Warrior

The de Lohr Dynasty:
While Angels Slept
Rise of the Defender
Steelheart
Shadowmoor
Silversword
Spectre of the Sword
Unending Love
Archangel
A Blessed de Lohr Christmas

The Brothers de Lohr:
The Earl in Winter

Lords of East Anglia:

While Angels Slept
Godspeed
Age of Gods and Mortals

Great Lords of le Bec:
Great Protector

House of de Royans:
Lord of Winter
To the Lady Born
The Centurion

Lords of Eire:
Echoes of Ancient Dreams
Blacksword
The Darkland

Ancient Kings of Anglecynn:
The Whispering Night
Netherworld

Battle Lords of de Velt:
The Dark Lord
Devil's Dominion
Bay of Fear
The Dark Lord's First Christmas
The Dark Spawn
The Dark Conqueror
The Dark Angel

Reign of the House of de Winter:
Lespada
Swords and Shields

De Reyne Domination:
Guardian of Darkness
A Cold Wynter's Knight
With Dreams
The Fallen One
Black Storm

House of d'Vant:
Tender is the Knight (House of d'Vant)
The Red Fury (House of d'Vant)

The Dragonblade Series:
Fragments of Grace
Dragonblade
Island of Glass
The Savage Curtain
The Fallen One

Great Marcher Lords of de Lara
Dragonblade

House of St. Hever
Fragments of Grace
Island of Glass
Queen of Lost Stars

Lords of Pembury:
The Savage Curtain

Lords of Thunder: The de Shera Brotherhood Trilogy
The Thunder Lord
The Thunder Warrior
The Thunder Knight

The Great Knights of de Moray:
Shield of Kronos
The Gorgon

The House of De Nerra:
The Promise
The Falls of Erith
Vestiges of Valor
Realm of Angels

Highland Warriors of Munro:
The Red Lion

Deep Into Darkness

The House of de Garr:
Lord of Light
Realm of Angels

Saxon Lords of Hage:
The Crusader
Kingdom Come

High Warriors of Rohan:
High Warrior

The House of Ashbourne:
Upon a Midnight Dream

The House of D'Aurilliac:
Valiant Chaos

The House of De Dere:
Of Love and Legend

St. John and de Gare Clans:
The Warrior Poet

The House of de Bretagne:
The Questing

The House of Summerlin:
The Legend

The Kingdom of Hendocia:
Kingdom by the Sea

Regency Historical Romance:
Sin Like Flynn: A Regency
Historical Romance Duet

Gothic Regency Romance:

Emma

Contemporary Romance:

**Kathlyn Trent/Marcus Burton
Series:**
Valley of the Shadow
The Eden Factor
Canyon of the Sphinx

**The American Heroes Anthology
Series:**
The Lucius Robe
Fires of Autumn
Evenshade
Sea of Dreams
Purgatory

**Other non-connected
Contemporary Romance:**
Lady of Heaven
Darkling, I Listen
In the Dreaming Hour
River's End
The Fountain

Sons of Poseidon:
The Immortal Sea

**Pirates of Britannia Series (with
Eliza Knight):**
Savage of the Sea by Eliza Knight
Leader of Titans by Kathryn Le
Veque
The Sea Devil by Eliza Knight
Sea Wolfe by Kathryn Le Veque

Note: All Kathryn's novels are designed to be read as stand-alones, although many have cross-over characters or cross-over family groups. Novels that are grouped together have related characters or family groups. You will notice that some series have the same books; that is because they are cross-overs. A hero in one book may be the secondary character in another.

There is NO reading order except by chronology, but even in that case, you can still read the books as stand-alones. No novel is connected to another by a cliff hanger, and every book has an HEA.

Series are clearly marked. All series contain the same characters or family groups except the American Heroes Series, which is an anthology with unrelated characters.

For more information, find it in **A Reader's Guide to the Medieval World of Le Veque**.

About Kathryn Le Veque

Bringing the Medieval to Romance

KATHRYN LE VEQUE is a critically acclaimed, multiple USA TODAY Bestselling author, an Indie Reader bestseller, a charter Amazon All-Star author, and a #1 bestselling, award-winning, multi-published author in Medieval Historical Romance with over 100 published novels.

Kathryn is a multiple award nominee and winner, including the winner of Uncaged Book Reviews Magazine 2017 and 2018 "Raven Award" for Favorite Medieval Romance. Kathryn is also a multiple RONE nominee (InD'Tale Magazine), holding a record for the number of nominations. In 2018, her novel WARWOLFE was the winner in the Romance category of the Book Excellence Award and in 2019, her novel A WOLFE AMONG DRAGONS won the prestigious RONE award for best pre-16th century romance.

Kathryn is considered one of the top Indie authors in the world with over 2M copies in circulation, and her novels have been translated into several languages. Kathryn recently signed with Sourcebooks Casablanca for a Medieval Fight Club series, first published in 2020.

In addition to her own published works, Kathryn is also the President/CEO of Dragonblade Publishing, a boutique publishing house specializing in Historical Romance. Dragonblade's success has seen it rise in the ranks to become Amazon's #1 e-book publisher of Historical Romance (K-Lytics report July 2020).

Kathryn loves to hear from her readers. Please find Kathryn on Facebook at Kathryn Le Veque, Author, or join her on Twitter @kathrynleveque. Sign up for Kathryn's blog at www.kathrynleveque.com for the latest news and sales.

www.ingramcontent.com/pod-product-compliance
Lightning Source LLC
Chambersburg PA
CBHW070749190726
48292CB00002B/469